LEGEND OF THE
DRAGON SOUL

Dedicated to

All those who sometimes feel lost in the dark.

Shadow Dragon Saga

Curse of the Dragon Shadow

Legend of the Dragon Soul

Rise of the Dragon Sworn

Blood of the Dragon Throne

Reign of the Dragon Born

Secret of the Dragon Crown

First Edition
Published by Fairies and Fantasy Pty Ltd 2024

ISBN: 978-1-922390-87-5 (paperback)

Legend of the Dragon Soul copyright © 2024 Selina Fenech
Cover art and interior illustrations © 2024 Selina Fenech
Editing by Zero Alchemy

www.selinafenech.com

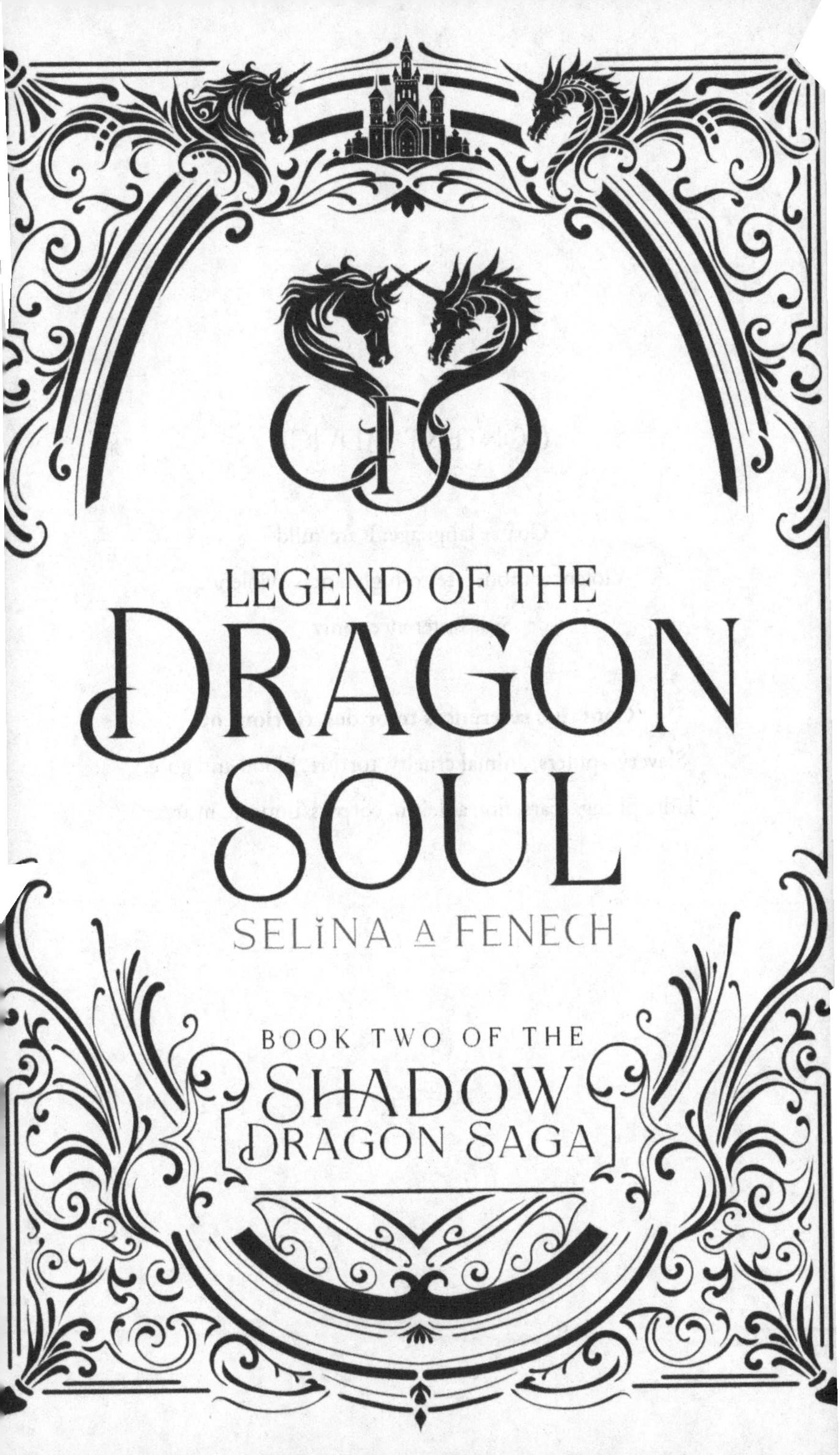

LEGEND OF THE DRAGON SOUL

SELINA A FENECH

BOOK TWO OF THE

SHADOW DRAGON SAGA

CONTENT ADVICE

Coarse language: Rare/mild

Violence: moderate-to-high fantasy violence

Sex: References only

Contains references to or descriptions of:

Slavery, spiders, animal cruelty, torture, blood and gore,

kidnapping, scars, fire, ableism, corpses/undead, murder.

CONTENTS

ELUNDRAE
EIGHT WINDS OC
TAEN HIGHLANDS
Nord Halfort
Heithorn Estate
EYLE TAENESK
Tree W
Eldisun Grove
The Gre Wing
Vesland Plains
Longtail River
Dragon Keeps
1. Braigwenkeep (Trade Hub)
2. Nevrynkeep (Mining)
3. Ardahnkeep (Trade Harbor, Old Rolanian Capital)
4. Tjollaskeep (Mining)
5. Salixkeep (Fishing)
6. Ulfrenkeep (Mining)
7. Ylvakeep (Farming)
8. Leskakeep (Farming)
9. Pryshakeep (Farming)
10. Dastmyrkeep (Glass)
11. Tarrickeep (Mining)
12. Gerichkeep (Lumber)
13. Skaellakeep (Farming)
14. Idrakeep (Penal)
15. Hjelzahnkeep (Training)
16. Eslindekeep (Incomplete)
EYLE TAENUSH
Abandoned Quarries
(1)
(11)
Lorg Cornis
Unicor
WESTERN ALDERKIN DEPTHS
(Ewess Deemfret)
Midsun Dale
Snowshimmer R
(2)
Yeonard's Passage
Vasthome Reach
Sturmfell Peaks
Lorg Blessn
(12)
Lorg Nisk
(10)
Tallesis Shores
(16)
Sut Myrr
EYERSUNN SEA

EYLE NORDCREST
(14)
NORTHERN ALDERKIN DEPTHS
(Nerrun Deemfret)
Nord Myrr
(8)
Lorg Sesstra
(9)
Gris Hofen
(15)
Seasong Shores
Lorg Eldstrom
Lorg Draeka
Serpents Run
Mestra's Horn
EASTERN ALDERKIN DEPTHS
(IlstDeemfret)
Draeskull Crags
Sunborn Range
Stonewing Crest
DRAEKHAN'S REST
(4)
Starris River
(7)
CENTRAL ALDERKIN DEPTHS
(Luns Deemfret)
Etherflame Plains
Eishowl Peaks
(6)
(3)
Bovin Steppes
Grand Hofen
DRAEKHANHELM
Unicorn Tears River
(13)
SKYBREAK SEA
(5)
Erst Hofen
The Red Cliffs
SOUTHERN ALDERKIN DEPTHS
(Sons Deemfret)
Talon Bluffs

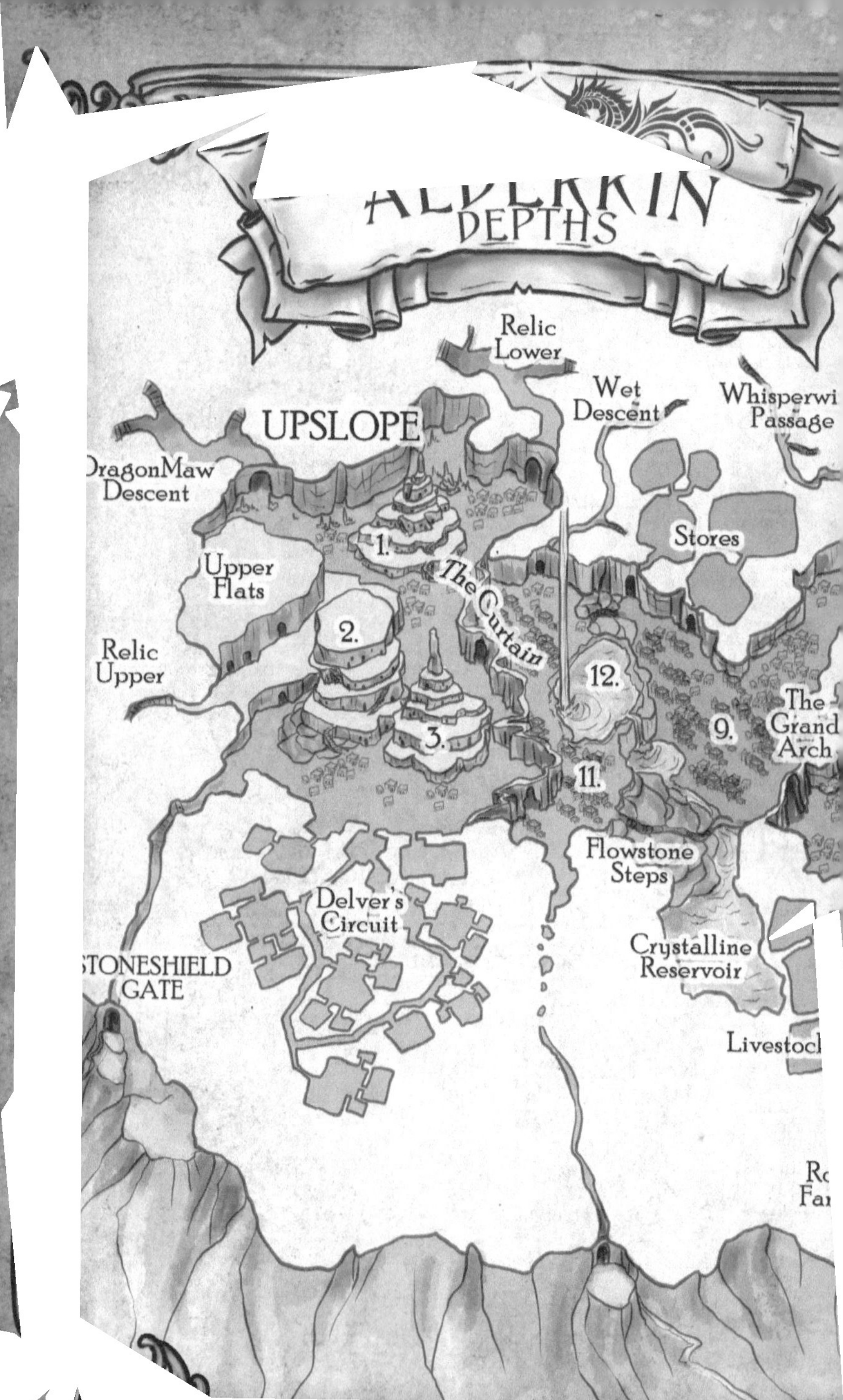
ALDERKIN
DEPTHS
Relic Lower
Wet Descent
Whisperwi Passage
UPSLOPE
DragonMaw Descent
Stores
Upper Flats
1.
The Curtain
2.
Relic Upper
12.
The Grand Arch
9.
3.
11.
Flowstone Steps
Delver's Circuit
Crystalline Reservoir
STONESHIELD GATE
Livestock
Ro Far

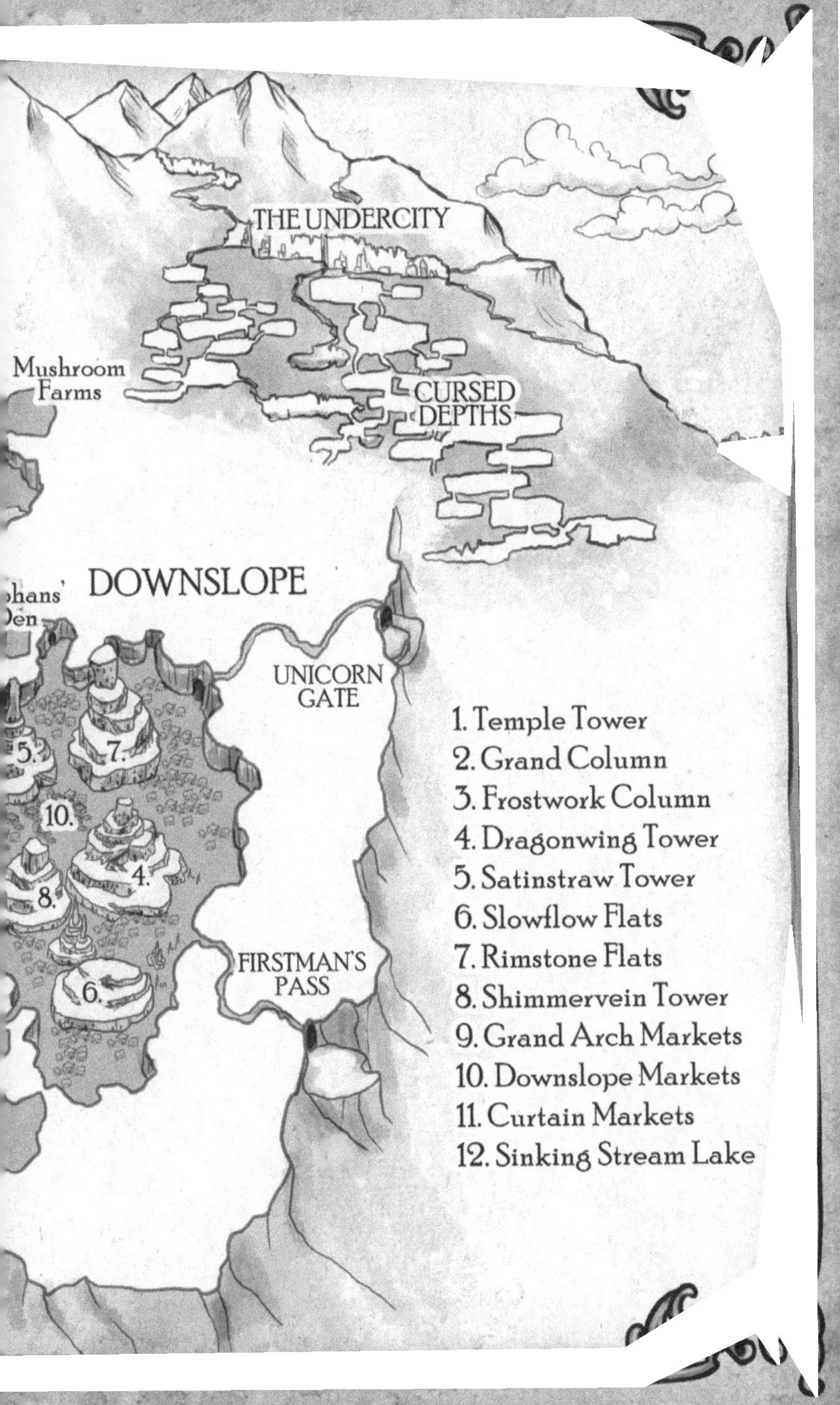
THE UNDERCITY
Mushroom Farms
CURSED DEPTHS
DOWNSLOPE
phans' Den
UNICORN GATE
FIRSTMAN'S PASS
1. Temple Tower
2. Grand Column
3. Frostwork Column
4. Dragonwing Tower
5. Satinstraw Tower
6. Slowflow Flats
7. Rimstone Flats
8. Shimmervein Tower
9. Grand Arch Markets
10. Downslope Markets
11. Curtain Markets
12. Sinking Stream Lake

ONE

Kessara Heithorn had dreamed of flying for her entire life. She knew she belonged on the back of a dragon, soaring through the iron-gray expanse of sky, high above the cinders of the world. She yearned for it, right to the core of her bones.

So being underground, prowling through stony, lightless spaces, left every part of her feeling twitchy and irritated. The dank air caught in the back of her throat, the threat of suffocation trying to drive her from the caverns.

She and Griskin had been searching for weeks through this cesspool of cowards who hid from the perils of the world above.

What should have been an easy hunt was spoiled

by the overcrowding of the undercity and because the underground disagreed with her wolf, Griskin, as well. There was something in the musty air, making Griskin a snuffly, drooling mess. His clogged nose was unable to pick up the scent of their prey.

Kess had to follow her own eyes and ears instead, hoping to catch a glimpse of the redheaded monster or the small girl with the bright-blue eyes that Pony called 'sister.'

Her hunt was also complicated by the fact she couldn't risk Pony knowing she was in the caves until she had her hands on the dragonling. And gossip of a girl riding around on a wolf was sure to spread.

Kess wasn't much less conspicuous when not on Griskin either. She had sat on a corner alone once or twice, face hidden, pretending to beg, trying to get some information that way.

But as just one of many beggars, few people had stopped to show her any kindness and certainly hadn't stayed long enough for her to ask questions.

So she had to keep herself hidden, mostly on rooftops and skirting around the shadows of the crowded slums.

The way the buildings were stacked on top of each other in flowing tiers, carved into clusters of stalagmites—some as large as mighty keeps—made it easy for Griskin to leap from one roof to another, staying off the streets below. The constant hum and bustle from the dwellings covered the sound of Griskin landing on their stone roofs.

Kess kept her body low, pressed close to Griskin's back, his fur fluffing out around her. The smoky scent of the world above hadn't yet left his coat. Kess's hood remained over her head to hide the bright sparkle of white streaking her dark hair.

Then if anybody saw them, they'd mostly just see Griskin and assume it was just another of the weird creatures that inhabited these caves beside the humans. Kess had already seen some shockingly large otters, feasting on scraps they had stolen from a marketplace.

The otter Pony had in her backpack back at the slavers' camp must have been a baby. And the intolerable woman had been so close to tricking Kess into thinking that was all she carried. But she also had another baby in her backpack that day, the one Kess intended on taking for herself.

Kess perched behind a row of thin limestone spikes, watching the ground level below. A natural archway of majestic proportions was formed between curtains of stone there, central within the vast cavern, and the main way to travel between the upper and lower areas.

It seemed to be a major thoroughfare, from what Kess could work out of the layout of the ramshackle community. She'd spent all of yesterday there, but an entire day of surveillance yielded nothing, despite the sheer number of people pushing through.

There were some possible sightings. But flashes of scarlet always turned out to be some other red-haired Rolanians. Tall brutes that caught Kess's eye, that matched the build she sought, were more often men. Never Pony. Perhaps she never even came through this part of the caves.

"Come on, Gris." Kess squeezed her fingers lightly against his neck, and he stood up.

It was time to move on, try a new location.

Griskin sniffed and wheezed as he carried her on soft, silent paws.

Although the temperature in the caves was even and comfortable, Kess shivered. *What if Pony's taken the dragonling and moved on already? What if she isn't even here underground anymore?*

She'd tracked Pony and her group of liberated children back from the slavers' camp to here but couldn't go in the gated and guarded entrance like the others.

Kess had to climb back up the snow-capped ridges of the mountain above and sneak in through the tunnel that Pony had come out of before, when she screwed up all her plans with the mother dragon and the eggs.

That extra travel meant she lost track of her target.

Kess hadn't realized how big this underground community had gotten. She hated the place, but she could see the allure for people who didn't have the stomach or skills for

surviving aboveground.

The refugees had adapted well to the Alderkin ruins, learning how to use their magic and technology that remained in the abandoned homes.

As Griskin padded across a flat-carved roof, Kess wondered at the magic of these caves, the way cyan crystals brought a pleasant, cool glow to the craggy cavern. Through a window across the way, she spied a family cooking over compact stone crucibles that lit up with the heat of a bonfire. The scent of spiced food made her stomach grumble.

Smooth mechanisms slid below as stone doorways opened and closed. It almost matched some of the technological luxuries found in dragonkeeps.

If it weren't for the overcrowding, it could be a very comfortable life, for people who could live without seeing the sky. Food was harder to come by down beneath the earth. But the refugees had worked out how manage a semblance of farming underground, everything from goats to roots to fungi to worms. People would eat anything when there were no other options.

Kess had even spotted someone eating what looked like fried giant spider legs. Kess shuddered. No, this place could never be comfortable for her.

I better not be wasting my time here.

She shook her head, disagreeing with her own fears.

Pony would still be here, somewhere. She'd run back to hide underground again as fast as she could, as soon as she'd gotten the kid she called sister back. The only reason she'd leave was if she knew Kess was there looking for her, and Kess had been too careful for that.

Kess just had to *find* her.

The leap to the next rooftop was long, and Griskin slowed. A low whine came from the back of his throat, and he sniffled and looked back at her with weeping eyes.

"Keep moving." Kess squeezed her fingers to encourage him forward.

Springing off his hind legs, they sailed across the open air between buildings, like ghosts in the cyan light.

As they landed on the rooftop on the other side, a shape emerged from the gloom in front of Kess. A low-hanging stalactite, right in their path.

Griskin went under it. Kess tried to dodge, but there wasn't time.

The spear of stone clipped Kess's shoulder. The impact twisted her around and tossed her off Griskin's back. Her feet came free of the stirrups, and she reached to catch hold of her makeshift saddle.

She missed, toppling off onto the damp, cold stone of the rooftop.

The fall sent her rolling uncontrollably in a bone-jarring

tumble down the slope. Kess clenched her teeth and twisted her torso, trying to right herself. They were a few stories up. She couldn't take that fall.

Scrabbling her arms out, she clawed her fingertips into the clammy limestone. Skin scraped raw and fingernails broke as they dug through the soft, silty layer of dust and into the rock below. Belly down, her fingers hooked into the stone, swinging the rest of her body in an arc from that catch point.

Her legs went out into the air. Hands tensed like steel around their hold. Kess skidded to a stop, right over the eave.

She was bent at the waist, chest on the roof and legs dangling down. With a great heave, she dragged herself up.

Kess rolled onto her back, taking in hard, shaking breaths.

Clutching her stinging hands into fists, she swallowed away the threat of tears.

Her voice was a hissed whisper of a scream. "Raze this whole place! This entire stars-damned, unblessed place!"

Griskin appeared beside her, whimpering between sniffles, his wet nose pressing to her cheek.

"Get away from me, you horrible beast!" Kess pushed his face away from hers. Her bruised shoulder twanged painfully, and she stifled a cry.

"How dare you drop me? You're a useless, worthless fleabag! I don't want you! I ..." Kess choked as tears burst

in a hot wave from her eyes.

Griskin slipped around the shield of her hands, licking at her cheek.

"I was *born to ride a dragon*!" She tried again to thrust him away, but he remained beside her, and then her hands were around his neck and she was clinging to him with all her strength and pressing her shameful tears into his fur. Between sobs, her words caught. "Not you. Not you … A dragon."

Griskin folded into her, paws lying over her lap and head nuzzling her chest. She held him like that as she fought down her tears. Whether from frustration, pain, or any other cause, she couldn't let herself be weak like that.

As her emotions calmed, Griskin tilted his head up again, lapping his tongue and wiping his mucus-dripping snout over her face.

"Stop! You're gross." Her lips twisted up, but she didn't push him away again. She leaned her forehead against his and scratched him behind the ear. "The sooner we find that dragonling, the sooner we can be out of this miserable place, and you'll feel better."

We'll both feel better then.

The tumble down the rooftop had knocked Kess's hips and knees too, leaving them feeling bruised. She'd once met a dragonrider who had lost the use of her legs after a fall and had lost the feeling in them too. But Kess felt everything.

She could move her legs too, only barely. She'd just never been able to stand on them, never been able to walk on them. Born that way, nobody could work out why or fix the problem.

And how her family had tried to fix her.

Kess knew she didn't need to be *fixed*. And if only she could get herself onto a dragon, she could show everybody else, too.

She shifted farther away from the roof's edge, then used her hands to move her legs into a better position to get herself back onto Griskin.

Soon they were dashing silently across rooftops again, searching for a new vantage point to hunt from.

Taking a turn south—or what Kess thought was south but worried she was too turned around without the sun as a marker to know—she headed into a new area she hadn't properly explored yet. One even filthier and slummier than the busy main market district.

The squeals of playing children drew her attention, and she nudged Griskin that way, slowing their pace. The buildings and pathways ahead were carved into the cavern walls rather than built up within open spaces or larger stalagmites. She wouldn't be able to stay above them when

there were no roofs to be used.

But she could see well enough from the final high point she ended up at and watched as a group of children milled around and played. She recognized a couple of their faces. They had been behind slavers' bars the last time she'd seen them.

Children that had only made their way back here with Pony's help.

Kess patted Griskin and he lowered down onto his belly, then they settled in to watch. This was the closest she'd gotten to a connection to Pony. She could spend some time there, listening and watching.

Voices drifted up from the pathways below.

"No, *you're* in! I got you! Stop cheating!" a tiny voice growled.

Kess leaned to the side and reached into one of her saddlebags, pulling out the bundle of strapping she'd been working on and some leather tools.

A woman muttered softly, "Fifty more yesterday! A whole town. Stars know how they kept a settlement going so long up there, but their home's gone now."

Kess examined the makeshift muzzle and bindings. The dragonling looked freshly newborn when she'd seen Pony with it. Even smaller, since it had hatched sooner than it should have. It was a few weeks old now. Dragons grow fast, since they have a long way to go from their tiny starting size to full-grown.

Kess pictured in her mind how big a dragonling of that age might be and decided to punch a couple more holes into the buckle strap just in case. It was the offspring of a seasong after all.

A man grumbled, "I heard it's a lot worse up there now than it was when we last saw it. You should hear some of the stories. Revenants coming back a second time, they're saying."

"Oh, I don't believe a word of that nonsense."

Kess huffed. She'd heard that rumor aboveground too and hadn't believed it, until she saw the terrifying truth of it with her own eyes. *But if you can kill a rev once, you can kill it twice. And soon, I'll be able to burn them all with my own dragon.*

The woman added, "Don't know how they think we're going to fit any more orphans in here if they keep letting them in, though. Whole undercity is ready to pop. Maybe they should open up some lower levels."

Kess switched to her hunting knife and trimmed another strap of leather off a spare skin. Once she had the dragonling, she couldn't risk rushing the taming process. She'd have to get it out of there first, go somewhere quiet and do it right. The wild beast would need to be subdued until then.

The man guffawed. "You think anyone is crazy enough

to go down lower? Whole place is cursed from the way the delvers talk. We're lucky they've cleared all the traps up here. Hey! Watch it! Go play over there!"

Giving the leather a tug-test, Kess felt satisfied it would be enough to bind a young dragonling's legs.

The muzzle was done too, and Kess checked the herbs she'd stuffed inside remained in place, careful not to inhale their scent. Having the dragonling writhing and whipping around as she carried it wouldn't do. But luckily, she'd learned a thing or two about herbs from Pony, back when they were kids.

She took the remaining skin and a leather needle and worked on creating mitts to cover the dragonling's claws.

A child peeped, "Yeah, Lyrrin's sister! The one who helped get Cammi, Leeu, and the others back from the slavers."

Kess's hands stilled.

"Na-ah. Mira said it was that delver Aishena who saved the kids, all by herself!"

"No, it was her, and her brother, and that other girl. The big one, with the red hair. She wasn't a delver before, but she's a delver now!"

Her head shot up, and she sought the owner of the voice. A stick-thin brat with a tumble of ruddy brown curls that were matted in tangles at the ends. The nearby glow stone cast a cool blue light over him as he continued boasting in his high, squeaky voice to a few gasping runts.

"Aw, I wanna be a delver."

"You're too scrawny to be a delver."

"You're too dumb to know what I can be."

Kess stuffed her leatherwork away and took in her options. She could just snatch the kid and make him show her where to find Pony, but that was too risky. Despite the unkempt appearance of the ragged children, at least a couple of adults kept an eye on them.

There was one unlit pathway across from where the children were playing. It would only be a couple of big leaps by Griskin across the street to get down there. There was a small risk of being seen, but Kess was tired of waiting.

Nobody called out as Griskin bounded off the roof and dashed into the shadows of the narrow pathway. Kess's pulse raced regardless, driven into a frenzy by the feeling of being close to her prey.

The kids were separating from their circle, and Kess whistled to get the boasting kid's attention. He turned to look, squinting into the dark alley with beady, uncertain eyes.

"Hey, kid, can I ask you something?"

"Umm ... I probably shouldn't." He looked to one of the watching adults, but their backs were currently turned, separating a nearby scuffle of squealing toddlers.

"I just want to have a little chat." Slipping a gold sov

from her belt pouch, Kess held it up high, letting it glint in the light.

The boy's eyes widened.

"Yeah, it's all yours. I only want to ask a couple of questions." Kess rolled the coin around her fingers.

He stepped closer, into the shadows of the alleyway. He flinched when Griskin became visible, seeing that he approached not just a strange young woman, but one who rode on top of a wolf. Kess could see the war of desire versus flight in his eyes. But the piece of gold flicking between Kess's fingers kept him moving toward her.

That piece of gold was probably worth more than an orphan like him could dream of. He'd spill everything Kess needed to know for his chance at owning it. And it meant nothing for Kess to spend a gold sov on that.

Because Kess always dreamed bigger.

And for those dreams, she needed to steal a dragon.

Two

The explosion rattled the herb jars on the shelves and buffeted hot air over Riony's bare arms. Jagged pieces of burning hot crystal rained all around the room.

Riony grabbed Lyrrin, leaning over her as her sister leaned over Dracuni, sheltering from the hail of searing shards.

Loud! Scared! The unidragon curled into a ball, hiding her snout beneath a translucent, iridescent wing.

"Oops," Lyrrin said, as the pattering stopped.

"Oops?" A crystal chip burned the tip of Riony's ear as it fell free from her hair. She shook her head, swatting at it to clear her hair of any other embers, worried it was about to catch on fire.

"Oops? Lyrrin, it's *my first day.* Is oops going to clean

this up? Is oops going to stop time for me? Because I cannot afford to be late."

Lyrrin didn't offer an answer. She had the intense, bright-eyed expression she often had while messing around with Alderkin runes. She stepped away from under Riony's shadow and huffed at the source of the explosion. "Okay, so I can't add a burn rune onto a light stone. I know that now."

"We're learning. Yaaaay," Riony muttered. She kicked glowing fragments away from Dracuni and checked the young unidragon over for burns.

Dracuni peeked out from under her wing and blinked large, lilac eyes. **Was loud. Was scary.**

"I know," Riony replied quietly. Dracuni's thoughts, which somehow found their way into Riony's head, had been changing. No longer a simple rush of emotion alone, they started to have more nuance. Past or future tense. More range. Names.

Something more like language, which felt crazy to Riony considering everything she'd ever learned about dragons said they were ferocious, thoughtless creatures if they weren't tamed.

Although Dracuni wasn't a normal dragon.

"Not hurt?" Riony asked softly.

No hurt.

Riony patted the pale scales on the unidragon's neck.

"The crystal must overheat too much when combining those two runes." Lyrrin looked at the sharp claws on her fingers, moving them as though tracing runes in the air.

"Yeah, I'd say so." Riony smelled burning. She hissed as she flicked a crystal shard out from where it had stuck into the waist of her new delver leathers. A singe mark smoldered and Riony licked her fingers and tried to wipe it away. It remained blackened. Riony glared at it.

She had only just been fitted for the sleek, clever armor that delvers earned after their training. The soft leather was designed to be close-fitting and flexible for squeezing through tight gaps. The trousers and vest had a heap of useful straps and harness points, and most importantly, Riony was sure she looked extra hot wearing it.

And now it has burn holes before even starting my first official day. What worried her more though, was that the smell of burning was only getting worse.

Riony followed her nose, searching around the room for the source of the smoky scent.

Lyrrin's eyes were on the collection of out-of-charge artifacts and almost out-of-charge glow stones they had collected over the last few weeks. They were spread out across the carved stone counter, piled in the corners of the room, lined up in between clothes and kitchenware on the shelves. An abundance of worthless and soon-to-be worthless Alderkin relics.

When they had returned from their overworld adventure, Riony had sought out a couple of spent athames. They were easy and cheap to obtain since they were practically worthless without any charge left. She kept them with her, hoping to discover how to recharge them.

Her cutting athame had miraculously recharged, so she figured there must be a way.

Like maybe she had a special magical essence unique to her that switched the artifacts back on again when she carried them around for a while. But realistically, she figured it was probably Dracuni that was the special one.

But no matter whether she kept the athames with her or with Dracuni, none of them glowed back to life. Whatever had renewed the cutting athame, it wasn't something she was able to replicate again.

Then grateful orphans had noticed her collecting the Alderkin junk and had decided offering more as presents was a wonderful idea. Riony suddenly had an army of children picking through waste to bring her every tossed and worn-out relic they could find, and her rooms were now filled with the useless things and not one of them had recharged.

No new athames for Riony.

She'd really been hoping to show off a collection that

could rival Aishena's on her first day at delving. Now she would just have to impress the other delvers with her good looks and wit alone. Aishena didn't seem into that, but maybe the other delvers had taste.

Lyrrin had been the one to benefit most from the supply of Alderkin crystals. Glow stones were plentiful and often swapped out before they lost their charge entirely, so Riony was gifted a lot of those as well. That was when Lyrrin saw her opportunity to start experimenting.

"I thought I put it over here ..." Lyrrin searched through the artifact collection.

Riony continued her own search for the source of the burning smell.

Where is it coming from?

Looking through the curtain to the bedroom, Riony's eyes widened, and she rushed over to their blankets-on-the-floor bed.

Crystal clinked as Lyrrin sorted through, reaching for something toward the back of the shelf. "Let me just show you the other combination I worked out last night. It's much better."

"Lyrrin. Lyz. My darling sister. Are you not seeing the fire? There is a *fire* in our *bed*." Riony grabbed handfuls of blankets, folding the coarsely woven wool over itself on top of the burning sections and smacking it with her

hands to smother the flames.

"It looks mostly put out now."

"And even worse, I am going to be *late*."

"It will only take a moment. It's really great, I promise." Riony stopped patting down the blankets and looked Lyrrin dead in the eye with an expression that slammed Lyrrin's mouth shut. "*You could have hurt Dracuni.*"

A silent *oh* formed on Lyrrin's lips. She solemnly slipped the carved crystal away into her pocket and turned to the unidragon. "I'm sorry."

Dracuni inhaled, then snorted breath out sharply twice in a row, nostrils flaring. **WAS LOUD. Hot loud. Scary loud.**

Riony winced and rubbed her forehead. "You still can't hear that?" she asked Lyrrin.

Pouting with the depth of how not being able to hear Dracuni's thoughts was the very worst thing in the entire world, Lyrrin shook her head.

"Dracuni forgives you," Riony replied.

Dracuni lowered her horned head and growled at the closest piece of shattered glow stone.

As though not wanting to be left out, Sir Butterfur Spelunkychunks popped out from under a corner of blanket that hadn't combusted, chittering angrily.

Lyrrin folded her arms. "I'm sorry, okay? But—"

"You're really bringing out a but? Right now?"

"*But* just listen to me! Can't you please trust me for once?"

"You just almost blew us up." Having thought she'd gotten the fire under control, Riony straightened out the blankets to inspect the damage and a glowing ember puffed up into flame again.

"It was an important experiment! It could have worked out really well. I had to try it. Like Pabba used to say, big dreams, bold deeds."

"Pabba didn't know about magical runes that could blow us up."

"And now I know what will happen next time I put those runes together."

"There will *not* be a next time." Butterfur pounced on Riony's hands as she returned to swatting out cinders, as though she were playing a game. To get him out of her way, she said, "Lyrrin has the treats."

The pale-furred otter zipped over to Lyrrin, who absentmindedly dropped a treat from her pocket into his mouth as she stared Riony down with an immovable glare. "I want to be able to help. I want to be able to make things to help protect Dracuni. And maybe not all my experiments are working, but you just haven't seen the good one yet. I worked out this new rune—"

"You're trying out new runes? I don't know about that."

"Just ones the delvers and other trades use but keep secret for themselves. It's good, trust me! And if I can work out one good one, maybe I can work out others even better, and if you just let me show—"

"I DON'T HAVE TIME!"

Lyrrin's eyes glossed over with tears in an instant.

Swearing softly to herself, Riony confirmed that the blanket was no longer on fire. Her nose still held the bitter scent of smoke, but it seemed as though nothing else was burning anymore and the shards had cooled.

Lyrrin glared, red-faced, as Riony checked her one working athame was in her belt pouch, then strapped on her belts with their ropes and pouches and her beloved dragonguard sword.

She went and knelt in front of Lyrrin as she did the buckles, then she took Lyrrin's hands in hers, giving them a small squeeze.

"I'm sorry. I'm sorry I yelled. But I have to go."

Dracuni perked up as Riony moved to the door. A wave of worry and longing washed over her and the unidragon mewled questioningly.

Go? Safe here. Stay!

Everything Riony had communicated to the unidragon since they had arrived back home was how the hatchling had to stay in their rooms to stay safe, and so Dracuni had developed a high level of anxiety at the idea of any of them leaving their home for the dangerous world beyond those rooms.

Poor little thing. How much longer are we going to be able to keep you couped up in here?

Apart from the logistics of keeping a growing part-dragon-creature alive and hidden, another worry had grown in Riony's head. The thought that maybe, once Dracuni was big enough to look after herself, she should be released into the wild. But that freedom would only come with other risks, of being hunted by dragonlords, tamed, and her special blood being discovered.

No. No way can I let that happen. Dracuni needed to be protected from them, and all dragon-obsessed psychos, including Kess. Riony had been on edge since running into the wolf-riding gremlin, but thankfully hadn't seen hide nor hair of those two beasts since getting home.

She waved to Dracuni and Lyrrin, a small ache in her heart at having to leave them, even for a short time.

"I have to go. This is going to be good for us. I'm coming home rich today, okay?" *As long as I don't get kicked out up front for being late.* Riony locked eyes with Lyrrin. "Clean up. No more experiments while I'm out. Look after Dracuni."

Lyrrin's mouth twitched but she didn't argue. She

moved beside Dracuni and wrapped an arm around the unidragon's neck. With how small Lyrrin was, and how big Dracuni was growing, they were almost the same height standing together like that.

Even Butterfur was growing, able to reach up to Lyrrin's hips as he begged for more food.

Lyrrin grumbled barely audibly. "Of course I'll look after Dracuni, and Riony has the treats."

Riony watched the approaching otter, shaking her head at the creature that had been smart enough to train into this game but not smart enough to know Lyrrin still had treats in her pocket.

It seemed to think the sisters had a magical pocket that the treats traveled between, only existing with one of them at a time, when they both kept plenty of treats on them. At least for now.

The initial outpouring of goodwill from the community that had fed the three of them well after returning as heroes had all but dried up, and with it, their pantry stores.

They wouldn't have to worry about going hungry again after today though. Riony had achieved her goal of becoming a delver; now she was going to be the best delver there was.

She was already mentally spending all the riches she intended on unearthing. Good food, a real bed, a larger dwelling for a growing family that included a dragon that seemed to be doubling in size every time Riony turned around.

Maybe a place big enough to have a separate, strong-walled room just for Lyrrin's experiments.

More otter treats. She dropped one from the now ever-present collection of crumbs in her belt pouch into Butterfur's awaiting grabby hands.

Riony pressed the mechanism to open the door. It rolled smoothly. Fixing that sticky mechanism was one small improvement in their lives, but after today, they could have many more.

Butterfur twirled around her ankles, sniffling up at her hands.

"Lyrrin has the treats," Riony said, and he ran back the other way again as she stepped out the door.

Lyrrin called out, "Wait! Riony?"

She turned back.

Lyrrin frowned, pouted, then lifted her chin. "Don't be late."

Riony huffed out in exasperation as the door closed between them. "Are you sparking kidding me?"

THREE

Riony took the fast way down from their high-level dwelling. And she took it faster than she ever had before. She skidded down carved limestone and vaulted over rooftops at a frantic rate. Muscle memory took over, knowing each tilt of slope, each point to kick off, each handhold to catch her landing.

She still scared herself when the sheer momentum she'd built up barreled her right off a rooftop she intended to land on, her body soaring through the air, momentarily weightless, before landing onto the next level down.

Holding on to a decorative column to steady herself, she smirked, laughed off the near miss, and then took off again.

Riony's face felt flushed, her heart pounding in sync

with the rhythmic beat of her footsteps. The underground city spread out beneath her, a labyrinth of narrow alleyways and makeshift dwellings stacked together between the stone-carved homes left behind by Alderkin.

The cavern echoed with the bustling of its inhabitants starting out their day, the dusty cave air thick with scents of mushroom-heavy meals cooking.

The familiar route down from Dragonwing Tower felt like an extension of herself, an intimate dance with the cyan-tinted undercity. And a strange sensation grew in her chest as a grin spread on her face. A feeling of belonging. A feeling that this place had finally become *home*.

The undercity. It had its own stark beauty, a starry sky of cyan lights spread over the rocky backdrop, made soft by all the inclusions humans brought to their life in the cave. Pennants, curtains, and tapestries brought splashes of color to the creamy-brown world.

Human refugees had only taken homes and tried their hands at underground farming in this one upper level of the Alderkin depths, but delvers had not yet found the end to how many lower levels there were. Some believed the Alderkin ruins burrowed right down into the center of the earth.

As Riony dropped off the final rooftop to street level, she thought she glimpsed some other shadowed form dashing over the roofs nearby, but she couldn't slow down to look again or question it. She raced on, propelled by a sense of urgency to not lose the thing she had long dreamed of and only just achieved.

She was a delver now. One of the brave few able to search the Alderkin depths for hidden riches. Riches that made life better for everyone in the undercity, who needed the glow stones and cooking crucibles and other Alderkin tools that made life underground possible.

Getting paid handsomely for providing those artifacts was just one of the perks. Perks Riony and her family desperately needed.

Ugh. I shouldn't have yelled at Lyrrin. But I can't screw this up.

The streets were more crowded than ever, but as she hurried through in her delver leathers, people took notice and moved out of her way.

In her haste, she caught glimpses of familiar faces—neighbors and friends she had come to know so well. The fried worm vendor, the baker with the crooked smile, the old lady who always had a kind word for her.

But there were many new faces in the undercity now.

More beggars took up residence on corners than ever before. Pained expressions were etched around their eyes. Wounds sustained during their flight to this sanctuary marked their bodies.

Wounds that had come both from the undead and the dragonriders' indiscriminate attempts to cleanse the world of those revenants through fire.

Every wounded or diseased person Riony saw felt like a stab of guilt. The anguished cry of a burned child, cradled in his begging mother's arms, seared Riony's conscience as intensely as if she stood before the full force of a dragon's burning breath.

Because she held a secret that could alleviate their suffering.

Because she guarded Dracuni and the unidragon's precious blood.

She yearned to share the miracle of Dracuni's blood, to offer solace and hope to those who suffered.

But how could she do that to Dracuni? How could she bleed that innocent creature to alleviate the pain of others?

That didn't feel like her decision to make, and the more she got to know Dracuni, sensing the creature's growing emotions and intelligence, the more she felt it was a choice the creature could and should make for itself.

Not to mention the utter chaos that could result in anybody discovering Dracuni and the existence of a living creature with unicorn blood. Riony was not prepared for an army to come knocking on her door to take Dracuni away. That didn't sound like a good time.

The decision that Dracuni must remain hidden, concealed from the prying eyes of those who might exploit her, still weighed heavy on Riony. Doubt gnawed at her, questioning the ethics of withholding something that could heal and save lives.

For now, though, Riony justified she had to focus on her own and her small family's lives. Honestly, Riony figured they were enough lives to be responsible for.

But still, when faced with the pain on the faces she passed, Riony had to look away in shame.

When I have plenty of riches from delving, then I can help those people out in other ways. Then I'll have enough to share.

The crowds thinned as Riony passed Curtain Market and went into the richer Upslope sector. The sound of the thin waterfall of the Sinking Stream pouring through the cave ceiling into the pool below echoed behind her.

At the far back of the cavern, the ceiling seemed much lower and the tunnel ahead was lined with thin, sharp stalagmites and stalactites—Dragon's Maw Descent, the deep-run access tunnel that was the planned starting location for today's delve. She broke into a full sprint then.

Dust puffed under Riony's pounding feet as she bounded down winding staircases, carved at a time long before Riony was born or could even fathom. The cool breeze that swept through the descending shaft whispered tales of forgotten ages, and excitement pulsed through Riony.

Rounding a corner, she saw teams of delvers lined up in groups of two and three. Pale-aqua light spilled around them from the bright glow stones held within netted pouches on their belts. Only about half the delvers Riony knew of remained, and another team split off and left as Master Brishan called out a location off his roster.

The head of the delvers loomed tall, even over Riony's height, a solid block of body draped in a thick cloak. One of the few Taens in the depths, his charcoal hair had a hint of silver, even in his beard, but Riony figured it was likely just due to age, rather than the use of silvernix in himself or his bloodline.

He didn't hold himself with the same royal arrogance as the steel-haired Hjelzahn siblings. But he did still braid his hair in the traditional Taen way.

Riony's breath caught, looking over the impressive sight of the delvers standing together. They ranged in age from those similar to Riony, up to a few grizzled veterans. Their entire vibe was built from well-defined muscle and pure grit.

All wore a similar set of leather armor, but those who had been in the profession longest had fitted theirs out with more accessories, more of the expensive cave silk ropes, finely crafted harnesses, Alderkin athames, and crystal artifacts.

Most of them had sleeves on their armor, but Riony opted for a sleeveless fit. A decision born from style rather than function, and the undying hope that Aishena may one day look at her with physical desire.

Yoskar was there with his stone-encrusted staff, Benjin close by his side. The younger brother was not yet a delver; however, he had remained with his older siblings regardless. Riony was starting to get to know some of the other delvers, but as she'd only just finished training, the proper delvers hadn't yet deemed it worth giving her the time of day.

Spotting Aishena and Niskina standing near the back of the group, Riony dashed forward in a crouch, skidding into place, then straightening up between them.

"You're late," Aishena hissed from behind a sheet of steel-toned hair.

Chest still heaving from her run, Riony shrugged. "I've been here this whole time. I'm honestly upset you didn't notice me."

Aishena sneered. "Maybe you should have been later. Or not shown up at all."

"You're cute when you're annoyed."

Niskina snorted.

"Hey." Riony winked at her.

"Hey," Niskina whispered back, beaming. "Am I cute, too?"

Riony leaned back as though to take in the large, curvy

young woman beside her. Niskina was something of the odd one out in the group of sharp-edged, grizzled strength. More softness and pouty smile with playful golden eyes and waves of chestnut hair tumbling around a glowing face.

A mix of Taen and Rolanian features gave her a striking appearance. She wore delver leathers, new and not yet scuffed from use, and unfastened down the front, showing a white shirt decorated with fine lace beneath.

"Cute? Yeah. But really more drop-dead gorgeous. Straight up dream material. Do I want to be you, or do I want to be with you? It's not even a question. It's both."

Niskina tittered a hushed giggle. "You're good for a girl's self-esteem, Ri."

"I could be good for a lot more if you were into girls."

"I know. It's a tragedy, honestly."

"Must you persistently flirt with every woman you see?" Aishena grumbled.

Riony tilted her head her way. "Aw, are you jealous?"

Aishena turned her back on Riony.

"Here, thanks for the lend." Riony reached into her largest belt pouch and pulled out a bound wad of worn papers. She handed the *Rebel Riders* chapters she'd borrowed during training back to Niskina.

Niskina clutched the serial to her chest. "Did you love it? Did you love the scene between Rider Jaym and his soul mate in the hot springs?"

"I learned things I didn't even know I needed to learn."

Brishan sent away a team with Jonna, Caed, and Daymora. Caed and Daymora hadn't given Riony much attention yet. Jonna, a V-shaped chunk of man-chest with a strong jaw and button nose combination that made him rather adorable, had made an effort to get to know Riony very quickly though, until it was clear she wasn't interested in men.

He didn't mind and suggested his access to plenty of other options was another perk of being a delver that Riony hadn't yet considered. That opened up a world of heart-racing possibilities in Riony's mind. Possibilities that the books she shared with Niskina detailed and added to in ways that made her flush hot all over.

Because while Riony liked to talk game, her position as a kid's sole, full-time carer didn't give her much opportunity to act on those words.

The way Daymora's eyes longingly followed Jonna as they walked away gave Riony hope of romance within the delver ranks as well.

Niskina tucked the booklet away, then pulled out another, handing it over to Riony. "Just wait until you see what happens next."

Riony took the offered serial reverentially, blushing as Niskina made a gesture more lewd than even Riony would consider making in their current company. Niskina was quickly becoming her new favorite person.

The exchange lured Aishena's judgmental attention back to Riony. She kept her voice low as Brishan continued to send away delvers to their work locations. "Why are you late? I thought maybe you'd chickened out."

"Chickened out?" Riony gasped, appalled.

"Lost your nerve, gave up the ghost, bailed faster than a pirate with a chest of gold and a hole in their rowboat," Niskina clarified.

"My shock was based on the idea that I would be scared of this, not from lack of understanding the term."

"You should be scared," Aishena spat. "If you aren't, maybe you need to go back into training because clearly you didn't learn anything. It's dangerous down there. The Alderkin traps are one thing, then there are the cave spiders, giant olms, ghost snakes ... And why did you bring that ridiculous sword of yours along?"

Riony patted her sword in its sheath and the end bumped against the wall behind her. "I don't go anywhere without my good luck sword."

"It's too big. It's going to get in the way."

"You'll change your mind when I'm chopping up those spiders and olms and snakes with it."

More delvers around them left for their allocated

delving sites, thinning the group down even more. Brishan checked his papers, then looked over the remaining delvers. "Yoskar, you can be on cataloguing today with me, since you have Benjin with you."

Yoskar nodded solemnly, and Benjin, by his side, glowered over a puckered mouth. The Hjelzahn siblings hadn't left the youngest brother alone for a moment since his recent kidnapping. They moved from the remaining delvers over beside Brishan.

Glancing at the remaining few delvers, Brishan met Riony's gaze.

"Riony Eyfarr, glad you decided to join us."

"Very glad to be here, Master Brishan, and I'm very sorry for being late."

Brishan's lips twitched beneath his bushy mustache. "I noticed you still had time for trading those trashy stories with my daughter."

"I'm sorry, Mast—"

"Call my stories trashy one more time and you've lost any chance of me participating in this stupid job." Niskina folded her arms and pouted her full lips at him like pointing a weapon.

Riony's eyes widened. She knew Niskina was Brishan's daughter, and Niskina had made her rebellious dislike of being pushed into the delving profession clear during their training. But to see her talk back to Master Brishan so openly made Riony's eye twitch.

"They are dangerous propaganda. *Rebel Riders*? Riding untamed dragons?" Brishan scoffed.

"Riding untamed dragons *and* protecting their soul mates with the power of their chiseled chests," Niskina said.

"It's utter nonsense."

"That's it. I'm leaving."

"Nisk!" Brishan looked more embarrassed than anything. His cheeks reddened around his facial hair and he took a step toward her.

Riony averted her eyes. They were the last delvers left now, the Hjelzahn siblings, Niskina, Brishan, and Riony, but it still felt like too many people to be witnessing the standoff between father and daughter.

Niskina turned back. "It's not nonsense. It makes more sense to be up there fighting for something like the Rebel Riders, than hiding down here digging around in this cursed Alderkin grave to make ourselves rich."

Brishan folded up his papers slowly and put them away, his shoulders lifting, then sagging. He fixed his daughter with a firm gaze. "Niskina, you're on cataloguing as well with me today."

Niskina looked longingly toward Riony and Aishena. "Can't I at least—"

"No. Aishena, you're with Riony. Take Section Thirty." He pointed to a narrow tunnel just across from them.

"Yes, Master Brishan," Aishena barked, standing straight.

Riony echoed her a moment afterward, awkwardness delaying her tongue. She had done her best to study the delvers' maps but hadn't yet memorized the different locations in the confusing three-dimensional maze of tunnels and caverns beneath the undercity.

Although she *had* laughed for a solid half hour over finding out one of the delving tunnels was called Wet Descent. *Wet Descent.* Riony snorted.

But Section Thirty sounded promising. The higher the number, the more recently the area had been opened up to delving.

Niskina stared at her father for a moment, then leaned against a nearby wall, pulled out another booklet, and started reading.

Waving a dismissive hand at her, Brishan reached out and tapped Aishena's shoulder, then beckoned her and Yoskar away from the others. "A word before you go."

Riony pretended not to listen as he spoke softly to them. She only heard every few words. *Cousin ... He ... Brought ... Dead ... News ... Heir.* Aishena's face paled, but she didn't seem surprised. Yoskar just nodded grimly and met Aishena's searching gaze.

"Back to work. We can talk later," Yoskar said, flashing a look at Riony's unsubtle eavesdropping.

Aishena nodded. She chewed her lip for a moment as she watched Yoskar return to Benjin's side, then came back to Riony.

"Is ... everything okay?" Riony asked.

"Perfectly fine," Aishena growled. "Stop gawking at me. Get moving."

"Great. Love the energy. Excited to spend the day with you."

As Riony and Aishena stepped toward their allocated tunnel, a warm glow lit the stones before them. Then a buzzing sound echoed up the passageway.

"Glowflies," Aishena grumbled. She stepped back out of the way, leaving Riony in the path of the swarming insects.

The bright bugs fluttered past Riony like a rush of warm air, ignoring her in their apparent haste. Each golden glowing abdomen looked like a flying ember as they flew by, tangling in Riony's hair and butting up against her face and hands when she tried to ward them off.

The air was thick with them. Riony had to close her mouth and eyes to avoid the finger-sized insects flying into them. The critters were common enough in the depths, normally hanging around, unlit, on the rough ceilings of the caves. Riony had never seen so many, all flying together with some common purpose.

The humming eased and Riony opened her eyes to see the last few bugs zip by.

Brishan watched as the insects cleared out. "Scratch Section Thirty for today. You two head over to Section Three."

"Section Three?" Aishena practically whined.

Gaping, Riony asked, "What? Why?"

Without lifting her eyes from her book, Niskina said, "You never head down a tunnel glowflies are swarming away from. It's always a sign there's something down that way you don't want to mess with."

"That wasn't covered in training," Riony muttered.

"Section Three?" Aishena questioned again. "There's nothing in Three. We cleared it out ages ago."

Brishan leaned over her, raising an eyebrow. "Then clear it out again. Unless you and the tardy new recruit would rather sit out the next few weeks?"

Riony winced at the word *tardy*. And *sit out*. And *weeks*.

"We'll do Section Three, Master Brishan." Aishena grabbed Riony by the elbow and dragged her away down the tunnel in the other direction.

When they were far enough away that their voices wouldn't echo back to the others, Aishena grumbled, "Look what I get for vouching for you. Section Three? This is glorified babysitting."

"When you said cleared out, do you mean nice and safe from nasties but still filled with treasure?"

"I mean empty, bare, lucky to find a rock left to refill the ones in your head that you seem to use for thinking."

Riony's heart sank. She was supposed to come home rich today. If she came home empty-handed, it was going to be even harder to face Lyrrin after yelling at her.

She looked over her shoulder to see Brishan leading Niskina, Yoskar, and Benjin away into another nearby tunnel. "Then let's do Section Thirty. We just sneak back that way and—"

"Were you not listening, or do you just not believe that we could actually know something more than you? You *do not* go down a tunnel glowflies are flying from. You go down that tunnel, you don't come back alive, you ridiculous tame-brained lout."

"I'm so glad you warmed up to me and respect me so much more now after our life-threatening adventure together."

Aishena glared.

"Okay, okay. We'll try to make the most of Section Three then. There must be something still around there that we can dig up."

"This is such a waste of time." Aishena sighed but continued moving to their designated area. "At the very least we can show Brishan that you can follow orders and

do as you're told. Then maybe next time he'll give you a better area, and me too if I'm stuck with you again."

"You think there will still be a next time?" Riony asked with more vulnerability in her voice than she wanted to display.

"Look, Brishan seems to like you. Stop preening! The sun only knows why he's taken a liking to *you*. But sort yourself out, because one more screwup and you're out. And he doesn't abide disobedience or risk-taking. So ... good luck with that."

"What? I can be obedient and not take risks."

Aishena laughed bitterly. "Your *very first* impulse was to sneak around his orders and run down the tunnel of imminent death. Sparks, you're probably going to find some way to get yourself killed in the boring empty rooms we're stuck with."

"We *could* make the time in the empty rooms together more interesting."

"And it's probably going to be me that ends up killing you."

Faced with the threat of death on all sides, or even worse, the risk of losing her new job, Riony made her one smart decision of the morning and stopped talking.

Instead, she turned her mind to the impossible challenge of how she was supposed to follow orders, not take risks, but somehow miraculously not go home empty-handed.

FOUR

"Sparks," Riony huffed. "I really am sorry I was late. Do you think if we go back to Brishan and beg—"

"Because Niskina has obviously left him in a good mood to be doing favors for us." Aishena gave Riony the driest of glares.

Section Three was as bare as Aishena's levels of tolerance for Riony's flirting. Surveying the space, a cold, hard lump built in Riony's chest.

There's nothing here. Although the walls of the interconnected chambers showed beautiful carvings that may have once been the framing of a richly furnished Alderkin dwelling, everything else had been cleared away.

Every sconce had been stripped of glow stones. All

furniture, tapestries, rugs—gone. All shelves lay empty except for strands of dusty webbing. Not even enough of that to gather up and sell to the rope makers.

Riony ran her hands up over her head, turning to take in the barren space. They were only one floor down beneath the undercity, barely far enough away that Riony felt as though she'd delved at all. She could practically still hear Niskina and Brishan's arguing echoing down the stairs from above.

They'd quarreled during training too, as Niskina debated all the reasons why she didn't want to become a delver like her father, but it was worse today, now that Niskina had officially been made one regardless.

Niskina seemed to be quite smart, smarter than Riony considered herself to be, but on the other hand despised delving and loudly dreamed of returning to the overworld, so Riony couldn't entirely be sure if the girl was sane of mind.

Delving had been Riony's goal for so long that the current situation felt like being smacked in the face with her own dismembered hand—both painful and humiliating. The chambers around her were as simple and domestic as the ones humans had taken over on the top level. Not one bit of the treasures and adventure Riony had dreamed of.

Aishena had already done one quick turn around the sprawling interconnected rooms of what must have once been a grand dwelling, decided it really was empty and without even any nasty cave creatures to take her anger out on, then had dumped herself down on a raised block to sulk.

Riony had followed her, a few steps behind, taking in the flat stone surfaces of each room, hoping she'd see something new that had been missed before. There was only one closed door they didn't go through, which Aishena ignored, and all Riony saw besides stone walls, stone floors, and stone ceilings was the layer of dust over those surfaces.

As Aishena had said, not even a loose stone that Riony could have kicked in frustration. So she had to settle for pacing up and down in front of Aishena.

She chewed her lip and looked sideways at Aishena. The Taen probably-Dragon King-heir really hadn't warmed up to Riony much after getting back to the depths.

Yes, she and Yoskar had vouched for Riony with Brishan, but they had been more closed off than ever, the three siblings a silent, secretive unit.

Riony tried to be respectful of their privacy but couldn't help being entirely curious ever since the revelation their mother was out there looking for them.

Maybe if she couldn't dig up any treasures that day, she could at least discover something new about Aishena.

"Sooo ... Brishan seems to like you and Yoskar, too. Does he know, you know, that you're a Hjelzahn—"

"Shut it!" Aishena snapped, eyes darting for unlikely eavesdroppers. "Yes, he knows. He used to be a grayglim, worked with my mother. But a very long time ago."

A grayglim? Riony stifled a *phwoar* sound. She had only seen one of those elite royal bodyguards once in her life back at Heithorn Estate. They were as good as ghosts, the kind you were only likely to see when it meant your own imminent death. If the Hjelzahns' mother was one, then Aishena's stealthy proficiencies made sense.

"Does he know why you three are down here?"

"If that's your awful way of trying to find out for yourself why we came to the undercity, then you're thicker than I thought."

"It is nice to know you think of me." Riony rested her hand on her sword, making the sheath swing behind her. "I guess I'm just trying to understand, you know, why you three would leave home? I know the delving life is pretty good—usually—but only if you're not already coming from something better."

Aishena pushed her hair away from her face and stood up to glare at Riony. "You have no idea what we came from. You have no idea and no reason to need one and no right to ask. We are not friends and you are not my confidant so just mind your depths-damned business. There's nothing for you to know."

"Got it." Riony held up her hands in surrender. Clearly, nerves were too raw to be prodded. "I'll leave it. But ... If you do ever need someone to talk to, I am here for you. And I can keep a secret. Sometimes it can be good to share the load."

Aishena turned away, taking her turn to stalk back and forth within the room. Riony watched the tight, high shoulders and tense neck of the delver and knew that whatever secret she and her siblings were keeping, it certainly wasn't nothing.

If they really wanted to remain hidden, they should have dyed their hair like I do with Lyrrin. Hair that color screamed wealthy lineage and was rare in the undercity. Aishena flicked her silky-straight silver hair over her shoulder so she could turn back and glare at Riony some more.

Riony desperately sought around for a rock to kick again. This was going to be a long, painful day.

"Hey," she called over to Aishena. "What about that closed door? What's the story with it?"

"Jammed."

Riony headed through to the next room where the closed door was located and looked it over, testing the opening mechanism and trying to give it a bit of a push. The stone didn't budge.

Aishena appeared beside her. "I told you, it's jammed.

Which means it's been purposefully sealed and most likely trapped as well. Doors like that are better left shut."

Riony ran her fingertips over the large round slab. "You're telling me this has never been opened?"

"Because it can't be and it's too big of a risk to open even if it could."

"But there could be anything on the other side." The prospect of untouched riches practically had Riony salivating. She tried pushing at the door again.

"Yes. Exactly. Bad anythings. Trying to get that door open could trigger this whole place to collapse."

Riony shook her head, undeterred. She pulled her cutting athame from her belt. "Then we cut our way through."

Aishena rubbed her forehead. "I know training mostly just covers basic safety, survival, and knot tying, but you can't really think you could cut through there, even with your athame. That stone would be almost as thick as your head."

Riony held out her hands, measuring. "That's not that thick. Oh. Okay. Yes, very funny."

"So glad you're amused."

Riony sniffed, darting her gaze over the blocked doorway. "Look, it's not my fault. No mention at all about glowflies or jammed doors. How much else wasn't I taught?"

"Delving consists more of on-the-job training. Like getting to know the limits of your tools and that the athame would run out of charge before you cut something big enough to fit a normal person through. Let alone something your size."

"Been sizing me up, have you?" Riony smirked.

"Only in your dreams."

There was the slightest hint of red over Aishena's ashy-tan cheeks that may have just been Riony's wishful thinking.

Aishena shook her head at Riony and her continued investigation. "There are plenty of other spaces to search, when Brishan isn't choosing to punish us, rather than waste time trying to get through a jammed door."

"But I mean, we're here anyway ..." Riony moved across to the side, feeling around on the hollow wall beside the door that the stone would slide into, if it opened. She thumped her fist against the cold limestone in a few places, listening to the returned sounds.

"What in the depths are you doing?"

"I managed to fix my sticky front door." Riony turned and grinned back at Aishena. "I just had to find where the mechanism was jammed and reach it."

"You really got it working again?" Aishena sounded skeptical.

"Yeah. It was easy. It just took some trial and error." Then Riony added in a quiet voice, "And almost losing my arm."

Riony turned back to the wall, then traced the cutting rune on her athame. It activated with a yellow glow, and Riony again marveled how the object had somehow recharged itself during their trip aboveground.

She found her target site and pressed the tip of the crystal blade into the limestone. It sliced in as smooth as butter and slowly, Riony worked to cut a rough circle, just large enough to fit her arm into.

It took a couple of minutes, during which Aishena huffed and Riony fretted that the charge of her athame would be spent, but soon the line of the circle closed and Riony juggled the resulting plug of stone from the wall.

She gave Aishena a smug look as she deactivated her athame. Holding her glow stone up to the hole, she peered inside the hollow double wall.

The insides were a marvel of stone and crystal mechanisms, from fine, weblike cogs and wheels to solid counterweights and moving levers. Most had been marked with harden runes, used to make the limestone behave more like steel. Riony couldn't identify the other runes, but imagined they might be used to make the parts run smoothly together without lubrication or weigh more than usual, and stars knew what other Alderkin magic.

The runes didn't matter though, as clearly they weren't intended to be manually activated. Like the harden runes, maybe they never needed to be reactivated after the initial function.

"Yeah, there it is! It's basically the same problem I had with mine, but worse. I just need to ..." Riony wriggled her hand into the hole, getting it in past the wrist, twisted around, and pressed in up to her elbow, turned again, shuffled closer, and pushed until her shoulder was pressed against the wall and the cut circle cuffed tight around her biceps.

"I should have cut this a bit bigger. Didn't realize my arms had gotten larger. I've been training more lately, can you tell?" She looked hopefully back at Aishena.

Aishena pinched the bridge of her nose and looked at the floor. "Please get your arm out of there before you set off a trap and bury us alive."

"I've got this. This is easy and doesn't count as risk-taking at all." Riony felt around inside the hollow wall, squeezing her hand down through the complex carved stone mechanism. It was tight, and her fingers scraped and caught. "Certainly not a big risk, anyway."

"Riony ..." Aishena growled warningly.

Riony ignored her. She groped blindly down through the labyrinth of stone shapes, feeling for the piece she needed to adjust.

There was just one line of bearings that had been pushed off track, whether by accident or design of someone

trying to block this path for good. Riony pressed her cheek against the cold stone, reaching farther. Her fingertips rolled over the smooth bearings, rounding them up and bringing them into the groove they belonged in.

The final one slipped into place and they rolled together down the line.

A harsh, scraping sound filled the room. The stone door rolled.

Very quickly, right toward Riony's arm.

"Riony!" Aishena cried.

"Sparks!" Riony tugged at her arm, hoping it would just slip right out, but it was twisted and turned down though the gaps of the mechanism.

Riony eyed the approaching stone as it vanished into the wall, right toward her stuck limb. She breathed slowly and worked on reversing the path she'd woven her fingers down through.

Her bicep scraped clear, and she twisted to adjust her elbow to bring it through too.

Aishena grabbed her other arm and pulled, causing her elbow to bend the wrong way and block up the hole.

"That's not helping!" Riony cried.

Aishena's face went gray, and she let go, running over to the rolling door and trying to grab hold of it there. Her wiry muscles and slim figure had no chance of anchoring the massive rock.

Riony felt the approaching stone brush the back of her hand, pushing against it. With one final yank that bent bones in her wrist the wrong way, Riony's hand came free from the hole, and she fell backward onto her bottom.

Riony examined the scrapes and reddening skin around her hand, then chuckled. "Told you I could get it open. And I didn't lose an arm! That's two-zero for me versus doors!"

Aishena didn't reply. She stood in the now opened doorway, staring into the room beyond.

Riony got up to her feet, dusting herself off and wincing at her aching wrist. "Okay, so it was a bit of a risk. Sorry. I was only joking before about losing an arm. My door back at home wasn't nearly that close a call. Losing an arm really isn't something I want to do."

Aishena still didn't reply. Riony stepped over next to her and looked into the revealed room. Her jaw dropped.

"I take it back. I would have happily lost an arm for this."

The modestly sized room before them was pristine, a perfect time capsule, preserving a window into the forgotten Alderkin era. Statues, paintings, and ornate weaponry adorned the walls.

Glittering jewelry and ancient tomes were laid out on shelves, and a large, low bed sat right in the middle of the room, embroidered blankets tossed back, unmade, from the last time the inhabitant of this space had woken up, never to return.

"I am going to be so stinking rich!" Riony crowed.

Aishena raised her eyebrows. "We. We are."

"Shut up. You're already rich and who risked their arm for this?"

"Delver hauls get split evenly and don't you dare mention anything to Brishan about risking an arm when this gets reported."

Riony huffed but couldn't shake the grin off her face. Even splitting the value of what was before them, she was going to be rich. She and Lyrrin and Dracuni, and even Sir Butterfur Spelunkychunks would have everything they needed, everything they wanted.

We're having fried rope worm tonight!

She took a step into the room.

"Careful," Aishena warned.

"Come on, let's see what we can carry out of here! Try to show a little positivity sometimes!" Riony rested her hand on her sword hilt and spun around to pull a face at Aishena.

The tension of something catching against the end of the scabbard then snapping was so slight, Riony almost dismissed it as her imagination.

Then the entire room trembled. Dust cascaded from the ceiling as a low rumble built through the chamber.

Panic flashed in Aishena's eyes. "We need to get out, now!"

Riony broke into motion, dashing back to the newly opened door. The ground tremored beneath her, and the walls groaned, and the thunderous slamming sound of ceiling hitting floor came from right at her heels.

The destruction didn't end at the threshold.

Dust and debris engulfed Riony and Aishena. They ran together back for the entrance through a landslide of crumbling stones.

The walls closed in on them, and Riony's heart pounded in her ears as loud as the falling rocks. She could barely see though the choking haze as they made a frantic scramble for the exit.

With a final, desperate leap, the two of them burst through the collapsing entrance, landing sprawled onto the stairs leading up.

Gasping for breath, Riony turned to see what remained. The rooms behind them were filled completely with rubble and dust, the ancient treasures entombed once more.

A million nasty, sweary thoughts raced through Riony's head as she stared at the destroyed chambers. She felt even worse when she saw Aishena's wrathful expression.

"Oops?" Riony muttered.

Aishena glared, open-mouthed, at Riony for a long moment before covering her face with both hands and lying back on the steps.

Riony wondered if it wasn't too late to throw herself back under the rubble and hope for a swift death. Her heart pounded from the race to safety, aching with each beat at what they'd just lost.

It wasn't long before the sounds of destruction brought the clamor of footsteps rushing their way. Brishan and Niskina, along with Jonna, Caed, and Daymora, raced down the stairs toward them.

"Is everyone okay? Any injuries?" Niskina was first beside Riony, checking her over in the cyan light of her glow stone. She touched gentle fingers to Riony's temples and neck. Even her beautiful, tender attention wasn't enough to console Riony.

"What in the depths happened?" Brishan demanded gruffly as he waved away the dust and stared at the collapsed chambers.

Riony winced. "We, aah, *I* opened a jammed door."

"What? How?"

"You just have to reach into the wall and jiggle things around and then pull your arm out in time once the door gets moving again." Riony demonstrated the actions with her arm, and Brishan's gaze followed the swelling redness on her wrist.

Niskina noticed too and grabbed it, pressing to check for breaks.

"Scratch that. Why? Why did you even open it?" Brishan swung his anger over toward Aishena. "Didn't you tell her that would be dangerous? Not to open jammed doors?"

"I did try," Aishena grumbled.

Riony shrugged off Niskina's attention, flushing hot from her ears to her collarbones. "It was fine, really, and it would have been worth it. You should have seen the room we opened up!"

"Except unfortunately the interior of the room was also trapped. Which I'm sure I also warned you about," Aishena added.

"It might have been mentioned." Riony finally found a rock to kick, one of many now, and pushed it off the stairs with her toe. Gently. Not wanting to set off any more disasters.

It was bad enough that Aishena glowered so disapprovingly at her, not to mention Niskina's pitying eyes and Brishan's gruff stare. But it was even worse to have the additional audience of the more experienced delver trio casting judgment over her too.

Jonna folded his arms over his chest and leaned toward Daymora as though gossiping. "Gonna take months to excavate all that out if we want to go through there again. Access to three other sectors, gone."

She shook her head. Brown hair, cut sharp at her jawline, swung like a hangman's rope. "A big sparking mess. Could also destabilize Section Twenty-One. It's right under here."

Caed simply turned his back on Riony, which felt like the harshest reproach of all.

"I'm sorry," Riony said.

Brishan grumbled incoherently and then crouched down in front of her. "Kid, listen, I know you're keen. But you've got to be more careful. You can't just deal with problems by throwing your body at them as though it's expendable. Because you'll spend it real quick down here. It's not worth it. And until you can understand that, I can't let you down here again. I can't have that on my conscience."

Riony's eyes glossed over as she locked them with his. "Master Brishan, please, I've already learned my lesson. I'll be so much more careful next time."

He shook his head and stood up, turning away from her too. "Go home."

Home. Home with nothing. Home, having lost everything she'd dreamed of. She couldn't.

Riony sprang to her feet beside him. "I need this. I can't … You don't understand how much I need this."

Niskina rose up beside her. She gave Riony a long look, as though pondering why someone would so desperately want this career she seemed to despise. Then she whispered softly, "Fadda, please?"

Exhaling a loud groan, Brishan turned back around and looked Riony over with a scowl. "Go home."

Riony's heart felt frozen solid.

Then Brishan continued. "Sort yourself out. And come back tomorrow. You've got one last chance. If you even slightly screw up again, you're out for good."

FIVE

Riony thought things couldn't possibly get any worse. She moped her way home, sore inside and out, empty-handed except the weight of her shame.

Delving wasn't what she thought it would be. She'd imagined the delvers plunging through the ancient depths with brave, reckless abandon, snatching treasures from the grasps of great peril.

But her attempt to take a risk in return for the chance of a reward was met with everybody sneering at her as though she were the dumbest stack of rocks they'd ever seen. It had also almost ended with her and Aishena being flattened by a stack of rocks too. Which might have been less painful.

Riony's cheeks burned so hot they were probably the color of her hair.

Recklessly throwing her body at problems had served her well in the past, and it felt like a betrayal that it had failed her now.

She passed by Curtain Market, the richer, Upslope trading area where she could have sold the Alderkin artifacts she'd found, if they weren't buried under a mountain of stone. Where she could have bought every tasty treat the vendors sold, come home the hero with two fried rope worms each for her, Lyrrin, Dracuni, and Butterfur.

I have another chance tomorrow. I'll do it all right tomorrow. No risks. No mistakes. I'll even leave my sword at home. Riony didn't like the idea of that final thought. The weight of the dragonguard sword at her hip felt like part of her body. She felt safer with it.

Another sensation washed over her as she meandered down the Flowstone Steps and toward the Grand Arch that led to her home district. A jab of fear, distant and strange. She could feel it tug at her insides, like a pull in the direction of home.

It felt almost like Dracuni's fear, but Riony knew she was still too far from the unidragon to feel that now. She wrote it off as her own feelings of fear at returning home empty-handed.

Lyrrin is going to be so disappointed.

Riony paused, almost turning to head back to the markets. Maybe she should sell off her cutting athame and say that was what she'd earned that day? Then nobody at home would have to know how bad she messed up.

Unless she screwed up again and tomorrow was her last day of delving ever. Then they'd know, and know she lied as well. Riony didn't like being dishonest with Lyrrin and generally was awful at delivering convincing lies anyway. She just didn't have the face for it.

One of the many reasons she'd receive whippings back in her days with the Heithorns.

And what if the sovs she got from selling the athame were the last she'd ever get and she and Lyrrin and Dracuni would all starve? Riony didn't count Butterfur. The tricky little fur-sausage would abandon them in a second once the treats ran dry and would be fine on his own.

Another wave of emotion rushed Riony. More worry, but also a bone-deep tiredness. Riony's shoulders slumped. All she wanted to do was get home and curl up with Dracuni on their singed and smoky blankets and feel sorry for herself. She ran her hands over her face, and when she looked up again, there was Lyrrin.

The child, hood up and gloves on, was running straight toward her, Butterfur chasing after like a streak of caramel silk. Lyrrin's cheeks were pink, and a worried look widened her bright eyes.

"Riony!" she cried out when she spotted her big sister, then—

"Are you okay?" they both gasped together.

Riony shook her head. "Fine. What are you doing out here? You should be with *your new pet*. Is your new pet okay?"

Lyrrin nodded vigorously, her expression still anxious. "She's fine. Darris came, ran a message to me, said something happened at delving and that you were hurt!"

Riony scanned over the crowd and spotted the boy about a block back, watching from a street corner with pursed lips before he dashed out of sight.

Riony frowned. How did the gossip spread so quickly? Did everyone know? She worked her lips to force out the shameful truth. "There was an accident. I made a mistake, but I'm fine. Everything is okay." *As long as I don't screw up again.* "You didn't need to leave your pet. You should have stayed with her."

"Darris said it was bad, that you were hurt bad, and I had to come right away."

Butterfur stood up on his back legs, nipping at Lyrrin's gloved fingers and trying to reach his paw into her pocket. With an annoyed huff, she picked him up and dropped him inside her shirt, patting him through the cloth to settle him.

Confusion crinkled Riony's brow. "Well, he was wrong. And you still should have stayed home. Your new pet comes first, always."

A red tint flushed around Lyrrin's eyes and they glossed over. "You're my sister. You matter too."

Riony simply shook her head.

"Dra—"

"Shh! *Your pet*," Riony shushed, wishing she'd given the unidragon a less obvious name for use in public discussions.

"She's okay. She was sleeping anyway. Are you *sure* you're okay? You don't have to hide it to make me feel better." Lyrrin had her clever eyes on the red swelling on Riony's wrist.

It was Riony's turn for her eyes to water. She wanted to vent everything, to swear and cry and be told she hadn't messed up despite knowing she really, really had. But she didn't want that comfort from Lyrrin.

She wanted that from her amma and pabba who she could never see again. Who would never comfort her again.

Riony opened her mouth to again express her okay-ness, when a bustle of children from the orphanage raced by, giggling and gasping.

"No way you saw a wolf," one of them huffed from the back of the pack.

The leader called over her shoulder, "I so did! Let's find it! Let's hunt the wolf!"

Every nerve inside of Riony caught ablaze. Dread curled within her. The sensations from Dracuni, a fear so strong it had reached her all the way out here …

She and Lyrrin stared at each other for a long heartbeat.

And then they ran.

Riony forged a path through the crowds, breaking ahead of Lyrrin on her longer legs. Bystanders swore as her shoulders crashed against them, but she didn't slow down. Rounding one corner, then another, the stairs leading up and up and up to their home were in sight.

Riony bounded over them, legs burning as she leaped three steps at a time. She had ascended more than halfway up the huge stalagmite when Lyrrin cried out in alarm from back at ground level.

"There!"

Grasping the low stone balustrade, Riony leaned over, casting her gaze to where Lyrrin pointed.

A shadowy form prowled below, jumping from rooftop to rooftop. Passing through a lit section, the form of the large gray wolf became clear and so did his wretched rider, and the limp, bound form of Dracuni, lying across Kess's lap.

"No," Riony breathed the word.

The wolf's ears twitched, and Kess turned back. She

smirked as their eyes locked, then her wolf pounced down again, out of sight onto ground level.

Lyrrin was already running that way, just a street off from where Kess went, from her closer starting position on the ground.

Riony vaulted over the low stone wall, off the steps, racing down the steepest part of the immense stalagmite structure. Her feet skidded, and she leaned back, sliding down in more of a fall than a run, her palms grazing against the stone as she steadied herself.

Her heart raced, worried she wouldn't catch Kess in time. Worried Lyrrin wouldn't catch Kess in time. Worried Lyrrin *would* catch Kess before her and it wouldn't end well for Lyrrin.

The shadowed shape she'd seen before on her way to delving must have been Kess and her wolf. If only she'd slowed to look then, if only she'd had time. Riony cursed under her breath.

The point Riony had left the stairs at wasn't her usual route down. The melted wax formations of stone bumped under her feet, threatening to buck her off and send her tumbling headfirst to the ground.

The slope plateaued below her where a natural limestone pool had formed and dried. Riony leaned into the rock, grasping at it to slow her descent before she hit the flat section.

It came up fast, and her legs buckled beneath her when she hit. She rolled across it, missed catching the rimstone edge, and plummeted down to the ground level below.

The short fall ended quickly in a puff of dust and spores. She found herself in the back of a small goat cart, filled with mushroom waste headed for the livestock.

"Where in the stars did you come from?" the elderly woman leading the goat sputtered.

Riony shook off the fall, got her bearings, and took off again, not even sparing breath for an apology.

More voices went up as she left a trail of stinking brown dust in her wake. Teeth gritted, she ran on, ignoring the indignant stares and the ache in her jarred bones. Nothing mattered other than reaching Dracuni in time.

She was not letting that miserable goblin steal the unidragon. Because she knew exactly what Kess wanted, and exactly what that would mean for Dracuni. Riony wasn't going to let that happen, no matter what.

The way Dracuni was draped, bound and drowsy over the wolf's shoulders, Riony worried she might be too late. *No. Kess wouldn't need to tie her up if she'd already been tamed.*

Riony had lost sight of both Kess and Lyrrin by then, despite getting down from Dragonwing Tower faster than she ever had before. She dashed down the narrow pathways toward where she'd last seen them heading. It led to the back entrance toward the Orphan's Den.

Speeding down that narrow tunnel, Riony saw Lyrrin far ahead, running out the other end toward the mushroom farms.

I've almost caught up. I've got you, Kess.

She followed Lyrrin's path, through the gasping crowd that obviously just had a front row view of a wolf running by, and into Whisperwind Passage, the same tunnel that led up to the hole into the mountains.

As Riony reached the entrance, she could only see the barest glimpse of gray fur ahead in the tunnel, where it split in three directions.

Lyrrin pulled a glow stone from her pocket. The one she'd jammed in there before, that had some alteration to it that she'd wanted to show Riony.

Riony had almost reached Lyrrin as the girl stopped and traced over the two runes on that stone.

"What are you doing?" Riony gasped.

"We can't catch them! We have to slow them down." The glow stone shimmered to life with a hum of magic, and Lyrrin pulled back her arm to throw it.

"No! It might hurt Dracuni!"

"Trust me! Just close—"

"Lyrrin, don't! I can catch them!"

But the glow stone was already arching through the air.

Riony sprinted harder, heart ready to burst. She had to get to Dracuni before whatever those runes did went off. But the rounded chunk of calcite sailed through the air so much faster than Riony could move.

Kess turned back, frowning at the brightness coming her way. The crystal clinked on the stone floor, bounced, and rolled to a stop at the wolf's feet.

Lyrrin cried out at Riony's back, "Stop! You have to close your—"

Riony saw only white. She threw an arm up in front of her face a moment too late as the glow stone crackled with magic and filled the tunnel with a burst of light so strong it seared Riony's eyes, making them burn and fill with tears as though someone had carved them both out with a hot spoon.

She prepared to be hit with a hail of fiery cinders, but only the brilliant glow filled the air, pulsing again and again, each burst duller than the last, until the charge wore out and Riony was left in darkness.

It shouldn't be this dark. There should be light from my glow stone.

Somewhere nearby, the wolf let out an ear-splitting whine.

"What was that?" Kess growled. "Go. Just move, you dumb animal!"

Riony rubbed at her eyes, trying to clear them. She blinked and squinted around the glowing blobs that filled her vision. Blurry shapes moved nearby, and the wolf snuffled and whimpered. It was close, really close.

Riony lunged, trying to catch and grab the animal. Fur slipped through her fingers. Kess cried out.

"Razing ... ugh!" Something glanced off Riony's waist. It skipped over the leather armor, then clattered on the ground. A knife? Kess didn't normally miss. She must be blinded too.

That was a small relief.

"She's to your right. Grab them!" Lyrrin called out, her small footsteps pounding up behind Riony.

Riony threw herself in a wide-armed grapple, stumbling into empty air and landing on her knees.

"Go, go!" Kess yelled.

The wolf growled, and Riony felt the flick of its tail lash by, heard the muted patter of its running paws, heard the impact as it stumbled into a wall.

"They're getting away!" Lyrrin said from Riony's side.

"And I can't see a sparking thing!" Riony snapped.

"If you'd just listened to me and closed your eyes, we could have caught them!" Lyrrin yelled back.

Riony curled her hands into fists. She turned her eyes side to side, trying to will the blurry splotches away. She found that when she looked directly at something it was nothing but a distorted shadow, but she was starting to be able to see around the edges, the very periphery of her vision clearing.

But that meant it could be clearing for Kess and the wolf too.

"Which way did they go?" She pushed back up onto her feet, wiping her still leaking eyes and trying to feel for where she was in the intersection.

"That way."

Riony could barely make out the small, wobbly shape that was her sister. "*Lyrrin!* I can't see."

"The first on the left." Her voice was small and wavery.

Riony exhaled a low sigh. Kess and the wolf had gone the wrong way, taken the turn into a tunnel that headed downward rather than up to the exit. She might still get a chance to catch them.

Riony's morning had left her with a renewed wariness of the depths. She had never gone far down the tunnel Kess had taken and didn't know what perils it may hold. But she knew people who would.

"Lyrrin, listen. I want you to go and find Aishena and Yoskar, tell them Kess is here and took something from us and that I need help."

"But *I* can help. You're just trying to get rid of me!

71

I'm sorry the glow stone hurt your eyes, but if you'd just trusted me and listened, it would have worked."

"And if you'd listened to me and not thrown the thing, I could have caught up to them! They're getting farther and farther away with every moment."

Lyrrin sniffled and her voice caught. "It looked like you were too far away. I was just trying to help."

"You can help by going and getting the delvers. They'll be near Dragon's Maw Descent. My vision is clearing up. I'll stay here and make sure Kess doesn't get out of the caves. You go and get help."

The shadowy blur in front of Riony bobbed up and down. A nod. "I'm sorry. Be careful."

Riony reached out, feeling for the top of Lyrrin's hood, then down to her cheek. "It's okay. I'll get Dracuni back. No matter what."

Lyrrin whimpered, then disappeared back the way they'd come.

And Riony turned toward the dark hole before her and ran blindly into it.

SIX

Getting through the streets of the undercity was a
battle for Lyrrin. The crowds trading in the Grand
Arch Markets jostled her small body and blocked her path
as she ran the very fastest she could run. She ducked and
weaved through the small gaps between the meandering
grown-ups.

Butterfur fussed in the confined pouch between the
layers of her clothing, and she kept one hand on him and one
holding the neck of her shirt closed in case he spooked and
jumped out and ran away and she never found him again.

She didn't want to lose anyone she loved again. Not
Butterfur or Riony or Dracuni or anyone.

Lyrrin had only seen Kess and the wolf she rode on

from a distance, when they came into the slavers' camp not long after she and the other children had been locked in the cages. At first, Lyrrin had looked at her in awe. A girl, riding a wolf! There was more than a little jealousy.

She'd had no idea who Kess was to Riony. Lyrrin had never met Kess before that, but the way Riony had talked about her since then, she sounded like the worst person in the whole world.

And now she had Dracuni, all because Lyrrin had left the poor baby unidragon alone.

She held her bottom lip between her teeth and willed away the wetness in her eyes by blinking hard and often.

Because her legs were small and she still did her best, but she just didn't have the strength that Riony did, and what if because she'd tried to do something her way instead of Riony's way she'd messed up everything and now Riony couldn't see properly and they might lose Dracuni?

The flash crystal would have worked if Riony had just listened to me. It would have worked, wouldn't it?

Lyrrin had only tested the combination of the light and burst runes one other time before, and that first glow stone that she'd altered mustn't have had as much of a charge left as the one she'd thrown at Kess.

Her first trial had been bright, enough that it took a few long breaths to confirm that she hadn't permanently blinded herself, but then her vision cleared up quickly.

The one she'd thrown at Kess was much brighter. She didn't know that would happen, that the amount of charge left would affect the power, and that the rune combination seemed to use up every last bit of the charge remaining in its burst of light rather than having the same energy usage each time.

She hadn't tested enough.

And Lyrrin worried that was a mistake that was going to hurt them all.

Her lungs felt like crumpled paper bags by the time she reached Dragon's Maw Descent deep-run access tunnel. Riony had shown her some of the delvers' maps and Lyrrin could still see them in her mind, how the pathways twined around each other as they went up and down through the earth in different directions.

She kept running, although she had left the well-lit inhabited areas of the undercity behind. The tunnel grew darker and darker and Lyrrin didn't have a glow stone of her own. Not one she hadn't tampered with, anyway, and the rest of those were back at home.

The light had completely gone and a shrill zing of panic filled Lyrrin when she finally saw a glow up ahead.

A group of figures were silhouetted in the light, seven tall and big, and one small like her. The small one was talking enthusiastically and Lyrrin recognized Benjin's voice.

"Yoskar wouldn't let me bring it back. But it looked so cool. The rat bodies were all dried up like hard leather and their tails tangled in a massive knot. Cammi said she saw one like that once, but still alive! She called it a rat king."

"That is disgusting," said a woman with short brown hair framing her soft cheeks and large doe eyes. The repulsed expression twisting her lips was at odds with her pretty face. "I hope you burned it."

"I was about to, then all this mess happened. I'll go back and do it later today when Benjin is with Aishena," Yoskar said, because all things dead must be burned.

The group of delvers stood near a tunnel from which soft billows of dust were floating, catching in the cyan light. The occasional sound of settling stone also drifted up from that dark hole.

Lyrrin arrived, puffing at their side. She yelled in big gasps, "Kess stole ... something important. Here in the undercity. Riony chased her! They went downward. She needs help!"

Everybody turned to her, expressions a mix of eyebrows up and eyebrows down. Along with the three Hjelzahn siblings, Lyrrin also recognized Master Brishan and his daughter Niskina from Riony's descriptions of them. She didn't know the three others, but they wore delver armor too.

Aishena scowled the fiercest. "She's here in the caves? Kess and her damned wolf?"

Lyrrin fretfully patted Butterfur though her shirt and nodded. "Riony's chasing them. She needs help."

"Sorry, what? A wolf?" one of the other men asked. He had shaggy blond hair that fell in tight spirals over his warm-brown skin.

Aishena ignored him and turned to Yoskar as though ready to pounce. "That unblessed maniac almost stopped us getting Benjin back. She didn't honor our deal at the bridge. This is our chance for payback."

Yoskar's mouth pulled inward, and he looked toward Benjin, whose eyes were glimmering at the prospect of a chase. "I'm not sure it's our duty. We need to focus on keeping ourselves and Benjin safe."

"I'm fine. I can help too," Benjin said.

"That's entirely what we don't want you doing," Yoskar replied.

Benjin scowled in reply. Lyrrin caught his eye, and they shared a knowing look.

Brishan lifted his hands in a calming gesture. "Okay, slow down, little one. What's going on?"

Lyrrin whined with impatience as she started again, "Kess—"

"Kessara Heithorn. A nasty piece of work that caused

us some trouble up above on our way to get Benjin," Aishena clarified.

"I know of the Heithorns. Not a Kessara though," Brishan said.

Lyrrin raised her voice over them to continue. "She stole something really important of ours, and we have to stop her before she gets out of the depths."

"What would they even own that would be worth stealing?" a handsome dark-haired delver at the back said softly to the woman beside him, who chuckled behind her hand.

Lyrrin pressed her lips closed tight.

Aishena's pointy shoulders lifted higher, adding to her angular build. "Kess crossed our family. She's dishonorable and I'm happy to help Riony take her down. I'll go on my own."

"No," Yoskar said firmly.

Aishena's gaze dropped to the floor, and she took a small step back.

"Please," Lyrrin whined. "Someone needs to help her. We have to stop Kess getting away. We're running out of time."

It was in a small voice that Aishena added, "We owe Riony—"

"We've repaid that debt bringing her into the delvers," Yoskar countered.

"Fine, so she's a delver now, and delvers help delvers,

right?" Aishena turned that question to the others watching the argument.

"You should help," Niskina nodded, turning pleading eyes to her father.

"Delvers look after each other," Brishan nodded. "And I suppose Riony is technically still a delver. We'll all go."

The other three delvers, despite a range of mocking expressions, stepped forward beside him.

Yoskar turned hard eyes to his peers. "You're willing to help other delvers, now? Daymora, Caed, Jonna? Where was that camaraderie when Benjin went missing?"

The woman, Daymora, met Yoskar's challenge with a steely gaze of her own. "That was different. That was a problem up above. This is a problem below. This is delver territory. We're in."

Lyrrin rubbed the gloved fingers of her hands and shook her head. "It's okay, we don't need everyone. We only need Aishena and Yoskar. We just need help knowing about the tunnel Kess went down."

"Which tunnel was it?" Niskina asked. "Can you describe its location?"

"It was the one right near the mushroom farms." Lyrrin thought back to the delver maps she saw. "Whisperwind Passage."

Brishan folded his arms across his wide chest. "It

branches out a few ways, none of them particularly good. And after the morning we had, it would be better if we all go."

"No, it's really okay. Please, just Aishena and Yoskar is fine. I don't want to cause a big fuss."

"If there's a wolf-riding thief stealing from delvers, I want to see they are caught," Brishan replied. He turned to the others with a swish of his long cloak. "All ready?"

The delvers checked over the items on their belts, tightened buckles on their leather delving armor, and nodded. Aishena bounced on her toes as though ready to sprint. Yoskar still had a hard-lined frown marring his face.

"I'll see you all when you get back," Niskina said, twiddling her fingers in a light wave at the group.

"You're coming too," Brishan huffed.

Niskina folded her arms over her chest in a way that matched her father. "I mean, I love Riony, but I'm not sure I'm ready to die for her. I don't need to be involved. This is a delver thing."

"Yes, and you're a delver."

"Not that I want to be!"

"You're coming, and hopefully you'll learn something about duty and responsibility." The tension of keeping his voice level cracked around the edges of Brishan's words.

"You mispronounced *obedience*."

80

Brishan grunted, then his voice boomed through the tunnel. "We're all going. *Now.*"

Niskina continued to glare at him but didn't argue again.

Yoskar finally offered a nod of acceptance. "Fine. We will help Riony. Benjin, stick close to me and Aishena. Aishena, keep an eye on him."

"Maybe he should stay behind," Aishena said uncertainly.

"Whose idea was it that he should stay behind last time? The time when we left him alone and he ended up kidnapped? He's coming with us."

Aishena's lips pulled in tight, and she looked away.

Benjin shuffled over close to Lyrrin and whispered, "I'm coming with you!"

He flashed her a bright grin, as though this was his best day ever. First finding some weird tangled up dead rat, and now getting to go hunting a thief with a group of delvers, he looked ready to split his cheeks.

Lyrrin could only grimace anxiously in return. This wasn't what Riony asked for. This was too many people to bring along, to find out what Kess had stolen.

But they were already moving.

Oh no, oh no. Lyrrin chased after them, sprinting to keep up with their long, running strides. Getting help was good, but if they did catch Kess, they might all end up seeing Dracuni. And even if they thought the unidragon

was a normal dragonling, that was going to cause big trouble for them.

Riony must have decided she could trust Aishena and Yoskar with finding that out. Or maybe Riony thought she could get some information off the Hjelzahn siblings, then send them away again before they saw anything.

But all the others? And all determined now to catch the thief in their midst? Lyrrin clenched her jaw to try to stop the trembling there.

As they moved through the streets to the rhythmic pounding of the delvers' pace, crowds parted before them. People pressed themselves to the walls of the narrow passages to make room for the urgency of the delvers in a way they didn't even consider for Lyrrin's urgent flight on her own.

It made the return journey much faster. They crossed the bridge over the small stream feeding Moonmilk Pool, and the musty, heavy scent of the mushroom farms rushed in with Lyrrin's panting breaths. She checked her pocket for her handkerchief in case she started getting sniffly.

With the tunnel in sight, she tried to be hopeful.

Riony should still be there, at the intersection, standing guard until her vision cleared. She could say something, explain to everyone that they weren't needed. They might listen to her.

But when the group reached the intersection, Riony wasn't there.

The delvers came to a stop at the three-way split, looking to Lyrrin for direction.

She stared wide-eyed at the tunnels, willing Riony to reappear. "This, this is where I last saw them. Riony must have chased after Kess."

"Which way?" Aishena asked.

Lyrrin pointed, and Brishan tsked.

"It's a dead end, at least. If they haven't chased back out and into another tunnel already, we have the thief cornered. This whole section is dangerously unstable though. Riony better keep her eyes open and be careful down there."

If she can see at all. Lyrrin cringed and fidgeted with the leather of her gloves.

"Why didn't Kess follow the path to the exit?" Aishena asked, lifting her chin toward the middle tunnel. "She must have known about it to come this way. Why'd she go down instead?"

Lyrrin didn't think it would be good to share her rune experimentation with the delvers. She racked her mind. "They … they all got … dust in their eyes. Kess and the wolf couldn't see properly and went the wrong way. Riony got it in her eyes too."

Brishan dragged his solid hand down over his mouth

and beard, covering a sigh. "Riony is down there, charging around blindly, chasing a thief and a wolf?"

Lyrrin nodded a tiny nod.

The delvers exchanged glances.

Aishena pulled an athame from her belt and adjusted her glow stone. "Then we'd better hurry."

SEVEN

Kess couldn't tell whether she was still blinded, or whether it was simply so dark she couldn't see anyway.

She didn't have one of those glowing crystals that lit up the main sections of the undercity. She'd considered stealing one, but she didn't know how to make them start and stop glowing like she'd seen others do and didn't want a bright beacon on her as she prowled around the shadows.

I should have grabbed one. Shoved it down in my pack somewhere out of sight. But Kess hadn't expected to be lost in some lightless tunnel.

There was a torch and tinder and a striking steel in her packs for light and fire that she used aboveground, but she didn't have the time for that while being chased.

She should be heading up, out of this awful, buried world, with her prize claimed. From the angle at which Griskin moved, Kess could tell they were headed downward.

Razing Pony and that damned brat. What did they do to us?

Griskin whimpered again, sniffling wetly, and bumped into a wall. His eyesight still hadn't cleared either. And Kess knew his eyes were so much keener than hers. And may have been hurt so much more by that bright flash.

A couple of times they slipped and tumbled down rough flights of stairs, Kess cursing all the way. But they couldn't turn back. Even with her human ears, Kess could hear that monstrous oaf storming after them.

"Kess! Where are you, you miserable ..." The yell came from close around the corner Kess had just passed. "Turn yourself in, and I promise I'll treat you as nice as you treated me!"

Kess's back muscles tensed rigidly. She leaned over the dragonling and hissed into Griskin's ear, "Move!"

Griskin charged forward again, and again their path dipped, descending deeper into the mountain. The smells of the markets and fried foods, and even the cloying stink of manure and fungus that surrounded this passage's entrance were all distant now. The tunnels were cool and quiet and smelled of only dust and dried bone.

The dragonling stirred, wriggling weakly against Kess. She crouched low in her saddle, pinning it between herself and Griskin.

How was it shaking off the sedation already? It should have lasted at least until they got out of the caves. Of course, they should have been out of the caves by now.

Everything was going wrong.

Even the dragonling itself. There was something strange about it.

Kess had never seen a dragon like it.

The gangly creature was small, much smaller than what Kess expected from a seasong dragon mother. Even if the mother had bred with a different species—rare in wild dragons, but with so few left, it may have been a necessity—it would have been with a midsize variety, a snowshimmer or etherflame.

Treedarts were too small and hadn't had successful breedings with seasong dragons even in captivity. But based on the diminutive size of the dragonling, Kess couldn't rule it out.

The coloring didn't match that theory though. Even with the paleness of the mother, a treedart would introduce ochre yellows and rusty browns. Sometimes deep purples, like the dragonling she'd chosen as her favorite from the hatchery, the etherdart her brother claimed for himself.

There was nothing earthy about this dragonling's coloring. It shimmered in an unearthly iridescent rainbow, overlaying the pale, silvery sheen of its scales. And those scales were soft, almost velvety.

Kess supposed it was also possible the hatchling was smaller than usual because it should have only just been born. It had come out of its shell earlier than usual. From Kess's calculations, the hatching date would have been closer to now.

If she treated the creature as a newborn rather than one a few weeks old, it wasn't that much smaller than expected. But there were still oddities about it.

The flimsy wings, the strange, singular horn formation, the tufts of hair down the back of its neck and at the end of its tail were all things Kess had never seen on a dragon before.

That central horn is going to be a problem. That's where the taming spike should go. I might have to get more advice from a breeder or tamer before doing the ceremony. Why can't anything just razing work out?

There she was, finally with her hands on her own dragonling, and it was this weird and abnormal thing. Not at all the strong beast she'd dreamed of. Would it even grow into a dragon that could fly? That could be a worthy steed for a dragonrider? Or would it prove to be lame and useless after all?

Kess's heart felt as though it squeezed to a painful stop. She gritted her teeth and shook off the swell of emotion, fought away the deep ache that echoed through her insides as though they'd been scooped out and left hollow and bloody.

No. She had her hands on a dragon, and she wasn't letting it go, no matter what. She was going to see her dreams of flying come true.

She just had to get out of this razed and ruined cave. As soon as she was up under the sun's blessed touch again, she could do the taming ceremony. She had her vial of silvernix tucked away safe in Griskin's saddlebags, and she had her metal spike. She'd seen it done before. It looked easy enough, if done with care. She'd make it work, even if it wasn't the normal way.

By all accounts, the very first tamed dragon had occurred by accident, when the Dragon King's silvernix-coated spear pierced the brain of a wild dragon. A freak coincidence that changed the course of history, giving humans dominion over the fiercest of creatures and all others from there down.

Still, Kess didn't want to risk getting the ceremony wrong and having to start from nothing again.

The dragonling squirmed, getting stronger. The lids over its huge eyes lazily tried to open and a tiny, pitiful trill came from beneath the muzzle.

"I'm coming!" Pony yelled from somewhere behind.

Did she have such good hearing?

Griskin turned sharply, a moment too late. Kess's leg and shoulder bumped against a stone wall as Griskin's side collided with it. The wolf followed the wall along, close to his flank, then stopped and cornered again. He sniffled and lapped his tongue against his snout.

"What's wrong? Keep moving!" Kess ordered.

A shimmer formed in the darkness of her vision. An aqua glow, growing stronger. Thumping footsteps carried it her way.

Kess squinted against the light, her eyes scratchy and raw as though someone had rubbed a handful of broken glass into them. She could only make out the glow, and a tall, dark smudge that carried the glow. *Pony*.

There was a long, sheering sigh of metal being drawn. "Give the dragonling back. Now. And I might consider leaving your head on your shoulders."

Kess's hand whipped out fluidly, plucking a bone dagger from her bracer and sending it toward the light. It clinked off metal.

"Still can't see? Let me clue you in then. You're at a dead end. You're trapped. You're screwed every which way, like your mother last time I saw her."

Kess drawled, "You keep making these jokes about my mami, but I think we both know neither of us cared

for the woman."

"You get my point though. Or you will, and feel it sharply, if you don't let the dragonling go."

Through blurred vision and dim light, it did seem as though Riony had a point. Kess seemed to be boxed in.

Maybe she could get Griskin to rush Riony, leap past her. But even without clear eyesight, the redheaded monster could easily gut Griskin with that stolen sword. Kess couldn't take that risk.

The carved walls surrounding her were shadowed and blocky in her vision, and she couldn't be certain one of those shadows wasn't another tunnel or some form of exit. Her way into the caves involved going through a broken hole in a wall, so she had to assume more were possible.

Kess shifted her weight, urging Griskin into slow movement. He edged them along the wall again, and Kess ran her fingers over the cracked and crumbly stone, hoping to feel for an exit.

"I'm still the one with my hands on the dragon, and I'm the one with the wolf, so I don't hate my chances." She spoke with a loud, laughing confidence to cover the sounds of her actions. "I'm also guessing the reason you haven't jabbed me with your sword yet is that your vision hasn't cleared up either."

"Except your wolf is blind, too." The blurry smudge

that was Pony circled slowly, matching Kess's motion and angling closer. "Personally, I'm not minding the lack of sight so much. Means I don't have to look at your dumb face."

"Keep your distance. Griskin can still bite your throat out easy enough, blind or not." Kess's fingers pressed into a softer section of stone, and pebbles crumbled out around her hand. She drove Griskin toward it, hoping it was the edge of a natural gap they could escape through.

The barest low whine came from deep in his throat, but with another nudge from Kess, he pawed at the stone in a digging action.

Riony took a step forward.

"And if you try to swing on us, you'll hit the hatchling first." Kess pulled the weak creature up into her arms, holding its body against her chest like a shield. It mewled pathetically.

"Sparks, Kess! Please, just don't hurt her."

The tame-brain really had gone soft for the wild dragon spawn. Kess smirked. That was all the leverage she needed.

But then the pattering of many feet tumbled down the tunnel descent toward them.

Pony chuckled softly. "Listen to that. Here comes my backup."

Griskin growled at the loudening sound. He reared, digging at the wall with both front paws as Kess leaned close to him.

Far too many new blurry figures emerged into the space before Kess, bringing more light with them. She scowled and drew another dagger, holding it out as a warning with one hand as her other kept hold of the hatchling.

"When you said there was a wolf, I didn't think she'd be riding it!" said a man.

Another gasped. "What is she holding?"

Then a boy said, "Is that a ... no way."

A sharp, clipped male voice barked, "What's the wolf doing? Get it away from that wall! The whole place could cave in." Yoskar Hjelzahn. She remembered his terse tone from the bridge.

Kess scoffed. She wouldn't be so easily tricked. Griskin must be close to a way out. She just had to buy time. "Everyone back off!"

A thick rectangle of a man stepped forward. "You have to stop the wolf from digging. This whole area is unstable."

"You're unstable if you think we're not getting out of here. You want us to stop digging? Then clear the path and let us go the other way."

"Fine, fine! Everyone move back!" the man ordered.

"No! I'm not letting her get away with what she's stolen," Pony bleated.

Figures moved around in front of Kess, stepping back

and forward and into each other's spaces. She gritted her teeth, blinking furiously against the blobby dots that obscured them.

"We'll all be buried if she doesn't stop."

There was a genuine panic in the man's voice that rattled Kess. Griskin must have sensed it too, or something else, as he stopped digging and spun an anxious circle on the spot.

Kess's back hadn't been turned for even a moment, when a guttural cry cracked through her ears, and a shadow fell over her.

"No! Don't!" a woman screamed, too late.

A bulk of muscle and leathers collided with Kess's side, grabbing awkwardly at her middle. The thick arms bundled around both Kess and the dragonling, and all three of them tumbled off the back of the wolf.

Kess gripped tight to the dragonling, refusing to let it be snatched from her grasp, and she and her brutish attacker—Pony, no doubt about it—flew toward the wall.

Kess braced for the smack of her body against rock. On impact, it was the stone that gave way. The cracked wall smashed apart. Abrasive slabs and shards scattered around them. They broke straight through.

In a deafening tumble of dust and rocks, Kess prepared to be buried alive and wasn't prepared at all to be plunged into a rushing stream of frigid water.

Legs and arms and tied up dragon claws tangled and lashed as the three of them swirled about in the current. The thin channel plunged, taking them under.

Pony's grasp disappeared from her skin as the torrent tossed them mercilessly. But Kess kept her arms tight around the hatchling, refusing to ever let go, as the water took her under and down into a breathless darkness.

EIGHT

"Riony!" Lyrrin screamed. She ran, but her legs skidded beneath her as soft hands grasped around her shoulders, holding her in place.

Time seemed to move in a stuttering series of images. The moment Kess's wolf turned around. Riony, wiping her eyes on the back of her forearm, tensing to lunge. The tumble of flailing limbs hitting the wall. Dracuni's tail, flicking up between them. The unstable sheet of limestone, cracking like eggshell.

Riony, Dracuni, and Kess disappearing into the dark hole beyond.

"Riony!" Lyrrin cried out again.

"Whoa!" Niskina had Lyrrin gripped tight. Keeping

her from running into that same hole or the snapping jaws of the panicked wolf.

The huge storm-gray beast yowled and yapped, turning side to side in clear distress. Its icy-blue eyes spun wildly, unfocused and weeping, and it sniffed at the air with panting desperation, causing it to cough and sneeze. The stirrups of the rough makeshift saddle on its back swung wildly, empty of their rider.

"Get that thing out of the way," Brishan ordered.

Aishena moved first, activating an athame with a dexterous tracing with her thumb. It lit up red and hot.

She approached the wolf, holding the blade before her like a flaming torch, the wolf backed up into a corner, growling. It could at least see something then.

It raised its head as it sniffed toward the hole again, then howled loudly.

Lyrrin felt a pang of guilt for the wolf, that she had blinded it and Kess and Riony, and now their loved ones were missing and Lyrrin wanted to howl too.

Brishan pointed to the other female delver and the man with the thick eyebrows and kind green eyes. "Daymora, Jonna, help keep that beast cornered."

The two delvers drew athames as well, although they didn't activate them, and moved beside Aishena.

"I always wanted a dog. Think I could keep it?" Jonna

asked with a grin. He tentatively reached toward the wolf, who snapped, almost taking off his fingertips.

Daymora beamed back at him. "You're such an idiot."

With the wolf out of the way, the hole was clear, and Lyrrin stared at it, willing her sister to reappear, Dracuni in her arms. Only the rumble of rushing water emerged.

Benjin reached out and gently touched Lyrrin's arm. "It's okay. They'll find your sister. It's what they do."

"Then why aren't they doing something?" Lyrrin cried.

Niskina's grip on Lyrrin softened. She shook off Niskina and Benjin and dashed over to the still crumbling hole.

Yoskar's crystal-studded staff appeared in front of her face, a barricade barring her way.

"Stay back! It's not safe." His tone was gruff, and then quieter, he muttered, "As wild as her sister."

"Keep her out of the way," Brishan said. He leaned toward the break in the wall, staring in at the darkness beyond. He called out Riony's name, but the gurgles of rushing water were all that replied.

"Sparks and stars," he grumbled. "I know the new girl has impulse control issues, but to charge an obviously destabilized wall like that, she must have been blind."

She was. And it was my fault. Lyrrin bit her lip, and her nose went hot and sore. Butterfur ran circles within her shirts, matching the swirling sensation in her stomach.

She wrapped her arms around her middle, trying to still them both.

She leaned as far forward as Yoskar's staff allowed, hoping to see signs of her sister returning, climbing back from that gaping hole.

Through the dust and trickle of crushed limestone falling like a curtain, there was only water. A massive, churning channel of an underground stream, coming in from above and disappearing below. No glimpse of red hair within the splashing liquid. No strong hands gripping the edges.

There were other grumbling, crackling sounds and the world felt off-balance, as the water roared and the wolf growled and Lyrrin's heart pounded in her ears.

"We have to go after them," she pleaded, meeting the eyes of the delvers spread through the dead-end room.

They turned away, unable to hold her gaze. Only Aishena kept her eyes locked with Lyrrin's, and Lyrrin didn't like the way her dark eyes stared back.

It was the same expression the delver had held back when she'd said *let the kid say goodbye.*

Yoskar lowered his staff and said flatly, "What we have to do is get out of this room. Those cracks are spreading."

"No!" Lyrrin pushed away the staff, ducking under it to get closer to the wall, and Brishan caught her at the edge

of the hole. Her feet kicked out, catching the crumbling rocks, scattering them over the floor.

She squirmed within his grasp. "Let me go after them!"

Brishan held tight. His eyes softened as he looked down at her. "Listen to me. There's every chance your sister will wash through that tunnel to somewhere safe. We will go and check the maps and see where that might be, and we will send search parties."

It sounded like a plan, but also a slow plan. How long would that take? And what if Riony and Dracuni didn't have that time? Lyrrin stopped fighting, but Brishan kept a strong grip on her as his frown deepened.

"But there's just as much chance that she won't. And I'm not letting anyone else jump into a hole with a fifty-fifty chance."

Lyrrin's stomach churned. She studied the expression on Brishan's craggy face, both hard and soft, sympathetic, but firm. He wasn't lying just to scare her, and he also wasn't withholding the truth from her because she was a kid.

Lyrrin wasn't sure how she felt about that. Those weren't good odds.

She felt as though she had two paths split in front of her leading into her future, and down one of them her sister was already dead.

Caed loped over beside them to look into the hole as

well. He sniffed and frowned. "Clean water, and cold. One of the melt streams rather than warm springs. Natural channel, not Alderkin carved, so it's unlikely it will be safe or come out somewhere we've mapped."

Lyrrin felt her future swing further again toward the path she didn't want. Her face scrunched up as she tried not to cry.

Niskina sighed loudly. She came over and pulled Lyrrin out of her father's grasp and put an arm around her shoulders. "Sparks, both of you! Could you use less tact? I'm sure Riony's going to be fine. She's tough as dragon scales."

Somehow, Niskina's words made Lyrrin feel even worse, and she gulped away a sob.

Caed simply shrugged. "Speaking of dragons, what was that thing the wolf girl was holding? Looked like a baby dragon to me."

Yoskar pushed his glasses up his nose and stared down at Lyrrin. "You said Kess had stolen something from you. Was that it?"

All eyes turned to Lyrrin, frowning and questioning. Benjin seemed outright hurt at the evidence Lyrrin had a very exciting secret that she hadn't told him. Considering he already knew one big secret of hers, she thought that was probably enough.

Lyrrin muttered, "No. I don't know what that was.

She stole ... something else from us."

"What did she take?" Yoskar asked.

"*Something*," Lyrrin murmured. She couldn't think of anything, a lie to offer, over the turmoil of worry inside her that was as loud as the rushing water. Her eyes kept turning back to the hole. It had grown larger, and a jagged crack split downward from it, running into the floor.

Had it been there before?

"The creature looked like a dragonling to me. Dragonlords used to have me working their breeding factory, so I know what they look like. Was an odd one though," Daymora said, keeping her keen eyes on the wolf.

"Aw, I've never seen one before. And I didn't get a very good look," Benjin pouted quietly.

Niskina said, "Where did that thief get a dragonling from around here?"

Aishena shifted just enough to meet Yoskar's gaze. Then they both looked at Lyrrin.

She could see them adding it up in their heads, the nest, the eggs they'd shattered, Riony being the last person in the cave.

"There was a dragon nest," Lyrrin blurted out before they could question her further. "Up in the snowy mountains. Riony found it, but Aishena and Yoskar went up after and broke all the eggs."

Benjin's mouth dropped and he looked at Yoskar the way he must have when he saw the Rat-King corpse. "You smashed baby dragon eggs?"

"I considered it a prudent course of action to deal with the eggs so the hatchlings didn't attract attention from people attempting to catch them. Especially the wrong people," he replied without a shred of remorse.

Benjin flinched a little, then grumbled, "But still ... baby dragons!"

Brishan huffed beneath his beard. "Probably for the best. We don't want dragonlords coming around and deciding that the undercity is theirs."

"That doesn't explain how or why the wolf girl had a hatchling though," Jonna said, leaning into Daymora as their expressions equally demanded answers.

"Riony said Kess is obsessed with dragons. And Riony said she saw Kess up on the mountain too, because she was after those eggs. So she must have found another one that didn't get broken, and that's why she has it," Lyrrin finished, hoping she sounded confident and convincing.

"Why did she come into the undercity with the beast, then? What did she steal from you?" Yoskar frowned and leaned in close, whispering to Lyrrin. "Did your sister have more silvernix?"

That might have been a good explanation, but Lyrrin

couldn't work out if agreeing or disagreeing would cause more problems. She just wanted Riony back.

Lyrrin balled up her hands and scrunched her face. "It doesn't matter! Can we please go and search for them now? They need our help!"

Yoskar gave her a long look like she was a particularly difficult passage in a book he was trying to understand. And still nobody sprang into action.

She couldn't understand how they were all standing around so calmly, as though the world didn't seem to be falling apart, as though her sister and Dracuni weren't gone and feeling less and less likely to get back with every second. As though they'd all already accepted the loss.

Aishena left her position guarding the wolf and crouched down beside Lyrrin. She deactivated her athame, and the absence of the red light left the room feeling chilled in the wash of cyan glow.

She seemed to struggle over her words for a moment, then said stiffly, "We can't go the same way your sister did. That's not a water channel that's safe for people. But we'll do what we can to get her back."

Aishena didn't sound even slightly convincing.

Lyrrin clung to Butterfur, hugging him through her shirt. She trembled with fear and grief and anger, and the earth seemed to shake with her.

The earth *did* shake with her. A thunderous crunching sound overwhelmed the roar of the water, and the floor they stood on lurched, dropping down a foot on one side.

There was a moment of silence afterward, as everyone steadied themselves, took in the new angle of the floor, and watched as newly forming fractures ran across the limestone like lightning.

Brishan bellowed, "Move! Get out of here, now!"

Everyone sprang into motion. The wolf was ignored over the larger threat of the floor breaking apart into loose slabs that wobbled and tilted.

Lyrrin remained still. She stared at the hole again. The channel that wasn't safe for humans.

Yoskar grabbed Benjin as Aishena reached for Lyrrin, snatching her wrist and dragging her into movement.

Lyrrin pulled back, slipping her hand from the glove and leaving Aishena holding the limp leather. She reached down into her shirt and pulled out Butterfur. She let him loose on the tipping floor, pushing him in the direction of the hole.

"Riony has the treats!" she cried to him, over the yelling delvers and splitting stone. The silky caramel otter skittered over the moving floor on sure, gripping feet. He sniffed at the air, snout and whispers twitching, then dove into the water channel.

Not safe for humans, but the natural habitat of cave otters.

"Back up! Back!" Daymora yelled. She grabbed Jonna by his shoulders as a wall of stone smashed down in front of them. The pathway out of the dead end was erased by the cavern closing in on itself.

The crumbling sections of floor under their feet felt like pieces of shattered ship on a sea, being drawn into a whirlpool, bumping into each other and sinking. With nowhere left to run, delvers pulled rope and tools and tried to lash themselves to something solid, but everything was crumbling away.

Lyrrin stumbled, falling onto her hands and knees. The slab of stone under her split in two beneath her belly, tipping her sideways.

The broken sections of floor tilted farther and farther, until they no longer had each other for support, and then they fell away entirely, taking everyone in the room with them.

NINE

Icy water rushed up Riony's nose as though it wanted to get intimate with her brain.

The current seized her like a vengeful spirit. Desperate gasps for air yielded nothing but mouthfuls of water.

Of all the ways Riony thought she may die on her first day of delving, drowning hadn't even appeared on the list.

Even then, drowning would be the second worst thing to happen, because in the initial confusion of hitting water, the very worst thing happened—she had lost her grip on Kess and Dracuni.

Scared, cold, help, scared, hurt, screamed through her brain, churning together with the roar of the water.

Which meant Dracuni was still alive, still needed her.

Riony just had to reach her. And not drown first.

Riony could only open her eyes for short bursts. Her vision was still damaged, but if anything, the washing of chilled water over her sore eyes seemed to help.

The walls of the tunnel rushed past in a blur of jagged rock, lit by the glow stone on Riony's belt, and the water's icy fingers clung to her, dragging her deeper. She couldn't see the others.

She struggled to orient herself in the rushing torrent. Her hands wanted to claw at the walls, end the relentless tumbling, pull herself up and out if there was even anywhere to pull herself up and out onto.

But she could feel Dracuni. Her pain, her panic, and she knew the unidragon was down, somewhere just ahead of her in the stream, still moving. She could *feel* her there, as though a string had been bound around each of their hearts, tugging Riony to her. So she let herself be dragged on.

Riony's chest burned and tightened from lack of air, but determination and sheer fury kept her from passing out. Because Kess had taken Dracuni and had tied her up, muzzled her!

Riony would come back from the dead to exact revenge on Kess for that. A little drowning wasn't an obstacle at all.

Tackling them had been Riony's mistake, but she'd been desperate and hadn't seen how fragile the wall behind

them was. She couldn't have known it would plunge them all into this splashing vortex.

But still her heart constricted with the shame that she had again thrown her body at something and caused a mess.

And Brishan was there, watching too.

Riony had more to worry about than whether she'd still be a delver when she got home, but she worried regardless.

The water's pull grew stronger, and Riony's body felt like lead, growing heavy with exhaustion from the effort to not be smashed against the tunnel walls and the inability to breathe.

She dropped suddenly again, sliding down stone worn smooth from the flow. Then she was expelled in a spraying fall of water, splashing down and plunging into a deep expanse of both darkness and light.

Bright streaks of moonlight blue stirred into existence at the motions of Riony's hands and feet. And out in the deep well surrounding her, other things moved, lighting their path as they went. Small things … and big things.

Chest bursting, Riony propelled herself in the direction she hoped was upward. She erupted from the surface in a spray of luminance, gasping for air.

She flicked her hair from her face and blinked the water free from her eyes. She could see clearly now except for two trailing blobs obscuring a small section of her vision.

Her heart pounded, a cacophony that echoed in her ears as she struggled to keep her head above water. The ropes and pouches and sword at her belts weighed her down. The cavern echoed with the rush of the waterfall she'd emerged from.

The current had eased in this larger body of water, no longer a crashing maelstrom. Only a steady tug now, dragging Riony away from a low shore she had almost washed onto, and toward an abyssal crack in the cavern ahead.

She exploded into motion, swimming toward that shore.

Because on it lay two shadowed forms.

And because one of the large things that moved in the water, brightening the luminescence in its path, was coming toward her.

Paddling wildly through the water and shooting glances behind her, Riony saw what hunted her. An olm.

The slithery, pale, legged eels had a nasty bite, even when small enough to emerge in the pools and reservoirs of the undercity. But this one must be ancient. It was huge, big enough to take most of Riony in its translucent maw.

And Riony did not have the time to be chewed on by a giant carnivorous water worm right now.

The creature lunged up at her, and Riony kicked out. Her foot met the slick skull and glanced off. Just enough to deter the olm, it turned the other way. But the kick also

pushed Riony off course too.

The current fought against Riony, and she had never excelled at swimming. She had to grasp on to a semi-submerged stalagmite to stop from being taken away into the next stream.

If Kess and Dracuni didn't lie waiting for her on the shore, and the olm didn't circle back around toward her, Riony would have clung to that pointed peak of limestone for a solid day as she tried to catch her breath.

Instead, she lunged forward again through the water. With a steely resolve, she dragged herself out onto the crystalline rimstone edges of the shore, her hands snagging and scratching against the sharp edges.

Drenched and battered, she pushed herself to her feet, her eyes fixed on the prone body of a monster and the precious creature she'd stolen, lying upshore.

She put her hand on the hilt of her sword, confirming it hadn't come free from where she'd sheathed it before tackling Kess. She'd be livid if she'd lost her lucky weapon in the bottom of the olm pool. Her fingers tensed and released, then tensed again over the scale-patterned metal.

Kess was up on her elbows, face down, busy hacking up a lungful of water. Dracuni lay on her side, shimmering chest heaving and breath gurgling inside that awful muzzle. Her legs were still bound, two by two, her front claws trying

to work together to scratch off the leather over her face.

Then she stilled, turning toward the light Riony brought with her. Dracuni trilled, and there was a surge of emotion that sounded painfully like **RIONY!**

I'm coming! Riony stumbled forward in a desperate rush.

Kess moved just as fast. One of her arms looped around the dragonling, pulling her close, and in her other hand she held a dagger and pressed it against Dracuni's soft neck, angling it up toward her jaw.

"Better think twice about where you're galloping, Pony."

Soft calcite crystals crushed under Riony's sodden boots as she came to a stop.

She could take Kess in a one-on-one fight, easy enough, without a wolf involved. But whether she could do that before Kess stuck that dagger up into Dracuni's brain or threw it into Riony's heart, was another question.

The way Kess's gaze tracked Riony's every action, the adjustment of her footing, the tightening of the grip on her hilt, made Riony think her eyesight must have cleared too.

Kess confirmed that with, "And don't you dare draw that sword on me." Then "No, take your fat-fingered hand all the way off it." And "*Now*, Pony."

She pressed the dagger harder, and Dracuni yipped. Any semblance of language coming through in Dracuni's thoughts was overwhelmed by *Scared, scared, scared!*

"Fine. No sword!" Riony lifted both hands up in a gesture of surrender.

Kess eased the dagger back, and Riony withheld her sigh of relief. She couldn't risk Kess even nicking Dracuni with that sharpened bone.

Because if Kess drew blood, the relentless psychopath would know she'd stumbled upon something far more valuable even than the dragon she'd always wished for.

Riony turned her hands palm upward, shrugging. "But let's just talk this through. How do you honestly plan on getting out of here alive?"

"I've gotten out of worse!" Kess's shrewd gaze flickered all around, regularly returning to Riony between taking in their shadowy, cavernous surroundings.

Riony took her chance to get her bearings too. The underground lake lay on one side, and the shore of crystal-veined limestone rose in shimmering tiers of ancient, dried out rimstone pools toward dark crevasses leading away in several different directions.

The ceiling of cracked and broken straws had fractures running through it too, small and large, mostly dry except for the one gushing water which had expelled them into this space.

It wasn't anywhere in the undercity or surrounding tunnels Riony had ever been before. It wasn't anywhere

Riony could identify from her brief study of the delvers' maps either.

A shiver ran down Riony's back, chased by the water dripping off her leather armor.

She could find a way out, couldn't she? Her delver training hadn't covered getting lost somewhere like this. It was all about how to not get lost in the first place. But Riony figured she just had to head upward. And if up led to a dead end, find another way up.

First, she had to get Dracuni safely back from Kess. Before Kess lost it and did something stupid. There weren't many people who could tell that Kess was panicking. The flat glare on her pointy face, framed by the tangled, gray-streaked braids, and still hands didn't give it away.

But Riony could see the sharp breaths swelling her chest. The whites around her enlarged pupils. She'd seen Kess's panic before and seen her hide it.

She leveled Kess with a solemn look and took a slow step forward. "Just hand over the dragonling. You know you're out of options."

Kess adjusted her position, leaning on her side by the water's edge, with Dracuni pulled in close. "We'll go back in the water, wash out somewhere else."

Riony tilted her head at the blue swish of light circling in the pool close by. "And trust your luck with the olm?"

"It would treat me kinder than you."

"Don't pretend you know anything about kindness. You've got a startling array of lacking qualities, Kess, and of them all, the inability to understand kindness is your worst. But I know you're smarter than dunking yourself into underground rapids again."

"Flattery won't get you anywhere, Pony."

Riony bristled. No one could get under her skin like Kess, even with one word. She took a soothing breath. "Listen. There's no way to be certain the stream washes out of the mountain somewhere. You're more likely to get stuck and drown and take the dragonling with you."

"I'll take my chances." Kess shuffled closer to the edge.

"Stop!" Riony grunted, frustration shooting through her like fire. She pressed her palms to the sides of her head and squeezed, shaking it at the awfulness that was about to emerge from her mouth.

The words came out, tasting like vomit. "We can work together. Just stop. I'll help you get out of here. Just don't hurt the baby dragon."

Kess stilled, keeping her eyes on the rippling surface. "Why would I ever work with you?"

"Sparks, I don't know! Maybe because we're down, stars know where, under an entire mountain, in dangerous, cursed, trapped, and unstable, uncharted Alderkin ruins.

And I have the only light source."

"You're just saying that to get close to me, get a chance at snatching this hatchling back."

"OF COURSE I AM!" Riony bellowed. "But what's it going to be, Kess? We all die here in a never-ending standoff? Or you get to keep leveraging an innocent life to order me around as long as you can until you screw up?"

Kess smirked, shifting back from the water's edge. "I don't screw up. My plans just keep getting screwed up by other idiots. Namely you, Pony."

Riony cringed and swallowed bile. "Stop calling me that."

"I thought you said I could order you around?" Kess pressed into a more upright sitting position.

She pursed her lips as she looked Riony up and down with a thoughtful gaze, then shook her head. "I think it would be smarter if you just throw me that glowing crystal of yours and me and *my* dragon find our own way out."

"And how long is that going to take you? The olm aren't the only things creeping in the depths that would love to eat some unsuspecting prey. You aren't prepared. You never know what could burst out of the shadows down here."

Kess rolled her eyes lazily. "Stop overselling it. It's a cave. How bad could it be?"

A guttural growl from above answered her.

Riony's eyes shot up, searching the cavern roof for

motion. A stream of rocks and debris trickled from one of the larger cracks. But nothing emerged.

She huffed and looked back at Kess.

Seeing how Kess regarded the ceiling with her widened eyes, Riony smirked and counted off her fingers, "Could be anything. Ghost snakes, cave spiders, stinging glowflies, diseased bats—"

"Revs?" Kess asked, eyes still turned high.

"Those are the one thing we don't have to deal with," Riony grumbled, annoyed at the interruption. "Kind of the whole point of living underground."

The growl emerged again.

Kess shimmied backward, dragging Dracuni with her toward the closest wall.

"Sounds like a rev," she muttered.

It did sound like a rev, but Riony was already exasperated from dealing with Kess and never expected a rev to appear in the depths. So she yelled, "It's not a sparking rev!"

Then a second later, the animated human corpse fell through the air and landed right in front of her.

TEN

The earth tried to swallow Lyrrin whole. There was a moment of freefall. Her hood flapped around her ears and her stomach felt like it floated up to her throat.

Then just as fast as the falling started, it ended in a thunderous crash.

The shattered stone floor landed on the floor of the level below, flattening onto it like slamming a book closed. Lyrrin bounced and rolled, the extra layers of oversized clothing giving her some protection. She collided with Aishena, who caught and steadied her.

Yoskar waved the dust away from his face, and Benjin squirmed in his overtight grip.

"I'm fine, you can let me go!"

Yoskar didn't let him go.

Aishena also kept one hand on Lyrrin's shoulder, but lightly, looking the other way as the dust cleared.

The delvers moved slowly, careful of injuries, but the fall hadn't been far. When Brishan and Niskina stood up, the floor above was only a little higher than their heads.

Jonna and Daymora shared a chuckle of relief that spread through the whole group. They clasped hands, helping each other up.

"That was quite a ride," Caed said with a relieved sigh.

The wolf had come down with them and whimpered in the corner, turning circles of distress as it looked up and down.

The new area they'd landed in had beautifully tiled flooring in multicolored calcite—now broken and mostly hidden beneath the chunks of ceiling—and the natural columns had been carved with spiraling motifs.

"Everyone okay?" Brishan asked, while looking to Niskina.

Mutters in the affirmative came from all around.

"I don't recognize this area," Daymora said, eying the columns.

"Are we going to be able to get back from here?" Lyrrin asked, but her soft voice was lost under the continued rattling of loose stones pattering around them.

"Yeah, I think it's uncharted." Jonna grinned widely. "Well, that's one way to open up a new sector."

Brishan snorted. "Not the right way. We were sparking lucky that wasn't worse than—"

The ground shifted again.

There was a single heartbeat of time as Lyrrin held her breath, hoping the quaking motion was her imagination.

With a skull shaking crack, the floor went out from under her in the blink of an eye. The entire floor broke through, and they all were falling again.

There was another thunderous crash as the rocks hit the next floor down. Lyrrin tensed, waiting to hit it as well. But with the combined weight of two floors worth of stone, that floor didn't even slow the cascading rush of rubble that time. It smashed straight through.

Shattered tile and chunks of stone filled the air. Aishena fell near Lyrrin, and through a swirl of pale, flying hair, she reached out and caught Lyrrin around her waist. Bodies of other delvers twirled and tumbled through the air beside them, the light of their glow stones strobing through the dark pit.

Some of them screamed. Lyrrin's own fear escaped in short bursts of uncontrollable shrieking, punctuated by paralyzed breathlessness.

Again, the combined weight of the landslide hit another

floor, and again pierced through. And again and again. The earthshaking rhythm boomed, boomed, boomed, with the crack and patter of smaller rocks and bodies ricocheting within. Gray fur flashed by. The wolf yelped and whined.

Aishena kept Lyrrin pulled in tight, and when larger slabs of stone caught against the rough wrought hole, threatening to block their path and bring them to a bone-jolting stop, she angled her body, kicked off, and rolled away from them.

She had a dim-green glowing athame in her hand, twice-hardened rune activated, and thrust it into any surface that came within reach. It slowed their descent a few times but didn't stop it.

Lyrrin held tight to the delver, looping her gloved fingers into the straps of her harnessed armor. Her other hand, glove gone, she tried to use the same way Aishena used her athame. Clawing at the walls or broken floors that flew upward beside them.

Her clothing buffeted around her, and it was so much more terrifying than the time she and Riony had jumped together into fire. Then, at least, she was with Riony. Then, she knew the ground had to be beneath them. Now, she felt as though they could fall into the center of the world.

Benjin had teased her about the dangers his siblings faced in the depths, including bottomless pits. Now, she was worried he might not have been lying.

The booming finally ended in a clattering earthquake. And it took Lyrrin a moment to realize that meant their fall would be ending too. And what that might mean.

Aishena seemed to work that out faster. She struck out with a mighty grunt one last time and sank her athame deep into the closest wall. It caught, slicing down through the soft limestone like cutting fabric. She and Lyrrin swung from the hilt of the dagger, wrenching violently from the sudden halt, and Aishena's grip slipped.

They fell again, clattering down a second later onto a steep pile of stone and smashed furniture and shattered crystals. Together, they slid in a rough landslide and came to a stop under a huge archway.

Dust filled the air thicker than smoke from a wet-leaf fire.

Lyrrin coughed and tried to sit up.

"Careful. Move each part of your body slowly. Make sure nothing is broken," Aishena choked out beside her. Then she cried out "Yoskar?"

Groans and skittering rocks came from all around.

"I have Benjin," came his reply from across the clouded space.

"I'm here. I think I'm okay," Niskina's voice came from nearby.

Brishan boomed the loudest. "Caed? Daymora? Jonna?"

The dust began to settle, and Lyrrin could see silhouettes moving within it. The delvers, and the shaggy form of a wolf, crouched at the edge of the landslide.

"Here," came Daymora's reply.

"Good enough," came Caed's.

And then nothing.

"Jonna?" Brishan called out again.

"Oh no. Oh no, no, no," Niskina gasped. "Keep the kids over there!"

"Stay here," Yoskar muttered.

"Mm-hmm," Benjin groaned from somewhere low down.

A few of the silhouetted bodies scrambled in Niskina's direction, bringing the lights of their glow stones together at one point. They looked as though they were moving through murky water, as the brown dust obscured all but light and shadow.

The delvers knelt down, keeping their voices low in a rush of whispers, pleas, and instructions.

Then Lyrrin heard Brishan say softly, "He's gone."

"No," Daymora growled in a slurred, drunken way.

Brishan muttered a few more soft words, sounding like a prayer.

"Gone?" Lyrrin asked Aishena in a trembling whisper.

"Just stay back there." Aishena gave her a soft push away from the landslide and toward the archway, then

went to join the other delvers. She knelt down into the huddle of them.

In the archway, the air was clearer, and Lyrrin gasped it in with shaking breaths. Her whole body felt rattled and bruised, and even her tough claws were red-tinted with scrapes and grazes. Her heart was going faster than a hummingbird's wings.

She turned her face upward, and the hole seemed to extend up into an infinite void above them. They were so far down. And one of them ...

Lyrrin couldn't look at the huddled team of delvers and the hole left between them. She turned away, looking instead at the space behind her, through the archway, and her breath caught.

Brishan's voice rumbled through the air. "Come now, up to your feet, all of you. We still have our lives, and the dead won't mind us doing what we must to stay that way."

Lyrrin turned back to them. All but one of the delvers stood.

"Get that wolf subdued!" Brishan ordered. "We can't have it running loose around us."

"On it," Aishena, Yoskar, and Caed replied together.

There was a scuffle nearby, and three bodies pressed the wolf against a wall in unison. The two larger bodies, Caed and Yoskar, kept it pinned there as Aishena's arms

moved fast, lashing strong cave silk rope around the beast. It growled and whimpered.

A figure stumbled through the clouded air toward Lyrrin. The dust had settled enough to see faces clearly when nearby, and Niskina's was shaken, streaked with dirt and tears. Brishan followed. Daymora remained unmoving, beside where Jonna had fallen.

Niskina took in Lyrrin's wide-eyed shock. "Are you sure you're okay, little one?"

Lyrrin's throat still felt clogged, so she could only point.

Through the archway, where the dust sifted like a low fog across the ground, there stood a vast, regal chamber, packed to overflowing with Alderkin riches.

Down there, in the heart of the earth, they had fallen into a place untouched by time or traps or plundering, where the air hung heavy with enchantment.

The vast room before them gave the air of both royal chambers and laboratory, a dwelling of a mad wizard from another race, lost to time and rumors, unknowable to those who now stood in their place.

Stone slab tables with legs carved into realistic animals were piled high in ancient tombs and scrolls and crystalline artifacts that gleamed beneath the soft light of the delvers' glow stones.

The walls were adorned with intricate carvings that

danced with iridescent light, as if the very stones still resonated with ancient magic. In the center of the room, up on a tiered platform, an immense slice of natural geode stood upright, casting fleeting rainbows upon the surfaces around it.

The chambers held a sheer volume of Alderkin relics and tools that could double what was currently in use by humans in the undercity. Every artifact held the whispers of a past imbued with both grandeur and mystery. Every one immensely valuable.

And all of it felt hollow, because behind them lay a body. Because they had just lost a life, and the delvers all looked at each other and the gaping pit above them as though they weren't sure it would be the only one.

With the wolf downed, Aishena, Yoskar, and Caed joined the others away from the rubble, taking in the sight.

"Isn't that something," Caed murmured, wobbling as he favored one leg.

"It's the Alderkin mother haul," Niskina replied, but her voice was flat.

"What is it? I want to see!" Benjin called.

Lyrrin turned to see why he hadn't joined them yet and saw he was still lying where he'd been asked to stay near the edge of the mountain of fallen stone. He shifted, trying to sit up.

"Ow," he muttered, and then seemed to think again and howled a second time, "Ow!"

He slumped onto his back again with a high-pitched cry.

Yoskar was by his side in a flash. "What is it? Where are you hurt?"

"My ... my neck. My head."

Aishena's expression turned stony, and she ran to join them.

Lyrrin wobbled awkwardly across the unstable rocks a few steps behind. She hovered at the edge of the boundary of the tight circle formed by the siblings.

"What's happening? Is he hurt?" she asked.

Benjin lay flat on his back on a large broken slab. There was no sign of blood marring his finely made clothes, only dust settling over his white shirt and embroidered vest.

Yoskar had his hands on either side of Benjin's neck, touching with the gentlest motions. Aishena held her glow stone up near his face, staring into his eyes.

"Can you wriggle your toes? No, don't nod, you tame-brain!" Aishena scolded.

Yoskar added, "Stay still. Don't move anything. You can talk but try not to move your head too much."

"Okay," Benjin whimpered. "Is it bad?"

Aishena and Yoskar shared a long, silent look.

Niskina moved in beside them, kneeling next to Benjin.

"If you can wriggle your toes, you're doing great. Falls can be really hard on your body, and breaks are far too common in delving." She shot a caustic look at her father. "But we're all here with you and it's going to be okay."

Benjin looked like he wanted to nod again, but after a glance at Aishena, he stayed still. He mumbled through a still mouth, "What do we do?"

"Is it his neck?" Aishena asked softly.

Yoskar nodded, glaring at her with unrestrained aggression. "You should have been with *us* during the fall. You could have helped keep him safe."

Aishena turned her face to the ground. "I'm sorry."

Lyrrin felt a pang of guilt too. Aishena had helped her, instead of her own brother. Whether that choice was made just based on how close they'd been at the time, or something else, it had cost Benjin. Lyrrin didn't want that.

She wished Riony was there with her, that Riony had been the one to help her, and that nobody had to have gotten hurt or fallen or died.

"I'm okay though, aren't I?" Benjin asked.

Niskina reached out and squeezed his hand. "You will be. We just have to get you safely out of here so you can get to work healing and get better."

Lying on his back, Benjin set his gaze straight, looking at the empty distance through which they'd fallen. The

delvers followed his gaze.

Lyrrin didn't. She'd already seen how far down they were. With one lost already, and Benjin's neck broken, and Riony feeling so far away, she didn't want to look again.

Over beside Jonna's body, Daymora let out a single, chest-cracking sob.

And the tied-up wolf loosed a long, mournful howl that echoed up and up to the world that remained so far above them.

ELEVEN

Kess had only a fleeting moment to decide whether she should let the revenant rip Pony to shreds or make any attempt to avoid that outcome.

The hideous, shaggy monster—the revenant, not Pony—dropped directly in front of the oafish woman, and the fool didn't even have time to draw her sword before the creature was lunging for her with clawing boney fingers and yellowed teeth.

Unfortunately, Kess had to agree that finding her way out of this premature grave was going to be an exercise in frustration on her own.

With a curse on her lips, she sent a bone dagger flying. It hit true, skewering through the rev where the base of the skull met its neck. It had enough rotting meat still on its bones for the knife to lodge in satisfyingly.

Sometimes getting a hit there was enough to sever whatever cursed connection a revenant had to life. More often, it just seemed to make them angrier.

The once-human undead gargled and hissed, spinning around to turn its attention to what had stung it.

Angrier it is.

Despite its eyes being bloated, milky spheres, it locked on to Kess. Jaw snapping, it raced for her with ferocious, inhuman speed.

Kess drew and threw two more bone daggers from where she sheathed them in her bracers. One went right into the target, lodging between hip and thigh bone. The other hit location mirrored on its other side, but bounced off, clattering away on the ground.

Bone daggers didn't have the weight to slow the creature down or the capacity to cut it into pieces small enough to end it once again. But Kess had faced enough revs aboveground to learn some tricks. How she could spike them in strategic spots, disable them, slow them down enough so she and Griskin could get away.

But without her wolf's speed, and with only one dagger causing the rev to limp unevenly, it still approached too fast.

Pretty certain now that she'd made the wrong decision

in helping Pony, Kess pushed her dragonling prize behind her and braced for the worst.

Claws up and jaw wide, the revenant froze in place as a steel blade skewered through its chest from behind with a loud *shluck*.

Kess exhaled roughly. "Finally got your sword drawn?"

"I really, truly, honestly wasn't expecting there to be revs down here!" Pony yelled from behind the rev. "Also, you're welcome!"

"Oh, we're counting who just saved who, are we? Because you're welcome first."

"Great to see you're still the spoiled baby I used to know."

Kess's cheeks flared. She was so much more than the person she used to be. That girl had died alone in the woods, and the woman who had crawled out of that grave on Griskin is something so much more, even if this worthless, intolerable woman couldn't see it.

"And don't think I'm dumb enough to think you were saving me and not this helpless hatchling." Kess shifted again, making sure her hostage wasn't squirming away.

Unperturbed by the length of steel through its gut, the revenant twisted and jittered on the horizontal sword. Its head flicked around, neck cracking as it turned entirely backward to face Pony.

Arms contorted, shoulder sockets popped, and the rev pushed itself farther up the sword to reach its sharp-nailed hands out for Pony.

"Ew, no! I don't like that at all!"

She balked at the disturbing, half-backward body but didn't release the dragon-scaled hilt of her sword. Leaning back, she kicked into the revenant, pushing it away and pulling the blade free with a grunt.

The rev clattered awkwardly to the ground, disjointed limbs and crooked elbows pointing in every direction. It landed far too close to Kess for her comfort, and she drew another dagger.

Its attempt to skitter across the ground toward her was halted by Riony swinging her sword with all the finesse of a lumberjack into the rev's side. The clumsy strike landed with a walloping impact, lifting the corpse off the ground and flipping it over in the air.

Kess flushed, involuntarily impressed at the strength behind that blow, then immediately disgusted with that emotion.

"Where did you steal yourself a dragonguard sword from?" she snapped.

"Pulled it out of my ass." Riony kept up the assault on the revenant as it rolled around, trying to right itself. "Seemed like a better time than ever seeing your face again."

"You're the one making a career of being a fool, a liar, and painfully unfunny all at the same time."

"Aw, thanks for acknowledging how multitalented I am."

Pony chopped the battered old sword down, straight through the rev and cracking onto the stone below. Kess cringed at the horrible abuse the once fine weapon suffered.

The swing severed through the living corpse between shoulder and arm, leaving that limb lifeless. But still the undead monster howled for their blood.

It wasn't one of the strange, ashy, re-raised ones Kess had seen recently, but without the use of fire, it would still take a great deal more dismemberment to put it down for good. Pony hadn't broken a sweat yet, but Kess wasn't certain she'd be able to put the monster to rest with that sword alone.

"Hit it into the water," she ordered.

"What?"

Kess pointed to where the midnight surface of the water rippled with blue glow as an olm swam beneath. "Knock that unblessed thing into the water!"

Finally catching on, Pony circled the revenant that skittered on three limbs like a demented spider, putting herself between it and Kess, and it between her and the water.

The monster took the opportunity to snatch Pony's ankle in its death-worn fingers.

Kess withheld a gasp when Pony went down, falling flat on her back as the rev scuttled up her. But the fool was smiling. She brought both legs up to her chest, pressed them into the revenant, and thrust them out together.

The stinking mass of skin and bones went flying, arcing high in the cyan-lit cavern, and then splashed down into the luminescent water with a bright splash.

"Saw a dragonrider do that once," Pony said.

Kess just scowled, her eyes on the rippling water.

There was a moment of stillness, with Kess and Pony's labored breathing seeming loud even over the rushing water. And then the water churned.

The cavern lit up, the strange, glowing water brightened by the splashing and writhing olm, tearing its meal from the bones of the undead.

And then Riony was back on her feet, and the point of the sword was at Kess's throat.

"Let go of the—"

Kess flung the dagger from her hand. It sliced across the fingers Pony had wrapped around the hilt of the sword.

"Sparks!" she hissed, and her hand spasmed, dropping the blade. It clattered onto the crystalline floor and tumbled down, disappearing with a plop into the water.

"No, no!" Pony raced after it. She landed on her knees at the water's edge and plunged her hands in, splashing

around, reaching deeper and deeper until she almost had her face in the water.

"I told you not to draw on me," Kess drawled and pulled another dagger. She adjusted her sitting position, pulled the dragonling back in front of her, and settled its squirming with the warning of the tip of the blade.

Pony continued to trawl through the water, lying flat on her stomach and angling out farther. "My sword ... I'm going to kill you if you've lost my sword!"

"You're the one who dropped it. It's just a sword. Let it go, unless you want to be second course to the rev."

A trailing blue glow headed through the water for Pony's reaching hands. She thrust herself out of the water again, rolling backward away from the snapping jaws of the olm. Smacking her soaking arms onto the surrounding rocks, she cried out in an echoing shriek.

"Wow. Who's being the baby now?" Kess raised her eyes.

"You have no idea, *no idea* what that sword means to me!"

"I'm sorry," Kess said, and Pony's eyes snapped to look at her with an intensity of skepticism that left Kess's lips curled. "It must be a hard loss. Almost like if someone had been carefully hunting a mother dragon for almost a year, then some imbecile stumbles in and destroys everything *I've been waiting my entire life for.*"

Pony pointed an accusing finger Kess's way, spraying an

arc of water with it. Red droplets spilled from her knuckles. "As if you couldn't have just picked a different dream to follow from your lap of luxury instead of wanting the only thing in the world that was denied to you."

Kess's voice dropped, low and dangerous and with a great effort spent to not let it break. "If you think owning a dragon was the only thing denied to me, you never spent a day at Heithorn Estate with your eyes open."

Pony had the grace to shut her mouth then. Her cheeks darkened and she turned away, rolling over onto her hands and knees and staring at the ground.

In a land where the symbol of wealth was a miraculous, healing fluid, strength and power were the pinnacle of status to dragonlords. Having a weakness like Kess's was a dishonor her family did everything they could to fix, and when it couldn't be fixed, it was hidden away. And then disposed of.

Before shame could creep hotly up her own neck, Kess grumbled, "So I've lost my wolf and you've lost your sword. I'd say we're even. But I still have the hatchling, and you still have the light. And we're still stuck down here, wherever here is."

Pony still didn't look at her, just shook her head limply.

Kess continued. "I want you to know I blame you entirely for this situation. So you had better get me out of here, in one piece, or I'll make sure this baby dragon doesn't stay in one piece either."

Pony laughed, almost hysterically. "And how are we supposed to make that work?"

"I keep my hands on this hatchling. And you carry me."

Pony convulsed as though gagging.

Kess hated the idea too. She didn't want to be beholden to that intolerable traitor ever again. The thought of being in such close proximity to her for any length of time left a horrible, hot, acidic feeling melting away her chest.

The only thing the two of them had was a shared history of immeasurable cruelties. She couldn't trust Pony for a second, no doubt as much as the woman would trust her in return.

She wanted Griskin back. She hadn't thought she'd miss him so sharply. They hadn't been this far apart since they'd met. Every aspect of her existence since that day had been shared with him, and her experience of that existence changed through him.

The way his skin would shiver or his ear would twitch. The tensing of a muscle in his shoulder or the raising of a paw. The subtle differences in growl or whine or sniff, it all felt like a language between them, as though he and Kess shared the same heightened senses.

She felt numb without him, cut off at the ears and eyes and waist.

Wherever he was, somewhere up above, those other cowardly cave dwellers better not have hurt him.

Pony was still shaking her head. "I don't even know the right way out."

"Up, obviously," Kess snarled.

"I know that much. I'm not as dumb as you look. But how? Which way?" Pony shifted up into a kneeling position, gesturing to all the dark tunnels leading from the craggy cavern.

Kess glared at the options as though she could intimidate a sense of direction out of them. None seemed any more promising than the others. She looked up, the direction she hoped to go, frowning at the toothy limestone ceiling.

"That rev must have come from aboveground. The stream could have washed us down to a point where we are only just below the surface. That crack up there could get us out. If we could get up there."

Pony stood and looked at the hole above them. She ran her hands through her short tumble of fiery hair, sending droplets of water showering around her. She reached a hand up and seemed a long way from the cavern ceiling.

"Looks too high up even for a monster like you."

"I could reach it," Pony said.

Kess scoffed.

Pony bounced on her toes a few times and took a deep

breath. Stepping onto the highest nearby point, she flexed her long legs and launched upward.

Fingertips scraped the cavern ceiling. One hand missed. The other caught, clinging by nails only to an outcrop at the lip of the crevasse high above.

Pony grunted and hung for a moment by one arm before swinging the other up to join it. Her leather armor was sleeveless, with just one strap around each bicep to hold the shoulder guards in place, which tightened and strained around her upper arms as she lifted her chest in a pull-up. Her head disappeared up into the hole.

Her voice echoed as she called back, "Not a lot of space up here. Can't see any sign of daylight. I might be able to climb out but couldn't bring anyone else with me. Not someone intent on using their hands to keep threatening a baby creature anyhow."

She lowered herself down, hanging by one hand again for a moment before dropping back to the ground in a fluid, effortless motion.

It took Pony winking at Kess for her to realize she was staring with her mouth open. She shut it promptly.

Getting out of this place with her is going to be a razing nightmare.

"One of these tunnels must get us out of here," she muttered.

140

"Are you going to pick? If we take the wrong one, we could be walking around in circles until we starve to death or strangle each other."

"I'm pretty sure what will come first."

"And," Riony continued, her voice rising in frustration, "there are no carvings or signs that any human or Alderkin has ever been down here before. This might be a dead-end natural cave that nothing but the occasional falling revenant and olm have ever seen."

She swung her arm back toward the water, where a slash of glowing luminescence streaked speedily toward them. It made no sign of slowing as it approached the shore.

"Those things don't come out of the water, do they?" Kess asked.

"This morning I would have said no, but then a rev fell from the ceiling, and I feel in uncharted depths now."

Pony's eyes narrowed and she reached for the empty sheath at her side. With a breathy, grunting curse, she raised her empty fists instead, as a slithery shape breached the water and launched itself at her.

TWELVE

The grown-ups spoke, making a plan and allocating tasks to get them out of the deep hole they'd fallen into. And Lyrrin was left by the side, hovering and hurting.

She and Benjin had gone through a lot together when they were taken by the kid snatchers. When they had been pulled from their underground home and had their lives and future threatened, Lyrrin had even shared her secret with him.

She had taken off her gloves and shown him the hard, sharp, blue-tipped nails she had at the ends of her fingers. They planned together how she could use those, cutting a trail of markings along their path for those who came to save them and sawing through the bars when they were caged.

And Benjin stood watch every time Lyrrin slipped off a glove to work with her sharp nails. And he hadn't shared that secret with anyone since.

He was still a braggart, but she liked being around him now, liked that they shared an interest in Alderkin runes and magic. He'd told her with sparkling eyes all about Yoskar's staff and all the cool things it could do, and Lyrrin didn't even tease him for boasting once.

Lyrrin wasn't sure what the neck injury meant but it sounded pretty bad. She also knew if she had never thrown that glow stone she had altered at Kess, they wouldn't be where they were now, hurt and lost and dead.

Daymora cried for a bit longer, then pulled off her scarf and laid it over Jonna's body. Lyrrin couldn't see him behind the pile of fallen rocks and was scared by even the thought of seeing him, so she stayed away.

While the delvers muttered their plan over to the side, Lyrrin took a step closer to Benjin.

"How are you feeling?"

Careful not to move his neck, Benjin turned his eyes up and as far from Lyrrin as he could.

"It really doesn't hurt that much. They shouldn't be making such a fuss," he said, but his eyes were red and puffy and his nose wet where he couldn't wipe it. His brown skin was coated in a layer of pale dust, except for a couple

of places where scrapes from the fall had bled through.

"Is there anything I can do to help?" Lyrrin was starting to notice the sting of grazes on her bare knees and one bare hand. Otherwise, her oversized clothing, hood, and glove had protected her.

Even her ungloved hand only had a few minor cuts, the skin tougher there than most people's hands. She kept it hidden, tucked up her sleeve. Her other glove was probably somewhere deep within the pile of rubble.

"I'm fine. I don't need your help." Benjin still wouldn't look at her, and his mouth closed into a thin, firm line.

Probably because he also knew they wouldn't be down there, he wouldn't be hurt, if it wasn't for Lyrrin.

"I'm sorry. I know I made some mistakes, but I'm not useless. I want to help."

Benjin's golden-brown eyes reddened more. "Just leave me alone!"

"What's going on?" Yoskar snapped, glaring at Lyrrin. "Stop disturbing Benjin."

"Okay." Lyrrin backed away, and said again, even softer, "Okay."

"All right." Brishan clapped his hands together, and the group of delvers began to move apart. "Daymora, are you ready to give it a go getting out of here? I'm sorry to ask, but you're our best climber and in the best condition

after the fall."

"I'd prefer to buddy with someone for a climb like that …" She looked to Aishena and Yoskar, who both shook their heads.

"We're staying with Benjin," Yoskar said.

Niskina tried to step forward, but Brishan held her back, and Caed leaned heavily on one leg.

Daymora straightened her shoulders. "I'm sure I can make it on my own."

Brishan clapped a hand on her back. "The others might come looking for us eventually, but they're at the other end of the undercity right now. Some of the mushroom farmers must have heard the racket this made, but unless we hear someone hollering from above, we have to assume we're on our own."

Yoskar nodded. "We need to take action now. We can't risk a delay."

Brishan waved to the others. "And we'll do what we can to prep Benjin for transport from down here. With that Alderkin hoard, we might be lucky and find something with a float rune."

Lyrrin's ears pricked up. She hadn't heard of a float rune before, but she knew the delvers kept a lot of what they'd discovered of Alderkin magic to themselves, just as the Alderkin themselves had.

"Niskina, can you—"

She turned her back on her father, heading into the grand chambers. "I'm going to find something to brace Benjin's neck."

Brishan flinched, but grumbled, "Good, fine, do that. Caed, have you got bandage in your kit to wrap that leg of yours?"

"I'll sort myself out." The shaggy blond delver limped across to take a seat next to Benjin and gave him a lopsided grin. "Might have a few candies in the bag with me too."

"Did you hit your head too? Benjin shouldn't be chewing anything," Yoskar said coldly. He'd already moved through the archway and was ducking and checking the sides of furniture.

Caed popped something into his mouth and muttered around it, "Didn't say they were for him."

Lyrrin looked over the separating group, and the sulking wolf bound up beside the wall, and Benjin lying still and flat and refusing to look at her, then ran over beside Aishena.

With a deep breath and scrunched-up face, she said, "Can I help? What can I do?"

Aishena moved into the Alderkin chambers as well without looking back, but she responded with, "Help us find a float rune."

"I don't know what that looks like."

The delver paused, then squatted down over the dusty floor. Her shoulders were hunched and angular as she scribbled in the dust.

Lyrrin craned her neck, but Aishena kept her work hidden until she was done and sprang up to her feet again.

The shape she'd left drawn in the fine dirt was an upside-down triangle formed from a zigzagging line, with a couple more lines scratched across it.

Waving a hand back at it, she walked away. "It makes things practically weightless. Alderkin sometimes put it on larger objects, ceremonial crystal platforms to carry other things on, because the magic slightly affects items in contact with the runed crystal too, making them lighter."

Lyrrin memorized the shape of the rune. She hadn't seen how to activate it, even if Aishena had drawn it in the correct sequence, but Lyrrin had a knack for working out a rune's sequence. No one had shown her how to activate a blast rune either—a *four-stroke* rune—and she worked it out in only twelve tries.

There was an obvious pattern to how to trace the lines, a way that just felt right. The float rune was only a three-stroke rune. Easy.

Aishena ran her hands over a spike of orange crystal as long as her arm, brushing dust off. She muttered, "Imagine having all of that magic and using it to move furniture."

"Oh, they used it for plenty of other things too," Brishan replied from across the cluttered space.

Lyrrin followed after Aishena, looking at the crystal she passed by. No float rune on it. No runes at all, so the crystal probably had no charge either.

If there was something though, with a charge, anything big enough, maybe I could add the float rune onto it myself.

Lyrrin fidgeted the fingers of her ungloved hand around the hem of the sleeve she had it hidden up inside. But she'd never tried combining a float rune with another before and couldn't be sure what the recipe would do. She knew from experience that some combinations were explosive.

And even the result of her best experiment, the flash stone, had gone very wrong.

"A lot of this stuff seems half-finished, crystals and items being prepared for later use," Yoskar said from beside a set of shelves that were carved into the cave wall and filled with calcite rhombohedrons and prisms in pale blues, yellows, and whites.

"That geode slab is something," Aishena said, passing it warily. "A lot like the one in the shrine we camped in aboveground."

"Most Alderkin shrines aboveground have something like that in them," Brishan said. "Not so unusual. But there are a lot of relics in here I've never seen before. The

Alderkin had trashed most of their personal belongings in the top level during their last stand. Even what we could salvage, it was never like this."

"Stop salivating, Fadda." Niskina stopped beside a table and picked up a thick ancient tome, assessing the binding. She wrenched the cover off, then tore it to pieces, pulling out some rigid strips.

Yoskar winced audibly, hissing in a breath.

Niskina didn't stop. "You'll get your chance to rob the dead later, once we all get out of here alive."

Brishan's face flushed red, even in the cyan light. "The work we do serves all the people of the undercity!"

"But you serve yourselves first. Always acting high and mighty that you aren't like the dragonlords, while you're doing the same thing, really. Making yourself rich off others. Others who often end up dead." She paused her destruction of the priceless relic to give her father a long, fiery glare through glossy eyes.

"I suppose you think a life aboveground as a rebel would be any safer?" He flung an arm up dismissively and turned his back on her.

"No, but at least then I'd be making a difference."

Lyrrin turned around, pretending to be searching along a low side cupboard. But a glint of light from the wall above caught her eye, and she looked up.

She had to move a few steps backward to take in and make sense of the flowing, carved shapes on the stone surface. And as she did, an image became clear.

"Whoa," she gasped.

In the corner of the room's shadowy depths, a mural sprawled across the expanse, a tapestry of realistic figures, carved in intricate detail and adorned with the shimmer of inlaid crystals.

At the center of the scene, a man on horseback reared, his arm poised in frozen action. His features seemed aflame with unyielding cruelty. A streaking arc of motion was struck through the stone, leading from his arm to a spear—a spear lodged into the skull of a dragon soaring above.

The dragon, wrought in tarnished gold and ruby reds, hung in midair, head bowed in agony, its serpentine form spiraling in anguish.

Poor thing was the first thought that came to Lyrrin. The injured dragon looked so deeply broken and sad.

"The leg's not too bad. Just sprained, I think." Caed hobbled into the room, catching up to the others.

"You should stay with Benjin. Someone needs to stay with Benjin." Yoskar headed back their way, converging with Aishena who made the same move.

"I ... I can," Lyrrin offered. She wasn't sure Benjin would like her company, but it was something she could

do without causing more problems. Although, despite her offer, she couldn't take her eyes off the mural.

A pale section of satin spar below the horse's feet caught her eye, and she gasped. A fallen unicorn lay there, its elegant form broken and sullied on the ground, its eyes empty and vacant. Swirls of silver were inlaid into the ground beneath it.

And standing witness to the tragic scene were tall figures in a style of clothing Lyrrin hadn't seen before. They seemed human, but taller, narrower, with mournful expressions and large, somber eyes of bright, glistening gems.

Caed had reached where she stood and turned to follow her gaze. "Yikes, did you all see this?"

Aishena and Yoskar, already heading their way, stepped closer to look. Brishan and Niskina also turned from where they had been searching the largest table, continuing their argument in whispers.

Caed pointed up high, and Lyrrin tilted her head back, seeing the final part of the design that she hadn't noticed before from her shorter vantage point.

Behind the flying dragon, another ethereal form unfurled its wings.

Captured with inlays of a dark, oily stone that Lyrrin didn't recognize, a specter of shadow and smoke mirrored the pierced dragon. Wrathful and disturbing, its presence even in the mural seemed to merge with the very essence of darkness itself.

"It's the curse." Aishena's nose scrunched up and she took a step away from the mural as though it itself was the cause of all that plagued the land. "It's showing when the Alderkin cursed us all with the shadow dragon."

Caed shivered. "Stars, this whole place feels cursed."

Aishena turned to him, wide-eyed. "You don't think this *is* the source of the curse? Some magic in this image?"

A cold chill shuddered down Lyrrin's back. Scanning over the mural, she couldn't see any runes or other Alderkin symbols that suggested this was some kind of spell wrought from stone.

Niskina tsked and took a step closer, letting her gaze wander over the artwork. "I really doubt it."

With her voice low so Brishan couldn't hear, Aishena muttered, "You're just being contrary because you think it makes you seem smarter."

Niskina tucked her tumble of chestnut curls behind her ear. "I seem smarter because I think critically about things instead of believing whatever some old idiots tell me. And just look at this! This could be an accurate Alderkin record of the first tamed dragon. They could have *been there*."

Niskina pointed at the figures surrounding the rider.

Were they Aldkerin? Lyrrin had never seen images of

them before. Anything in the undercity level had been destroyed, either by Alderkin themselves or the first humans to settle there.

Yoskar sniffed at the mural and those gawking at it once. He adjusted his glasses, then marched off. "I'll be with Benjin."

Caed raised his eyebrows at Niskina. "So you'd believe the old idiots that created this image instead, who were also our enemies?"

"They were only our enemies because the dragonlords were killing unicorns." She stared hard at where the magical creature in the mural lay with its life spilled out on the ground. She moved closer, reaching out a hand to touch it.

Everyone else at the mural tensed.

"Could you imagine, seeing one in person? Having lived while they still lived?" Her voice was soft, dreamy. She sighed sadly as her fingertips brushed over the image of the dead unicorn, but there didn't appear to be any other consequences, no trap or curse set off by her touch.

Emboldened, Lyrrin stepped closer too. She was fixated on the sparkling gemstone eyes of the Alderkin, in startling sapphire, emerald, and amethyst. They all wore hoods, and most stood gravely with their hands behind their backs. But one had his hand lifted, pointing at the tragedy before them.

And that hand had long, sharp nails. Not so much

longer or sharper than a regular human's, on first glance. Only as long and sharp as her own.

The chill that had shuddered through Lyrrin now rattled deep in her bones.

Niskina huffed violently, making Lyrrin jump and hurry away from the mural. Her heart pounded furiously, and she clenched her ungloved fist, throwing furtive, confused glances at the mural.

Niskina said roughly, "We should have been on their side. We should have fought alongside them to stop the dragonlords draining the land of every drop of silvernix they could get. Now all the unicorns are gone and look at the world we're left with."

Aishena lifted her hands in disbelief. "Yeah, because the Alderkin cursed us!"

"And maybe we deserved it!"

"Enough bickering," Brishan commanded with a sigh. "Emotions are high. We're all grieving and haven't been given room for that grief while we're still stuck in this situation. So let's work together and get out of it sooner rather than later."

Niskina sorted the strips and boards she'd accumulated from destroying ancient relics in her hands. Nodding once, she headed for where Benjin lay.

"I still think this place is cursed." Caed sighed and limped over beside Brishan, helping search the overflowing table.

Aishena tossed a final glare at the mural, then shook her head once. "The shadow dragon didn't even appear until decades after the first taming. Probably because that was when the Alderkin cursed us, when they knew they were losing the war. This is all rubbish."

Everyone moved away, continuing the search.

Lyrrin felt glued to the spot.

In that moment, she didn't care about the shadow dragon and who cursed who, or why or when.

She'd never seen anyone else like her before. She'd never seen anyone who came out different at birth because of silvernix being used in the pregnancy. It wasn't allowed for that very reason. It was a rule only rarely broken.

Amma had said babies born in the time before people knew better had a whole range of strange features, so even if she did meet another silvernix baby, they probably wouldn't be the same.

So how was she now looking at someone who felt so much like her? Bright-eyed, sharp-clawed. She wanted to reach out and pull down the Alderkins' hoods of stone and see their hair.

Did she really want that though? She felt so desperate for connection, but the Alderkin were an extinct, reclusive race that had struck the humans and land with magical warfare for decades and then left it behind, cursed.

They were evil monsters, and humans had only moved into their haunted, abandoned, underground city in desperation.

So why did Lyrrin's chest tremor with an overwhelming, yearning sense of belonging that she'd never felt so close to touching before?

THIRTEEN

The surface of the water broke in a spray of blue light, and a slithery, caramel streak launched upward.

Riony opened her fisted hands and reached for the flying otter. She snatched him from the air as the open maw of the huge olm bobbed above the water, seeking another meal.

"Butterfur?" Riony tried to keep hold of Lyrrin's cave otter, but he skittered up her arm and circled around her shoulders a couple of times, chittering angrily at the luminescent pool. The olm circled and disappeared into the depths.

"Oh. It's that thing again," Kess grumbled.

"You sound so disappointed you didn't get to watch me flex my fighting muscles again."

Kess scowled in reply.

Riony moved away from the water in case the olm really did decide to slither out to eat them. Sir Butterfur Spelunkychunks stopped nattering and sniffed a couple of times before climbing down Riony's chest and trying to break into a pouch on her belt.

Taking a moment to breathe and blink, Riony stared at the otter using her body as a climbing wall, wondering why and how he ended up there too.

"Did ... you come for treats?"

He snuffled, pressing his snout into the closure of the pouch and gnawing at the stitching with his pointy teeth.

"Okay, hold on!"

Riony dodged his bites as she undid the drawstring and pulled out a soggy piece of shroom jerky for the otter.

"Why did you come all the way here for treats? Did Lyrrin tell you I had them? If she did, and you found me ..." she said, mostly to herself.

Maybe he could help them find the right way back up again too, back to Lyrrin.

A tremor of heartache shivered through Riony.

Lyrrin must be so worried. At least she's safe up there with the delvers. I'll get back to her soon.

"I think I have a plan." She addressed Kess but looked at where Dracuni lay still and trembling in Kess's arms,

knife to her throat.

Her lilac eyes were wide open now, and water dripped from the muzzle.

Breathing hard.

Riony spoke directly to the dragonling. "We're getting out of here. Butterfur is going to help us find the way."

"That's your plan? We're going to follow a cave rodent?" Kess asked.

"He's got good senses. He might be able to sniff out the right way. Better that than choosing randomly."

Riony knelt on the ground, pulling off one of her belts and a coil of cave silk rope and laid them out in front of her.

Butterfur jumped off too, sniffing around the items on the ground in case more treats were being put out for him. Droplets of water beaded off his silky fur.

Riony looked over to Kess, sizing her up.

Riony's leather delving armor felt gross and squelchy, and she hoped the plunge through the water channel hadn't ruined it. The vest section, which extended down like a harness with straps that looped around the upper thighs, was going to be too big for Kess, but it would have to do. Riony undid the buckles and stripped it off.

The air in the cavern felt cold through the damp, thin layer of her remaining undershirt. She tossed the vest over to Kess.

"Put that on and do it up as tight as you can get it."

"I don't know what sort of fantasy you're trying to indulge in right now—"

"It's to carry you, dumbass. You wear that, I'll loop my belt and rope through the attachment points, and I can wear you like a backpack. That keeps arms free for both of us, since I'm assuming you're not letting go of my dragonling yet?"

Kess picked up the nearby vest with one hand and inspected it warily, all the while keeping her knife to Dracuni's neck. "*My* dragon. And I'm not exactly in love with the idea of being literally tied to *you*."

"What, were you expecting me to princess carry you out of here?"

Kess glared back as she put one arm into the vest, then switched hands holding the dagger to put the other arm through. "Do you really think you can carry us both all the way out of here like that?"

"Physically, no sweat. Emotionally, time will sparking tell."

Kess had always been on the smaller size, and whatever she'd been doing running around outside her estate like some wild girl on a wolf hadn't put any more meat on her bones. Dracuni probably weighed as much as her.

Riony frowned at Kess's thin but wiry arms. "Are you going to be able to keep holding the dragonling the

whole way?"

"Don't question my capabilities, Pony."

"Oh, I am loving the idea of being tied together for the foreseeable future as much as you are." Riony wiped the blood off her cut knuckles and approached Kess and Dracuni.

Kess tensed, keeping her dagger pressed to the dragonling and staring mutely as Riony adjusted the buckles even tighter and tied the rope and belt through the metal rings and straps on Kess's side and back.

Help, scared. Dracuni mewled, and Riony reached out a hand to comfort her.

Kess jerked the dragonling farther away. "Don't try anything."

Gritting her teeth, Riony turned around and pulled the makeshift straps over her shoulders, pulling her and Kess's backs together. Pulling the belt around her chest, she buckled it tightly.

She was going to get them all out of there, even if she had to bring Kess along too. Even if it the simple act of carrying her brought back flashes of trauma that left her sick to her stomach.

The scars on her back seemed to burn.

Giving a swift shake of her head, Riony huffed out a breath, pushing all of those emotions down. She tested the straps one more time, then pressed up to her feet. It

took a moment to readjust her center of gravity, leaning forward to make up for Kess against her back and Dracuni in Kess's arms.

"You good?" Riony checked.

"This is so humiliating."

"You smell like wet dog."

"You smell like cave dirt. Can we get moving already? Quickly?"

Riony agreed with Kess on that. The less time spent like this, the better.

"Hey, furry worm." Riony clicked her tongue until Butterfur looked at her. "Lyrrin has the treats."

His whiskers twitched, and he stood upright on his back legs, turning his snout up and around. Then without hesitation, he wriggled off toward the second tunnel on the right.

And Riony followed. Her footsteps fell heavier than usual, crackling over the crystal rimstone, but once she built up momentum, it wasn't much of a strain carrying the extra weight.

"This had better work out, Pony."

"If I had a way to kill you now before you stuck that poor baby with a knife, I would do it."

After a quiet moment, Kess murmured, "I know."

Riony grimaced and clenched her teeth.

There had been plenty of times when Riony carried Lyrrin around. It never bothered her, not in the way carrying Kess had.

But Lyrrin saw her as her sister, not as livestock to be worked hard and whipped for the fun of it. There was one time, though, when Lyrrin was only five years old. Riony had been playing a game and galloping around with her, and Lyrrin called her Pony in a shriek of joy.

She'd had to set Lyrrin carefully down on the ground and then go and sit alone for a long while until the rampant shivers of old fury and fear calmed.

Lyrrin didn't understand. But she never called her Pony again.

The tunnel they followed the cave otter into was narrow, and Riony worried it would scurry through a tiny crack and leave them. But he remained just ahead, sniffing the air and meandering along the rocky slope.

Riony's glow stone dangled from where her belt was now strapped across her lower ribs, and the cave silk rope dug into her shoulders, but she kept a sure footing on the uneven ground and loose pieces of ancient, crumbled stalagmites.

The slope became steeper, and Butterfur scrambled up a pile of smashed rocks and through a hole above.

The loose debris shifted under Riony's feet, but she grabbed the ledge of the horizontal opening and pulled

them all up through it, crawling out onto the level above. Kess and Dracuni flopped heavily over her back. Kess's tangle of messy braids tickled Riony's neck. Dracuni breathed roughly.

The ground there was flat. Unnaturally flat, and Riony looked up from her hands and knees to see a long tunnel with a paved floor and arched nooks and niches running up each side, carved into the stone.

Out of the natural cave system and into something else. That's progress, at least.

Turning to the niche closest to her, she found herself face-to-face with a humanoid skull.

Scrambling up to her feet, Riony checked the other alcoves. Ancient, cobwebbed skeletons lay in every one.

She held her breath for a long moment, waiting to see if they moved.

"They aren't revenants," Kess said, although her voice was hushed as though she still didn't want to risk waking them. "This may be some kind of burial catacombs?"

Riony also knew, from some talk of history somewhere in her past, that some races buried their deceased. But when burning the dead had been the only safe option for decades, the practice creeped Riony out in a wide range of ways.

Around the arched spaces, delicately twining designs of flowers and vines reminded Riony of the patterns sculpted

around her shelving at home.

"The carvings look like Alderkin work. And I can't believe I'm saying this, but finding a tunnel filled with skeletons is probably a good sign. At least people have been here before, which must mean they had a way to get out again too."

Riony checked for Butterfur, who continued to happily trot along through the halls of the dead. He'd never had to worry about revenants in his life, lucky critter.

Kess shifted, her knobbly spine rubbing against Riony's. "We keep going then."

"You mean *I* keep going. And you get the unmatched joy of riding me." Riony pressed forward again. Puffs of dust lifted from the ground with each footstep, and strange sounds, barely audible, echoed all around.

"Do you have to say it that way? Besides, I'd trade you for Griskin any day."

"Yeah. About that ... How did you end up with a wolf as your mount of choice?"

"What, you want me to share my story? Like that's going to make me open up and get emotional and change my mind about getting out of here with my dragon?"

"No, it's just that when a jerk from your past rides in on a sparking wolf, you get curious, you know?" Riony gave a beleaguered sigh. "I just, I never thought I'd see you again. I thought you'd never leave your estate, and I sure as stars wasn't going back there either. The fact that you're here is doing my head in."

"So sorry to disappoint you."

An unpleasant warmth had built up in the wet layers between Riony and Kess's back. It made Riony itch and ache, as though the old wounds there were reopening. She gritted her teeth, trying to stay focused on moving forward.

An intersection came up, and Riony stepped onto a fallen slab of stone to turn the way Butterfur had gone. Unstable, it tilted and Riony pitched to the side, knocking the three of them against a wall.

Ow! Dracuni whimpered.

"I'm sorry, Drac— Sorry."

Kess hissed, "Be more careful!"

Riony tucked her thumbs in under the straps at her shoulders and marched on. "Or what? You're going to whip me?"

Her footsteps and harsh breathing crackled through the silence.

"I ... Only once. I only did once."

"And the other million times you just got someone else to do it for you!"

Riony didn't know why she even said it. She didn't expect an apology, and how the silence drew on, she knew she wasn't going to get one.

Kess wasn't lying. The whip had only struck from Kess's own hands once. But that somehow made it so much worse. That Riony had been so far beneath care, beneath being seen as a person or anything of any value, that she wasn't even worth being punished directly.

It was such a screwed-up, awful thought, and everything felt wrong and confusing in her head, and she hated that Kess's presence made it all come out again, that feeling that she was less than nothing.

That cruelest oppression of simultaneously being owned and unwanted.

Kess's back sagged against Riony's. Her voice was soft and even as she said, "I left Heithorn Estate ... My brother ... He took me for a ride on his dragon."

"Nice. Doesn't sound like him at all." If Kess had always been an amateur psychopath, Kife had a heart so lightless it put the darkest of the Alderkin depths to shame.

"Then he dropped me in the charred wastelands and left me to die alone."

Riony swallowed hard. She fought down the chilling emotion creeping through her chest. *No.* She would not, absolutely would not feel sorry for the miserable gremlin that even at that moment held a knife to Dracuni's throat.

"I always hated him," was all Riony could say.

She trudged along, Kess's legs bumping against the backs of hers.

Kess sniffed aloofly. "I figured as much from the time you spiked his soup with a sprig of morass mercy at the harvest moon feast."

"You planned that! You made me do it!"

"And you executed the plan with more glee than I'd ever seen you follow orders with."

Riony's lips twisted viciously into an uncontrollable grin. "The way he passed out, face-first, right into the bowl in front of everyone ..."

Kess didn't laugh, but there was a soft tremor or convulsion in her back, and then she stilled again and cleared her throat. "Now, I've told you how I ended up with Griskin—"

"You did not."

"How about you? Have you been hiding underground since your family decided to commit murder and go on the run?"

Riony tilted her head. She often wondered what rumors spread around the estate after their escape. It seemed as though Kess didn't know it was Riony who had killed the dragonguard with his own sword, or why.

Riony sorely felt the loss of her sword again. She let that sadness flood her senses so that she didn't fall into the larger grief of the loss of her parents.

She chatted lightly, "We actually spent several lovely years living in a nice village in an old quarry with a beautiful waterfall nearby, which was everything that murderous fugitives could wish for."

"More than the noose that was waiting for you at Heithorn Estate."

Riony palmed her forehead. "I knew there was another reason we didn't go back, other than never wanting to see you again."

Riony could almost hear Kess's eye roll. "And who is that blue-eyed kid that you almost gave your life to save from slavers? Where did you pick her up?"

"She's my sister." Riony bit her lip. She couldn't trust Kess, but Kess had been there, at the estate, when the pregnant guest came to give birth. Neither of them knew who the young woman was at the time, but in the period after Riony and her family had fled with Lyrrin, maybe Kess had heard something.

Maybe Kess knew who Lyrrin's mother was.

"She's not your sister. Any fool could see that. But still you risked your life for her." Kess's voice dropped, almost confused. "Her, and now this dragonling too. Why are you trying so hard to save it? It's like you're still a slave to others, giving your life for everyone around you."

Any softness Riony felt fled instantly. She growled,

"At least it's my choice now."

"But why? What do you get out of it?"

Riony threw her hands up. "Helping the people I love and who love me? That's what I get out of it! Not that you could understand that."

"No ... No, I couldn't."

Kess didn't speak or move again for a long time. Riony kept up the path, following Butterfur as he led the way through a labyrinth of short, interconnecting corridors stacked with bones on either side. They reached some stairs and headed up them.

The ancient, dry limestone felt crumbly under Riony's boots. The new level opened into wider tunnels, with high ceilings and alcoves of a grander scale, columns and flourishes carved into the facades. With only a small pool of light to see by, it seemed as though tunnels led out into an infinite void in every direction.

A twittering, crunching sound came from down a side path, and Riony peered into the darkness. Shadowy, eight-legged silhouettes crawled over a still twitching corpse.

Bad bones, thought Dracuni with a whimper.

"So happy for us we aren't going that way." Riony turned sideways so Kess could look too.

"Is that another rev?" She shuddered. "More importantly, what are those things all over it?"

The revenant, something dog-sized and four-legged, snarled and gurgled as the spiders stripped the meat from its bones. Riony had seen the skull-sized critters before, generally only a couple at a time. But they swarmed en masse over the rev.

Carrion eaters were fairly common in the depths, scavenging on whatever they could get. But between the spiders and the olm, Riony was starting to wonder where they were getting all their food from down there.

She wondered how many revs had been falling from the ceiling.

It's probably something else. They're probably all just eating each other. Otherwise, there would be more bones around. Ones not neatly tucked into niches.

"Just cave spiders," Riony replied, relishing when Kess shivered again. "On the plus side, if we're down here long enough to get hungry, we know what we can eat."

"The *spiders*?" Kess balked. "You cave dwellers are disgusting. You probably eat worms."

Riony smirked and got moving after Butterfur again. "They're delicious fried. A bit of salt to bring out the flavor. So fatty the juices drip down your chin. Mmmmm."

"I'm not sure if I'm more worried about your diet or that rev back there."

"The spiders have it pinned; I don't think it's coming

after us," Riony replied.

"No, you tame-brain." Kess leaned back, turning her head to whisper into Riony's ear, as though what she was saying couldn't be said too loud. "I'm worried that if there are revs getting in down here, but they aren't going up and attacking you worm-eating cave dwellers up above ..."

Oh. Riony's heart sank as she caught up. "That there might not be a way out."

FOURTEEN

"I think I found one!" Caed called out from a corner of the Alderkin chambers close to the archway. He leaned into a gap between the wall and some tall shelves, hopping on his good leg.

Lyrrin turned from where she had been pretending to search the low side cupboard below the mural but had really been studying the Alderkin images with hungry eyes, hoping for any other details or clues about why their hands looked so much like hers. Why their eyes shone bright like hers.

"What do you mean *think*? Either you found it or not." Aishena stalked toward the delver, an anxious menace to her step as though suggesting he better have the correct answer.

Caed extracted a large sheet of pale-blue calcite from a stack of shining stones. It was as long and wide as his torso, straight on three sides with a couple of natural points at the top, as though it had been a slice cut from the center of a huge twin crystal.

"I mean, it's a float rune, but the final mark isn't right," he said, holding it up for Aishena to see.

Lyrrin moved closer to watch as well, the allure of seeing a new kind of rune activated enough to draw her from her obsessive staring at the mural.

Aishena ran her hands over it, wiping off dust and some strands of cave silk. "Hmm, it's like it's been chipped off in that section."

"I already tried activating it, but nothing happened," Caed said apologetically. "This whole stack here seems to be damaged goods."

"Any news?" Yoskar called from beside Benjin.

Niskina looked up too, pausing from her work creating a neck brace to keep Benjin's head still.

Aishena shook her head. "No, it's no good. We'll keep looking."

Benjin's cheeks were red, and he stared up into the hole above them with a huffy expression. "I want to see. What are they doing?"

Caed moved closer and held the slab up high for Benjin

to look at. "Sorry, buddy, the rune's damaged."

"Can't you fix it? We're spending too long down here when we should be helping Riony," he said, although he still didn't look at Lyrrin.

Brishan joined them in the archway and pulled a flask from his belt, taking a swig. "Don't have the tools. We've never successfully been able to carve our own runes. The crystal just doesn't seem to take to chisels or files. Not sure how the Alderkin made their marks."

Benjin's nose scrunched up as though in pain, then he blurted out, "Lyrrin can. Lyrrin could fix the rune."

Lyrrin's face flushed. She *had* been able to make those same marks. She had talked with Benjin about her experiments, and he'd even offered ideas for new combinations to try. But that was meant to stay a secret. "Benj—!"

"Please try. Don't you want to get out of here? Don't you want to go and help your sister?" His voice sounded rough.

"I do. But ..."

"Can you really carve runes? How?" Yoskar got to his feet and stared at Lyrrin. Everyone stared at Lyrrin.

Her first impulse was to lie. She'd lied and told half-truths her whole life to keep her hands hidden. It had been the one rule her parents and Riony had always enforced, not to be broken, lest the worst happen. Lyrrin was never told explicitly what *the worst* was, but she'd imagined plenty of terrible things.

Then the slavers had taken her and Benjin and the other children and that had felt like the worst had already happened, and sharing her secret with Benjin seemed like something she had to do.

Even Riony had said to her, *Sometimes taking action is more important than staying secret at the time. We'll work the rest out as we go.*

Maybe she could fix the broken rune. Maybe she could do the one thing needed to save Benjin.

Lyrrin's ungloved hand trembled as she lowered it down from hiding within her sleeve. She held it up in front of her. "I just ... I have sharp nails."

"Whoa," Caed gasped.

"Is that why you're always wearing gloves? I thought maybe you just had burn scars," Aishena said. She reached out an upturned palm and waited for Lyrrin to offer her own hand in return.

Lyrrin pulled her hand back closer to herself, bit her lip, and then extended it again to place it in Aishena's. Her skin tingled as Aishena brushed her fingertips over Lyrrin's clawed nails. It felt so wrong letting anyone see her hands, let alone touch them.

But Aishena offered a half smile and said, "It's like you've got your very own built-in daggers. I'm jealous."

A smile twitched on Lyrrin's lips too.

Brishan watched from above, brows set low over his eyes as he examined Lyrrin's hands.

"You can really cut crystal with those?" Yoskar ducked down beside his sister, the light of their glow crystals glinting off his glasses, lighting up his wide eyes as he studied her hands.

"Yeah. I've done it before."

"With runes? That worked?" Yoskar's tone was sharper than a knife.

"Uh-huh." Lyrrin didn't want to tell them all the details of the blast rune she'd added to the glow stone that had blinded Riony and led them to falling into this pit, so she chewed on her lip, hoping they wouldn't ask.

"Do you want to have a try fixing this up?" Caed asked, placing the sheet of crystal on the floor on one end and holding it upright in front of her. "It just needs this line extended down to here."

The glossy surface caught the light of the glow stones from the surrounding delvers. The float rune was carved large in the top center of the slab, surrounded by the usual hardening rune most crystal artifacts utilized to make the soft calcite more resilient and functional.

Lyrrin examined where a shell-shaped section had been chipped off, taking with it the end of one line. Another

crack spread from that impact point, running through the middle of the rune.

With all eyes on her, Lyrrin took off her other glove. She worked better with her left hand. Tentatively, she pressed her nail firmly into the crystal.

The grating, high-pitched screech sounded like the crystal screaming as she re-carved the missing line.

Caed winced and shuddered from his position holding the relic. "Ow, my teeth!"

"That's it, that's the complete rune now," Aishena said, one of her eyes twitching from the effect of the sound. "I'll try ..."

Lyrrin was already tracing over the rune with a soft brush of her fingertips. She knew that the line she'd fixed would be the last in the sequence, from what Caed said. And it just made sense that the spiraling triangular line would be first.

She felt the stone hum under her touch as her fingertip danced across the etched shapes. And the slab of crystal came to life with a cool purple glow, lifting from the ground.

Then it pulsed violently, and with a smacking crack, split apart right along the fine fracture line.

Caed dropped the broken sections. "Sparks, it must have been too damaged."

Yoskar kicked at one of the broken pieces. "We almost

had it."

"I'm sorry," Lyrrin said, looking up at the surrounding delvers.

"Not your fault," Niskina said. "You did great. That's a pretty amazing thing you can do."

Benjin coughed roughly from beside her. He was refusing to look at her again. Lyrrin didn't feel very amazing.

"Maybe we can find another one, less damaged, or hopefully not damaged at all. I'll keep looking." Caed limped off toward the back of the room.

Lyrrin tried to follow, wanting to distance herself from the failure, but a hand grabbed her shoulder.

"How did you know how to activate that rune?" Aishena asked. "I never showed you how to do that."

Brishan folded his arms, frowning at her as he waited for the answer too.

"I just guessed. It's only three lines, and Caed said which was the final one. I'm pretty good at guessing runes, and it's easy to know when you're right, because of how the stone sings to you."

"How the stone does what?" Yoskar had been walking away but turned back to Lyrrin then. His crystal-studded staff was strapped to his back and protruded over his shoulder as he leaned over her.

"You ... you don't feel that when you trace the runes

the right way?" Lyrrin replied.

The delvers returned a blank stare.

Lyrrin tried to make herself smaller. "It's just a feeling I get. Not a sound really, just like a warm humming inside. I thought ... I thought everyone did."

Aishena looked at Yoskar, and Yoskar shook his head and looked to Brishan, who hadn't taken his shrewd eyes off Lyrrin. Niskina shrugged. Benjin made an embarrassed choking sound.

"There are a bunch of runes I haven't seen before on some of this stuff. Maybe she could help us figure some of them out." Aishena pulled her larger belt pouch open, showing a mass of crystal chunks jammed in there along with some wadded-up parchments. She must have been collecting as she'd searched.

Niskina's eyes turned toward the large standing stone in the middle of the chambers, then back to Lyrrin. "Or the runes on the geode slice. Do you think you could try to work some of those out?"

"We don't know what those runes might do," Yoskar warned. "On something so big, that's a risk."

Niskina tilted her head toward Benjin. "I just thought maybe they could be healing runes."

Aishena's eyes popped wide, and she turned, pleading and hopeful, to her older brother. "She could be right. We

know Alderkin had healing magic, but they didn't like hurting unicorns, right? So maybe they had something else. Healing magic of their own."

She turned to Brishan. "Aren't there old stories from before humans worked out how to bottle silvernix, about how people would go to the Alderkin shrines to beg aid from the Alderkin when they needed healing?"

"There are," Brishan said. "And just about all shrines I've seen have one of these geodes in them, if they hadn't been broken already. But people went to the shrines to beg the Alderkin to get the unicorns to help them, from what I understand, and they rarely did."

Aishena wrung her hands, looking from Benjin to the large standing crystal. "We don't know for sure though. The Alderkin were so secretive."

Lyrrin watched and tried to work out how old Brishan was. He seemed very, very old to her, but a lot of grown-ups seemed very old to her. Even if he was only as extremely old as fifty, he would have been alive when Alderkin were still around, during the wars. She wondered if he'd ever seen one up close.

He bowed his head. "I don't know. Maybe it is worth a try."

"I can try," Lyrrin agreed. She wanted to do what she could to help, because Benjin was right. She wanted to get

out of there, then try to find Riony and Dracuni. And she wanted to get out of there without anyone getting more hurt.

Aishena moved over to the geode first and gestured at the engraved lines at the base. "I think this is the main rune here. The other markings surrounding the ring"—she pointed at more than vast array of smaller designs all around the circular crystal—"don't look like normal runes. They look more like pictorial symbols, maybe just decorative."

Lyrrin stood beside her, staring up at the huge crystal. The massive geode was a silvery blue, its sharp-toothed points angling into the hollow center and rings of deeper and deeper blue surrounding outward.

The gap in the middle was almost as tall as Riony, and if Lyrrin stood in the middle with her arms out, she didn't think she could touch both sides at once.

"That's a five-stroke rune," Brishan said.

Lyrrin jumped, startled. She hadn't realized he'd followed them over too.

"You think you can work that out?" he asked.

"Maybe. I worked out a four last week."

He raised his eyebrows.

"Try. I'm going to keep looking for another float rune," Aishena said. Her voice had a sharp, anxious edge, and she slipped away like a ghoul into the shadows.

Lyrrin crouched down, ignoring how the scrapes on

her knees pulled and split, and tried to take in the flow and pattern of the rune before trying to trace it.

"Riony," Brishan broached softly, kneeling down beside her. "She's not your blood sister, is she?"

"No?" Lyrrin replied like a question, wondering and a little scared that Brishan was going to suggest she start preparing not to see Riony again. That maybe them not being related by blood might make that easier.

"Do you know who your birth parents are?"

"My amma was a young dragonlord lady," Lyrrin replied confidently, because she felt it was best to tell the truth as Riony and her parents had told the story to her. "She didn't want to keep me because of how I was born different, probably because of silvernix used in the pregnancy, so Riony stole me."

Brishan raised his eyebrows, crinkling his forehead all the way up to his braided salt-and-pepper hair.

"They never saw who my pabba was, but he was probably an Elgarthian, considering my coloring."

"They do have your pale skin," he agreed, although he kept staring at her as though she was a puzzle to be solved.

He didn't say anything else as Lyrrin tried a few combinations for the lines of the rune.

It was definitely more complicated than any Lyrrin had tried before. The design was mostly symmetrical, with

one asymmetrical section in the middle where the lines swirled to meet each other. Two brackets and a V-shape surrounded that middle spiral.

Lyrrin let her fingertips play over the design, listening for the hum of the magic, trying each line in turn, one way and then the other, until she found one that sent the buzz of enchantment thrumming through her. Then she worked until she found the second, then third.

Did nobody else really feel that same hum of magic? She wondered how anyone had worked out any of the previous runes without having been able to feel they were on the right line. They could be guessing forever and never know if they had any part of the sequence right.

It didn't help much having Brishan watching her every movement with narrowed eyes. A couple of times she forgot the steps she'd already worked out, just due to nerves. But within only about ten minutes, Lyrrin reached the fifth line and completed the sequence.

At first nothing happened. A small glow to Lyrrin's left attracted her attention, as one of the pictorial symbols lit up.

"Is that all it does?" Lyrrin reached over and touched the shining glyph. And then the entire geode flashed with a silvery light.

Between the sharp teeth of the crystal, the hollow center shimmered and swirled and then reformed to show a sparkling image of another place. Ruined walls, a broken stone ceiling. A stream of dull light piercing down to a rough leaf-strewn floor.

"What happened?" Yoskar came charging over.

"Did you get it working already?" Aishena asked, appearing in a flash as well.

"It's doing ... something," Lyrrin replied. Although, heartbreakingly, it didn't seem to be the something they needed.

"That's ..." Aishena cast her eyes over the huge geode and the scene glowing from within. She stepped closer, holding her hand near the rippling surface of light. "It looks like somewhere aboveground. There are plants, things growing on the walls."

"I don't think this is a healing device," Brishan said. "I think this is a gateway, magic to take you somewhere else. There were rumors the Alderkin had such magic, but only ever rumors."

"You mean this would actually take us to where the image is showing us?" Aishena asked. "If it could take us aboveground, we can get out of here!"

Brishan clapped a hand on her shoulder, as though worried she was about to step through. "But we don't know where to. Alderkin shrines with these ring crystals are all over Elundrae. That could take you anywhere in the land."

Caed limped over, his face lit by the silver glow as he stared agape. "You mean we could travel to different places without having to fight our way through the revs? This could mean travel and trade with the dragonkeeps!"

"You say that like it's a good idea," Niskina scoffed. "If we bring the dragonlords into our business, they're going to want to claim the undercity for themselves."

She came closer to look at the portal as well. The light glimmered off her dark curls.

"I should go through," Aishena said. She was already adjusting and checking over her gear, making sure she had everything in place. "Then I can see where it comes out to, work out that location, and if it's close enough to the undercity, come back with help. I found these maps as well, when searching before. I can track my way with them."

She pulled out a large square of folded parchment from a side pouch, opening it to show the others the sepia ink lines in the shape of the land.

"No," Yoskar said. "It's not safe. It could be a one-way trip, and you could end up stuck on the other side of Elundrae. We stick together."

"I just, I really feel like it looks like the shrine we stayed at. Only half a day's hike from the undercity."

"They all look pretty much the same, I'm afraid," Brishan said.

"Deactivate it," Yoskar commanded.

Lyrrin looked to Aishena, but the lean girl just nodded solemnly. She refolded the map and tucked it away.

Lyrrin dragged her fingers over the lines of the rune again, and the glimmering window flickered out in a flash, and the sense of hope she'd felt a moment before flickered out just as fast.

Through the archway, Benjin coughed again. What had sounded before like him clearing his throat in distaste, now came out as a wheezing gasp for breath.

Yoskar and Aishena bolted between the stacked tables and cupboards to return to his side. Lyrrin followed but remained a few steps back.

Benjin's eyes reddened as he sucked air through a whistling throat. "It's just the dust. I'm fine."

Lyrrin reached for the handkerchief in her pocket, wondering if it could help him, but it was more for dealing with sniffles. Benjin didn't seem sniffly. He breathed as though someone had grasped his throat in a choke hold.

"The break is inflaming the surrounding tissue." Yoskar growled at Aishena. He adjusted the straps of the brace Niskina had patched together. Where he loosened them, the skin of Benjin's neck looked hot and puffy.

"What does that mean?" Lyrrin asked in a squeak.

She remembered Riony's broken bone, how her arm

had swollen, gone bad, fingers turned black as clean blood refused to reach them. If it hadn't been for Dracuni's blood, Lyrrin wasn't sure Riony would still have those fingers. And that was a break in an arm. Not a break in the bones of a neck.

"His skin is swelling up around his breathing pipe, closing it," Aishena replied flatly. "We have to get him out of here and find some way to treat him, before he loses the ability to breathe entirely."

FIFTEEN

By the fourth time Butterfur turned around, came back toward them, sniffed the air, then picked a different tunnel again, Riony was ready to take a seat on the cold, hard floor and join the skeletal masses around her.

Her damp pants chafed, and the rope cut into her shoulders, and Kess's horrible bony limbs kept banging into her, and her brain was a mess of painful old memories, tangled in with all of Dracuni's sensations of pain and fear.

It was only the hope of prying the dragonling from Kess's clutches and returning safely to Lyrrin that kept her burning legs going.

Sure, she had muscles for days, but carrying two bodies as far as she had was starting to hurt. She'd never admit that to Kess though, so she kept up the pace and channeled the heat from those burning muscles into a seething spite that helped her forge onward.

Even if it was starting to seem as though Butterfur was struggling to find a path back to Lyrrin.

Dracuni had looped her tail forward, wrapping it across the side of Riony's waist. Riony patted the soft scales and tuft of hair at the end.

Scared, the unidragon communicated again, but it was a sad, tired kind of scared. ***Want home.***

"We're going home," Riony replied with a soft determination.

"I'm not sure your rat knows the way out," Kess said, as though she'd been spoken to.

"His name is Sir Butterfur Spelunkychunks, and that's how you shall refer to him."

"He still doesn't know the way out. If there is one." There was a dull resignation in Kess's voice.

That was what scared Riony the most. That the relentless goblin that had stalked a mother dragon for months, maybe years, to get what she wanted, sounded out of hope. And that it had been Riony's choice to trust their salvation in the cave otter that had ruined them.

"And what's your plan? Which direction would you like to go?" Riony thrust her fingers out angrily at their

current four-way intersection, from which she could see the previous two intersections and more again up ahead.

The catacombs were a confusing labyrinth of inter-connecting tunnels and twisting pathways. And it didn't feel as though they'd been going upward in a long time.

Kess didn't offer any new options.

Riony put her head down and kept walking. "I'm following the rat."

"I thought his name was—"

"Shut it, Kessara."

"You're not in charge right now, in case you forgot." Kess's arms moved, and Dracuni keened. The sound rattled and gargled in the soggy muzzle.

Why? Hurt why? Dracuni's breathing sounded labored, and Riony almost felt the press of the dagger herself with how the fear and confusion pierced into her head.

Riony had no way to explain to the hatchling that hurting things was how many people got what they wanted. And that everyone would want Dracuni if they knew what she was. Everyone might hurt Dracuni. Kess, as cruel as the goblin was, wasn't an exception there.

But she was the one with her hands on the hatchling right now.

"Fine, yes, you're in charge! I am your devout peon, your obedient bondswoman. Oh, Exulted One. Beloved Ruler.

Glorious Mistress of Order-me-around-however-you-like."

"You always were the very worst at being servile."

"Hand me your feet so I might kiss them."

Kess tensed. "This is exactly the kind of behavior that got you whipped."

Riony's shoulders firmed up with a tension to match Kess's, pressed together back-to-back like two blocks of stone.

Riony grumbled out, "The point, that I lost somewhere along the way—"

"Because you just can't help running that giant mouth of yours."

"Is that you don't need to keep jabbing your knife at that poor baby to keep me in line. You've got me. You win."

"I don't believe that for a second," Kess said, but Riony could feel the pressure in her arms ease, and Dracuni snuffled a sigh.

Mouth trap, bad.

"Also, it would be super cool of you to take that muzzle off her as well."

"That sounds like a terrible idea."

"It's upsetting her and making it hard for her to breathe. If you want a nice, healthy dragon to steal at the end of this, you need to get that muzzle off her."

"She?" Kess seemed to consider this. "*She's* a wild, untamed dragon. She'll bite me if I remove the muzzle."

No bite. Want breathe.

"She said she won't bite you."

Dracuni mewled pitifully from within the confines of the leather.

"What do you mean 'she said'?"

Riony patted Dracuni's tail, soothing herself as much as the unidragon. "I can hear her. Her emotions and thoughts. I hear them right in my head."

She knew she was giving Kess more leverage against her, more insight into how and why she cared so much for Dracuni. But there was a part of her that also hoped it would make Kess realize the baby dragon was so much more than a dumb tool to tame and own.

Although she'd never realized that about Riony.

"Wow. You must have knocked your skull really hard when you jumped from the sky out of that slaver cage."

Riony remembered the silhouette in the smoke, watching as she miraculously landed on the taut tent wall. "You were there?"

Kess swallowed loudly. "I don't believe you can communicate with this wild beast."

"Yeah, well, if dragonlords weren't so keen to tame every dragon from birth, maybe they'd find all dragons were really chatty."

Riony walked them through the end of a narrow tunnel

into a larger space. A natural cave with the addition of sweeping staircases, high platforms, and massive, elaborately carved columns, rising into the darkness above.

"That's nonsense," Kess said.

"Dracuni, nod once if you understand me and won't bite Kess."

Riony felt the pull of movement as Dracuni's head bobbed behind her.

Kess muttered a low, whispered curse. "I don't know what sort of tricks you've trained this creature with, but ... I'll take off the muzzle if that will stop your delusional spouting."

Elbows poked into Riony's back as Kess juggled Dracuni. Then the dragonling sucked in a deep breath and huffed loudly.

Better. Better!

"She says that's better," Riony relayed.

Kess scoffed. "What kind of name is *Dracuni,* anyway?"

"Umm ... My sister made it up," Riony lied.

"As ridiculous as Sir Butterfur Spelunkychunks. I'll think of something more suitable for the beast." Kess thrust her hand back, holding the removed muzzle toward Riony. "Put this away somewhere in case I need it again."

Riony took the muzzle, staring at the wet mass of mashed leaves inside. A heady soapy and peppery scent made her nose scrunch. "You put morass mercy in here?

What were you thinking?"

"What's the problem? You were happy to use it on my brother."

"That was one tiny sprig, on one big monster. You've used way too much in here. No wonder she was having trouble breathing. You could have killed her!"

Kess shrugged. "I needed a way to tranquilize the hatchling. Although I expected it to last longer."

Riony dumped the contents of the muzzle out onto the floor with a splat and moved away from it quickly. The stuff was potent and dangerous. A strong hit of its scent caused rapid sedation, and prolonged use could have terrible side effects.

She tied the muzzle to a loop on her pants, but hoped Kess wouldn't ask for it back at any point.

Maybe it was something in Dracuni's strange hybrid makeup that allowed her to shake the effects off despite still inhaling the crushed herbs. Or maybe they'd had their potency washed away in the water. Either way, Riony hoped that also meant she wasn't suffering the headaches, hallucinations, and nightmares it could also induce.

Riony had learned about morass mercy in midwife training with her amma and shared the knowledge with Kess during a time when they had joked and plotted together about ways to torture her big brother.

And there was Kess now, using that knowledge to

kidnap innocent creatures. Tension surged from Riony's clenched fists, up her arms, and into her gritted teeth.

"I should never have shown you even a moment of kindness."

Kess's body shuddered. Her voice was flat and emotionless. "You were the only one dumb enough to ever make that mistake."

Riony's feet stopped, as though they'd simply forgotten how to put themselves one in front of the other. She felt so tired, and a painful strain ached around her eyes.

"Keep moving, Pony. I don't want to die down here with you."

Inhaling deeply, Riony growled, "If you call me Pony *one more time,* I will become unhinged in a way you've never experienced before."

But she started moving again. Marching forward. Legs on fire and heart sore.

Butterfur picked a winding staircase that led up far out of sight.

Riony's heart sank at the sight of the stairs. But they did have to go up, so up she went.

The staircase seemed endless, a winding spiral that coiled skyward, unguarded to the drop on either side. Built into the edges and walls around them stood gargantuan statues of solemn people. Alderkin, maybe. They looked human to Riony, but even when formed from rock, somehow more elegant and ethereal.

Kess stayed blissfully silent, and Dracuni's thoughts had calmed too. Curious, almost content to be carried through new and interesting areas. Riony's steps echoed against the weathered stone, each footfall an effort in determination.

Riony had no way of knowing whether Kess still had a knife to the young dragon's throat. But she had no way to strike out at her now either with Dracuni in Kess's arms, and both of them strapped behind her, and a long way to fall in every direction.

So Riony battled upward. Sweat poured down her chest and neck, making the thin fabric of her shirt cling to her. Her heart pounded a raging beat when finally, the end of the stairwell came into view.

The soft light of Riony's glow stone filtered through a narrow opening ahead, painting the chamber beyond with its muted cyan radiance.

The somber room before them was awash in swathes of cobweb, hanging gray and tangled from the ceiling and covering sculpted murals on the walls.

Riony stepped carefully into the space, listening for the scurry of arachnid limbs, but could only hear the deep gasps of her own breathing.

Butterfur ran across the floor, jumping and dodging

over the spread of dusty cave silk. He went straight for a larger tunnel but didn't continue along it. Only stood there, sniffing at the ancient air.

Three other passages led from that room, and Butterfur went to inspect them as well, dashing between each tunnel entrance.

While he was making up his mind, Riony turned her attention to the room around them. She had hoped they had left the halls of the dead behind when she saw no more alcoves stacked into the walls.

But in the center of the room, an imposing stone slab cradled the relics of a body long departed. Bones, weathered by time, rested upon tattered cushions, surrounded by the scattered remains of silver armor and crystal weapons. The tomb of a warrior.

And before that altar, veiled in cave silk, stood a massive crystal sword.

As if guarding its master's legacy, the sword leaned against the high platform. The sword's hilt spiraled upward, shaped like a unicorn horn. The skeletal hand of the body was stretched across from where it lay on the altar, holding the weapon even in death.

The blade, almost as long as Riony was tall, dully gleamed even below the layers of dust. It was thick, too, a wide and solid spike of glassy calcite, inlaid with sections

of lilac and sky-blue stones down the fuller. And on the largest of those inlaid gems were Alderkin runes. Standard hardening runes, plus something Riony didn't recognize.

Riony's eyes were transfixed upon the weapon.

"Oh baby," she exhaled with a greedy longing.

She beelined for it, approaching with a slow reverence as she got close.

"The rat's that way. Where are you going?" Kess asked from behind.

"There's a sword here." Riony didn't turn around to help Kess see what she was seeing. "Other artifacts too."

She could feel Kess angling, trying to see around Riony's back. "Don't touch anything. They could be cursed, trapped, full of dangerous creatures. Isn't that what you told me?"

"I'm just looking." Riony already had her hands on a glow stone that lay at the edge of the altar. A spare could be crucial, if it worked. She shoved it quickly into a pocket, because Kess didn't need to know. When no curses seemed to be set off, she light-fingered a few other artifacts small enough to tuck away.

Butterfur skittered back to the largest tunnel and sniffed at it again. He turned an anxious circle on the spot, then moved a little farther into the mouth of the tunnel.

Seems like he's made his choice.

Riony turned to follow, but her feet remained planted.

"I kind of want it though."

"Want what?"

"The *sword*. I need a new one, considering you made me lose mine. And it would be good to have a weapon other than one little athame." Riony twisted at the waist so Kess could see the sword in all its magnificence.

"That old thing? That doesn't even look functional. It's way too big to actually use."

Riony sighed. She should have known Kess wouldn't understand the rampant desire she was feeling for the weapon. Kess only got like that about dragons.

"I could swing it," Riony argued.

"It's *ceremonial*. And absolutely looks cursed to me."

Riony frowned at the weapon. She had never seen anything like it in use before, but it did have hardening runes on the crystal, so it couldn't be entirely decorative.

But with the previous owner's hand still gripping it tight, and the webs of cave silk enshrouding it, Riony did get a creepy, foreboding feeling about taking it. As sexy as it was, it probably wasn't worth it.

She turned away with a despondent sigh.

She was two steps away when Kess said, "The rat's getting away. Hurry up, Pony."

"Oh, *that's it*." Riony huffed and cracked her knuckles. She spun back toward the sword so fast Dracuni's tail

swished behind her. "I'm taking it!"

Kess groaned, "By all things blessed. Stop!"

But Riony marched to the sword, hot air snorting from her nose and her teeth bared. She grabbed the section of hilt not occupied by the skeletal hand and tugged.

The blade came away with the soft snapping of webs, and the boney fingers fell loose, releasing their claim. The knuckles and joints of the desiccated hand toppled off the altar, bringing with them an arm, a shoulder, a skull. The rib cage smashed down the tiered dais of the altar.

Sections of silver armor followed, clattering across the ground and bouncing into webs which vibrated in a disturbing hum until the whole room seemed to shake with the din.

"What under the blessed sun have you done?" Kess rasped.

Riony hefted the sword in two hands. "Mmmph. I think I found my soul mate."

"No! Listen!"

Riony stilled, lifting her eyes from her new treasure and focusing out into the space around them. A rattling, skittering sound came from the webs, from the walls, from the ceilings. *Everything* moved. The stone itself seemed to bulge and creep.

A massive swarm of cave spiders rushed for the source of the clattering sound, right toward Riony, Kess, and Dracuni.

SIXTEEN

"We should go through the portal." Aishena moved close to Yoskar, looking right up into his face and whispering not quite quietly enough.

A harsh anxiety rattled her words. "At least then we'd be aboveground. We could look for a healer, a settlement, some of those herbs Riony used on my ankle to reduce swelling. *Something*!"

The words seemed to rattle in Lyrrin's heart as well. Aishena was right. They had to do *something*. Benjin's breath whistled roughly beside her.

Yoskar shook his head. "If we use that portal, we could end up all the way across Elundrae, on our own, in revenant-filled wastes, and all three of us could die there.

It's not the right move."

"I can go alone, try to send help. Lyrrin can show me how to open the portal so I can come back from the other side, if that works, and bring help that way." Aishena glanced back and forth between the portal and Benjin.

"We stick together." Yoskar's expression was firm, but his voice remained calm. He put a hand on Aishena's arm. "His neck is braced. Daymora must be nearing the top soon. The other delvers will get ropes and pulleys set up. We just need to set up a stretcher for him now so we can lift him out, if no float runes can be found."

"And then what? How are we going to help him once we're back up there? Riony might have had some remedy but she's ..." Aishena noticed Lyrrin listening and dropped her voice lower, hissing in Yoskar's ear.

They moved a step or two away, continuing their argument.

Benjin finally looked at Lyrrin again, turning reddened and fearful eyes to her with a deep, wheezing sigh. He lifted a hand, just a fraction, angling his fingertips toward Lyrrin. She rushed over beside him and took his hand before his movement hurt him or he got scolded by his siblings for it.

"I'm here. I'm sorry," she said softly to him.

He tilted his head as though to shake it, and Lyrrin gave him a warning look.

He rasped a frustrated groan. "*I'm* sorry. Not you. Don't be."

"You aren't angry at me?"

"Not at you." His voice broke over the words as he tried to force enough breath into them. "At me."

"But it's my fault we're down here, I—"

"You tried to save your sister. You ... you're so brave, clever." He squeezed her sharp clawed fingers in his soft pink hands. "You're special, never useless. I'm the useless one."

Lyrrin leaned back on her heels, frowning. He was Benjin Hjelzahn, brother to some of the toughest delvers in the undercity, and most of the time he spent bragging, Lyrrin had to admit he had reason to be. Mostly. How could he think he was useless?

Benjin closed his eyes, and a tear squeezed from the side. "All I do ... is get kidnapped, hurt."

"No. That's not your fault. And I got kidnapped too!"

"Only 'cause ... punched Zade for us." His chest rose and fell sharply in incomplete breaths. He opened his eyes again and offered a lukewarm smile.

"Sorry ... I told your secret." He held her fingers tightly.

Lyrrin placed her other hand over his. It was scary, having her secret out. Nobody but her family, and then Benjin, ever knew. So far no one had treated her differently, but she didn't know if things would stay that way. Brishan

still watched her warily.

But she wouldn't let Benjin know her worries. Not now. "That's okay. I think it was the right thing to do. Anything that could help get you out of here, help you heal."

Anything? Lyrrin bit her lip. The words had come so naturally. But did she really mean *anything*?

Benjin's nose scrunched up. "Get us *all* out. Find your sister."

Lyrrin's eyes glossed over. She was more worried about Riony than she wanted to admit, because there were so many other things to worry about right now. She wanted her big sister back so desperately.

And if she could, if Lyrrin could find Riony, she could also find Dracuni. And the unidragon had the one thing in all the land that was guaranteed to save Benjin.

She wondered what Riony would do. They'd decided they didn't want to use Dracuni themselves. But what about when it came to saving someone else's life? Was keeping the secret worth Benjin's life? The only living creature with silvernix blood ... maybe it was a secret too big to share, for any reason.

But Lyrrin didn't have to tell the others *everything*.

"It's going to be okay." With a final squeeze of Benjin's hand and a confident, close-lipped smile, Lyrrin stood back up and stepped over to where Aishena and Yoskar

continued their hushed argument.

They didn't stop on account of Lyrrin's presence. So she took a deep breath and spoke over them in a fast rush of words.

"If we can find Riony we can save Benjin because Riony still has some silvernix."

The two delvers' mouths slammed shut and they swung to stare at Lyrrin.

"She has silvernix? How?" Aishena asked.

"Remember how she had some before, that she used when her arm was broken? She still has a bit more." Lyrrin felt wrong lying and had to look down at their shoulders instead of making eye contact.

Aishena angled her head up to look up the gaping hole above them as though ready to climb all the way back herself. "Could she have left it at home? Can we get it if we get back to the undercity?"

"No, it's definitely with her." At least Lyrrin hoped Riony had Dracuni with her still. "She always keeps it with her."

Yoskar kept his eyes on Lyrrin, studying her expressions. "This doesn't make sense. It's strange that she'd have any to start with, let alone enough for multiple treatments. Where did she get it from?"

Lyrrin did her best to face Yoskar and lock eyes with

him. "It's real. It was a gift from a dragonlord to my grandmother because she saved their wife during labor." That much was true, although that wasn't the silvernix they had anymore.

Aishena turned hopefully to Yoskar. "We should go and try to find her. One of the maps I pulled is of the depths, and if we are where I think we are, this area connects through to catacombs that the water channel runs through. I think I could find the way down there. She might not be far away."

Lyrrin frowned. How long had Aishena been holding on to that information for? Could Riony be nearby? "Can we go and find her?"

Yoskar scoffed. "It's too fantastical. Silvernix? A gift? She's making things up because she wants to find her sister."

Aishena's mouth opened, but she didn't speak. She looked down at Lyrrin and snapped her mouth closed again.

"We stick to the plan. Help will come soon. I'm going to find something to support Benjin on the way up. Don't waste time chasing ghosts."

Aishena's face darkened with hot red patches. But she nodded firmly.

Shaking his head, Yoskar walked away.

Lyrrin expected Aishena to follow, as she usually did, but the delver ran her hands up into her silver hair, tugging it at the roots. Then she dropped down into a crouch,

covering her face with her hands.

"I don't know what to do," she whispered.

"Aishena, please. Riony really does have silvernix."

The delver turned a skeptical, hard-edged face toward Lyrrin. "Even if she does ... I have to stay here. That's the plan."

Lyrrin clenched her fingers closed into fists as her nerves fired up. "That's Yoskar's plan. And maybe he's not right."

"He is. He looks after us. He does the right thing." The words seemed directed more toward herself than to Lyrrin.

"Did he do the right thing when he took you to smash the dragon eggs?" Lyrrin challenged.

Aishena winced slightly, then her face grew calm and stubborn again. "Yes. It was the right thing. For us." Her words held a bright, high edge. "He's the smart one. He's the planner. I can only follow well. Take action when told."

Behind her, Benjin's breathing grew louder, harsher. Niskina hurried over to sit beside him.

He needed silvernix, and he needed it soon.

"Why? Why can't you decide what you want to do?" Lyrrin pleaded.

"I can't," Aishena hissed. Her hands curled into fists and then loosened, and she stared at the open palms as though she hated what she saw. "I can't because the last time I didn't follow Yoskar's orders, I lost my father and my sister."

She crumpled forward, landing on her knees.

Lyrrin knew the pain of losing family that Aishena must be feeling, even if the delver didn't show it on her face. She simply sat on her knees, stony-faced, staring toward Benjin, but her eyes were distant, glazed.

"I'm sorry. I lost my parents too," Lyrrin said. But she didn't know what it was like to lose a sister. She didn't want to know what that felt like, when that was all she had left. "But your amma is still alive, isn't she? She was the one who put out the bounty for you."

Aishena's head shook slowly side to side. "Yes. My mother is still alive."

Lyrrin's heart hurt with a sudden strong wish that hers were too. "Why won't you go back to her?"

"It's ... we ..." Aishena struggled over her words, then her face scrunched up and she exhaled sharply. "You know we are Hjelzahn. My father, he was the one who was a Draekhan heir."

Lyrrin's eyes widened. Riony had once tried to explain to her about Yeonard Draekhan, the Dragon King, and all his children, and all their dragonkeeps and families and heirs. It was mostly just a lot of confusing and forgettable names to Lyrrin.

"So are you ... like a princess?"

Aishena laughed wryly. "No. We're still technically

heirs, but way, way down the line of succession by many generations, from Hjelzahn the First, who is still alive himself, thanks to plentiful silvernix. And my mother ... She's a grayglim who served my father and was training me to be one too, as Yoskar trained under Fadda. Until things changed."

"What happened?" Lyrrin knelt down in front of Aishena.

"On a mission, a couple of years back, my mother was downed, knocked off her dragon. She wasn't responding, out cold, right when the shadowdragon touched ground." A shiver shook Aishena's wiry form. "She survived. But ... she was different when she returned home from that mission. Refused to ride her dragon. Secretive. Cold and distant."

Aishena's lips twisted. "Or at least, more secretive, cold, and distant than she had been before. But she was a grayglim warden, after all."

Lyrrin hadn't heard the term before, but just nodded as though she did, because she didn't want to interrupt Aishena and the flowing stream of words tumbling from her.

Aishena's voice dropped to barely a breath. "And then ... heirs started dying."

"Naturally? Or ...?" Lyrrin whispered back.

Aishena raised her eyebrows. "Nobody knew at first. And at first, nobody really cared. It started with new heirs.

Fourth, fifth, even sixth generation. Still important people within their own family lines, but, well … in the grander scheme, there are so many of us."

The rattling sounds of the delvers searching through the Alderkin chambers echoed softly out to them.

"Rumors were spreading, though, and then Tarric the First was found, murdered in his own bedroom. The Dragon King's own son. Then the hunt was on for the Heir Killer. And then Yoskar, he told me he thought it was her. Our mami."

"Why? Why would she do that?"

Aishena lifted her shoulders weakly. "I don't know! I didn't know. And I didn't believe him. She was still training me, when she was home, and I trusted her, instead of him."

Aishena turned her eyes up to Lyrrin and reached out to squeeze her hands. Her eyes searched Lyrrin's face as though looking for something. Understanding. Forgiveness. "He begged me to leave. He told me she was dangerous, that our family were all at risk. And I didn't listen."

"And then one night … I found them. Fadda and Neif. Dead and bleeding in the library. Neif was … my little sister. I still can't understand. I don't know why … why would anyone …?"

Lyrrin shook her head and pressed Aishena's hands in hers, careful not to scratch her. She didn't know either.

She'd seen terrible things, even in her short years. Terrible monsters and terrible actions by humans, and she could never understand either.

Because why would anyone turn to cruelty when they could choose kindness instead?

Riony once told her that it was because those who suffered cruelty became cruel in turn, but that didn't make sense to Lyrrin. She wasn't born yet when Riony and her parents were still slaves, but she knew that someone had been very cruel to Riony because of all the scars on her back.

And Riony was still kind.

"Do you know who did kill your family?" she asked.

"Yoskar said it was our mother. That she had changed, she wasn't really our mami anymore, and we couldn't trust her. That we had to take Benjin and run if any of us wanted to stay alive. And we did. We fled our home and came to hide here, and I make sure I listen to Yoskar now."

"It's not your fault. It would have been hard for anyone to believe. What happened to your father and sister, you didn't do that."

"It all sounded so crazy ... I still don't know what really happened. But I could have *stopped* it happening if I'd acted on orders sooner. I am the hand and must act as the voice commands, not question it."

Lyrrin let go of Aishena and rose to her feet. She was

barely taller than the kneeling delver but looked down at her with piercing eyes. "I don't know what happened then. But Yoskar *is* wrong now. Riony has silvernix that could save Benjin. And you said she could be close to where we are now. We could heal him!"

Aishena turned to watch where Benjin wheezed and choked. His normally bronze face was blotchy gray and red. Niskina brushed his forehead and muttered soothing words.

Aishena turned back and her shoulders sagged. She remained kneeling, as though she'd forgotten how to move, and was slowly turning to stone like the stalagmites that had been smashed in the landslide around them.

Yoskar yelled at Caed across through the archway in the Alderkin chambers, and Brishan chided them both. Dust still settled and filtered through the cool cyan light of the delvers' glow stones, and it felt almost as though they were all already ghosts.

"Please, Aishena. You can listen to your own voice, your own instincts. What do you want to do?"

Aishena pulled her hands up near her face, studying them as though the answers were in the dusty lines and knuckles. "Something. I have to do something. Waiting ... feels like we've already given up."

Lyrrin extended a hand to help Aishena stand up. "Then let's get the silvernix and help Benjin before it's too late, so you don't lose any more of your family."

The weight of the whole mountain above them felt as though it weighed down, crushing the air in the space, making it solid and flat in Lyrrin's chest.

They had to do something.

Before either of us lose any more family.

SEVENTEEN

The pale, hairy legs of countless cave spiders skittered against the smooth floor, creating a nightmarish percussion in their multitude.

Little creatures? Dracuni seemed more curious than anything.

A star-filled sky worth of little creatures.

They wouldn't normally worry Riony when it was the odd one or two of them. But racing toward her now were so many it seemed as though the dull dusty stone that formed the room had burst into terrifying life.

Each scurrying creature was as big as her head. Their creamy shells gave them a ghostly appearance, and the cyan light glinted from the black, shining orbs of their eyes like fractured glass. Their strange mouths chattered and fangs twitched.

"Are you going to run or what?" Kess barked.

"Yeah, yeah, I think I will." Riony grasped her new sword tightly. It was heavy, far heavier than her old sword, and she didn't think she could even lift it one-handed. It certainly wouldn't fit into her scabbard. She hoisted it up and pressed it in a hug across her chest like a child carrying a doll. And she ran.

The point of the sword stuck up high over her shoulder, bouncing along with the two bodies on her back as she pounded across the room.

"Drop that thing, it's going to slow us down," Kess ordered.

"No way. Much like my undying hope that you will choke on your own vomit when you finally realize what an awful gremlin you have been, I will cling to this till my last breath."

"Can you for once in your ridiculous life shut your mouth and save your breath? You're choosing between a chunk of stone and our lives!"

"I'm choosing both, thank you very much, although your life is negotiable." Kess's demands only made Riony clutch the heavy weapon tighter. Rage still burned through her to the chanting echoes of *Pony, Pony, Pony.*

Grinding her teeth, she barreled for the largest tunnel that Butterfur had disappeared down.

The spiders flowed in from all sides around them, closing the gaps in which Riony slammed her feet down. She leaped through the vaulted archway of the tunnel as the floor disappeared entirely under the crowding arachnids.

The passage ahead was clear, although from beneath a shroud of webbing to her side came a soft growl that sounded like a revenant. Bones twitched out from the cave silk, as spiders stripped the monster of its flesh. She slowed to gawk at it, horrified to see another one succumbing to that fate.

"Ew, sparks. This is going to haunt me more than that time I saw you naked."

"They're still coming!" Kess cried.

Riony dared a glance back, seeing the creatures filling the tunnel behind them. The air reverberated with the cacophony of scuttling limbs. "Dracuni, if you could work out how to breathe fire, now would be a great time!"

Dracuni snorted. No flame appeared.

Riony continued her dash down the tunnel, desperately scanning for any sign of Butterfur. Cobwebs caught her face. An intersection passed in a flash, and she prayed the cave otter hadn't gone that way. Heartbeats thundered in her ears as her every muscle propelled her forward, trying to stay ahead of the wave of hungry scavengers.

"They're gaining on us!" A tremble laced Kess's words. She always did have a thing about spiders. If being eaten alive wasn't a real threat right then, Riony would have enjoyed the moment a lot.

She responded with a fierce grunt as she sprinted faster. The thought of those arachnid horrors closing in and hurting Dracuni was enough to ignite a burst of speed she hadn't known she possessed.

She wasn't too keen on being eaten by the creatures either.

The recollection of the rev, pinned down and being consumed alive—or undead—was still too vivid in her mind. They were taking every shred off its bones. Which may or may not actually kill the cursed undead.

The pale spiders raced after them with eerie agility, their hairy legs creating a clacking echo that built up within the tunnel walls like a horrific symphony.

They were right behind them, scratching at Riony's ankles, tripping up her feet. She caught the heavy crystal sword by the hilt again and swung the blade in a wide, low arc, taking herself around in a full circle.

The spiders scattered clear, only one getting caught up and hammered by the thick sword. The creature's abdomen broke like a cracking egg. Yellow ooze flicked up across the floor.

It was a slow swing, the weight of the blade dragging Riony's body with it and the tip scraped along the ground. She could barely bring it back up again on the other side as she spun around to continue running forward.

Her attack gave them only seconds of clearance before the spiders closed in again.

Kess let out a yelping scream, and Riony felt the smack of something landing on them.

Beast jumps!

There was a great wriggling and wrenching of bodies against Riony's back. She forced an extra surge of strength into her legs so the wrestling match tugging her shoulders didn't take them all down. Dracuni snarled, and there was a snapping, crunching sound.

Bit it! Dracuni thought with a strange surge of pride.

Good work, Riony thought back, even though she still wasn't sure the hatchling could hear her thoughts in return. But she didn't want Kess to think she was talking to her.

Kess sounded livid. "They can jump? You didn't tell me that!"

"Oh yeah. They can jump," Riony panted out between breaths.

"There's one on my legs!" Kess shrieked.

Riony pivoted, twisting fast so that Kess's legs swung out, smacking them and the spider into the tunnel wall.

The spider cracked against the stone, and Kess bit off her own whimper.

"Sorry! Sparks," Riony instantly regretted the spontaneous apology. *She doesn't deserve your remorse. If you show weakness, Kess will consume you as completely as the spiders did those revs.*

Kess's back had tensed like it could snap. "Better that than the spider."

Riony almost tripped and stumbled at the begrudging gratitude in the words. Gratitude was not something that Kessara Heithorn *did*. Riony must have imagined it. Because a version of Kess that could show appreciation rattled Riony more than the horde of spiders nipping at her feet.

But it also made her wonder whether Kess really was that desperate.

Riony called over her shoulder, "Cut Dracuni's bonds; she can help fight them off!"

Yes! I help. I scratch!

"I won't—"

Another spider flew at them from a wall. Riony managed to sidestep it, avoiding it landing on her or Kess's shoulder.

"Tell the beast it better not dare try to run," Kess huffed.

"She *can* hear you."

There was a quiet grumble, then a shuffling of elbows

and the snap of leather.

Free! Free!

Riony sighed inwardly.

"If the spiders come near you, kick them off! Don't let them bite you!" Riony called back. She couldn't risk Kess seeing any broken skin on the unidragon.

"You know I can't ... were you talking to the beast again? Wait, are these things *venomous*?"

A shadow flashed through the air on Riony's side. Sharp fangs flew straight for her, and a crackly cry nattered from the spider's mouth.

Then it collided with a sharp point in midair, a bone dagger, piercing right through the middle of its eyes. It dropped to the ground, swarmed over by the others.

"Nice shot."

"Always."

There was a swish as another of Kess's throwing daggers lanced out, and then the crack as it went through soft shell.

Through the flexible leather of her delver pants, Riony felt a scuttling presence that sent ice water shooting through her gut.

They were *on her*.

She glanced down, catching sight of two, maybe three of the arachnids. They clung tight with their creepy long limbs, pressing hooked paws through the leather as they

clung to their bucking prey.

Riony flushed hot and cold, her sprint turning into a leaping, bounding gait as she tried to shake them off. They shook and bounced but held tight.

"Can you run smoother? You're ruining my aim!"

The sounds of more spiders falling to Kess's daggers echoed through the tunnel. One by one, they fell to Kess's skillful throws, but there seemed to be no end to their numbers.

"They're on my legs!" Riony yelled back.

There was a scrambling sound and a weak yelp. "I'm out of daggers."

"Already?"

"The rest are on Griskin! Only got a hunting knife left."

Which she'd no doubt continue to hold on to to keep Dracuni under threat.

Even if Kess could have pulled a few dozen daggers from various hiding places on her body—something that wouldn't surprise Riony—there wouldn't be enough for all the spiders.

With a breathy grunt, Riony angled the big crystal sword downward, smashing it against her legs, and more preferably, at the spiders on her legs.

The first splattered with a bile-inducing satisfaction right across Riony's shin. She lugged the weighty blade up and down again, jabbing and smacking, while continuing her

attempts to move forward and away from being submersed under all the other spiders still chasing them.

A heavy, sharp pain surged into her thigh. Another burst of pain matched it at the ankle on the other side.

The walls on either side of them came to an end and the tunnel opened out. With one final surge of energy, Riony burst through into an expansive natural cavern beyond. The weights of the critters clinging to her legs disappeared.

"They've stopped! They aren't following us!" Kess yelled.

"What?" Riony turned to look over her shoulder but didn't dare slow down.

The cave spiders hesitated at the threshold, clinging to the shadows, some unknown barrier causing them to give up the chase and retreat.

Riony's relief was short-lived. The ground pitched steeply, falling away beneath her feet. She swung back around to see the steep slope ahead, sliding down toward a sharp edge and sheer drop.

Twisting her body just in time, Riony avoided toppling in a headfirst roll down that hill. Instead, she put herself face down onto the slick, silty stone as her feet went out from underneath her.

She let the sword fall free from her hands as she smacked down. It slid and clattered on the rock beside them, coming to a stop when it hit the remains of a broken stalagmite.

Riony, Kess, and Dracuni kept going.

Kess and Dracuni thumped down heavily on top of Riony's back as she fell, and the glow stone at her ribs jabbed into her chest, knocking the wind out of her.

They slid fast, feet first toward the ledge.

"No, no, no!" Riony gasped, digging her nails into the soft limestone slope, trying to halt their race toward doom. Her knees banged over the uneven surface and her shirt tangled and tore against her chest and dust filled her nose.

Her legs went out into open air as they hit the lip of the drop. Riony scrambled, arms clutching for any purchase. Her hands latched over the cliff edge and caught tight. Flying out into the air, her body jerked, then angled back, and with the smash of skin onto stone, they came to a dangling stop.

Riony let out a harsh whimper.

The pain of three bodies worth of weight shot like lightning into Riony's fingertips as she clenched them around the rock ledge. Kess's legs and Dracuni's tail swung behind her as they bounced against the side of the cliff. She stretched her toes out, trying to find purchase against the rough wall.

"Have you got Dracuni?" she bit out the words between waves of pain.

"I won't drop her," Kess replied. "Have you got us?"

"Mmmph."

"Then pull us up, tame-brain!"

Riony's arms trembled with the strain, and then she stopped, holding her body limply against the wall.

She pressed her forehead to the rough stone. Sweat poured over her heated skin. "I'm sorry. Maybe I regret taking the sword now."

"Really? Was it the imminent death by spider or the remaining chance to plunge to our deaths that finally inspired remorse?" Kess replied. "*Pull us up.*"

"I can't." Riony rolled her head to the side, leaning it against her upright arm that clung for their life. A shaking, anguished smile formed on her lips.

"Kess ... I got bit."

EIGHTEEN

Lyrrin waited, hand extended to Aishena, who stared at her with dark, troubled eyes, the silence broken only by Benjin's struggling breaths.

Then Aishena lowered her gaze away from Lyrrin's, shook her head, and stood up without assistance. "I can't leave Benjin here and run off to gamble on gut instinct. I have to do what Yoskar says. The odds of finding Riony are ... too low."

Lyrrin folded her hand closed, tucking the pointy nails into her palm and fighting off the tear-prickling feeling like she'd just been smacked in the face. She wanted to get Dracuni back, to save Benjin. But she also really, really wanted Riony back too. She was more scared than she wanted to admit.

She needed her big sister. And nobody was going to help find her.

Aishena had taken a step away when she looked back and frowned at the emotion she must have seen reddening Lyrrin's face. With a sniff, she moved closer to Lyrrin again and pulled a folded wad of parchment from her belt.

"Here, look."

Lyrrin's eyes widened as Aishena unfolded the crinkly, dusty sheet. Scratched onto the surface in fine sepia ink lines was a complex mess of chambers and levels and interconnecting tunnels. It showed the insides of the mountain they were deep within in flat relief and also from multiple angles, as though cut through with a giant knife.

Lyrrin's gaze flickered around the map, trying to make sense of the major landmarks. The largest cavern at the top, with the sinking stream waterfall running through the center, was the undercity where they lived. But there were so, so many more caverns below, more than Lyrrin had ever imagined.

"This is the most detailed map of the Alderkin depths I've ever seen. We have plenty of partial maps, and what the delvers have been mapping out ourselves, but nothing like this. I haven't had much time to study it yet, but look at this." Aishena's fingers traced paths across the parchment.

"That looks like Whisperwind Passage," Lyrrin muttered, absorbed in the carefully inked lines. Had they been drawn with a hand that looked like hers?

"Correct. I think this is the water channel Riony went into. And see this mark?" Her voice was low, almost a whisper, and Lyrrin strained to hear. "That's where I think we are right now."

Lyrrin gazed hungrily over the drawing, trying to map where that rushing stream could have taken Riony. The mark Aishena pointed to was like the rune on the gateway geode. And below it was a gridwork of smaller hollows, spaced out between some larger natural caverns and mazelike tunnels.

The water channel ran through there, pooling in one cavern before continuing down into the earth. That was the only place the channel expanded out into more than a narrow tube.

"She could be right there!" Lyrrin clutched the sides of the map, pulling it from Aishena's hands and trying to trace a path from their location to that cave. It was complicated, a few levels down and through the labyrinth of smaller chambers. "I could go ... if you give me a glow stone."

It could be a long walk, even if it was the right way, even if Riony ended up there, and not somewhere else, or if the map wasn't accurate. And if Riony hadn't moved on

to somewhere else. Or something else hadn't happened to her or between her, Kess, and Dracuni.

There were a number of routes leading away from that cavern too, and Riony could have taken any of them if she was trying to find her way back up again, which Lyrrin was sure she would be. Their paths might not cross at all.

There were just so many ifs, but at the same time it felt as though Lyrrin was so close to having her sister again, held back only by stone walls and darkness.

Hopefully Butterfur was with Riony and Dracuni too. It had been an impulsive action, sending the otter into the stream. The cave otters of the Alderkin depths were often found using both natural and Alderkin-fashioned water channels like fun slides though, and it took more ingenuity than the humans had managed so far to keep them out of the water reservoirs.

He would be okay. Because Lyrrin couldn't stomach the idea of losing him, and Dracuni, and Riony, at any point, let alone all in one day.

"No, it's too dangerous for you to go alone. And it's just speculation, just my thoughts. I could be wrong. Yoskar and the other delvers will have to look too and will know more. We can't split up right now, not with Benjin hurt down here. But as soon as he's safe, we'll start looking." Aishena eyed Lyrrin and the map with a frown but didn't try to take the parchment back again.

An ache twisted in Lyrrin's chest. She understood the logic, but she hated not being able to do anything. It made her feel so small and useless.

"Daymora must be nearly at the top by now too. She really is an excellent climber." Aishena looked up, squinting into the darkness. "There might already be help on the way. It shouldn't be long now."

Lyrrin nodded, but still her eyes filled with tears.

Aishena's shoulders twitched upward, and her mouth moved awkwardly without making a sound, and then she hurried off to continue helping the search of the Alderkin chambers.

A fat tear plopped down onto the ancient map, and Lyrrin rubbed it with her palm before it could soak in and blur the ink. She pulled the map to her chest and cuddled it, as her feet walked her backward into the shadows behind her, taking her to somewhere dark and private to cry.

She didn't want Benjin to see her tears, when he was being so brave, when he had said she wasn't useless. She sidled up the wall, out of the moving pools of light created around each delver, hoping to melt into the gloom and disappear.

A soft growl reverberated near her feet.

The wolf.

She turned warily, finding herself standing right between

where the animal's bound legs lay in pairs.

Lyrrin had forgotten all about Kess's ... pet? Companion? Mount?

Her body froze in place, expecting the gnashing of teeth to meet her flesh if she spooked the animal any further. She'd approached far more wild animals than Riony had ever been comfortable with and knew she had to avoid sudden movements.

The wolf lay on its side, motionless. The charcoal-gray coat was almost invisible in the shadows, and only its glossy eyes, wide and warily watching her in return, glinted through the dark.

Lyrrin's vision adjusted to the lower light, and she saw a lashing of silk rope kept its mouth closed. No worry of being bitten then.

Carefully folding the map and cringing each time it crinkled loudly, Lyrrin tucked it away in a pocket in her coat.

The wolf panted roughly through its shut teeth in a gasping, fretful way, broken by the occasional long snuffle through a running nose.

Lyrrin's heart immediately softened. "Oh ... poor pup."

In slow, gentle movements, Lyrrin knelt beside the tied-up wolf. It recoiled from her, long snout turning away while its eyes remained locked on Lyrrin's position. Front paws, bound together, scraped at the dust and rubble, but it couldn't shift its prone weight.

"I'm not going to hurt you," Lyrrin said softly.

The wolf's snout twitched, and wet nostrils flared. Whites showed around the edges of its eyes.

"You're all sniffly, huh?" Lyrrin said softly. She wanted to reach out and pat its fur but could tell it wasn't ready for that yet. "I got all sniffly too when I first moved underground."

She fished around in the inside of her oversized coat, checking the pockets. "It's the fungus farms. They spread spores in the air, and they make some people and animals sneezy. I know it feels really awful, like you want to stick a scrubbing brush up your nose."

Her fingers found what she was searching for, and she pulled out an old handkerchief that had been folded into a bundle.

"I don't get sniffly much anymore, but Riony makes me carry this around all the time anyway in case it comes back." Lyrrin held it briefly to her own nose and took a deep breath, inhaling the minty-green scent that chilled her nostrils like an icy breeze.

Lowering it down, she pushed it along the ground tentatively toward the wolf's snout. "She made it for me. But it might work for you too. I hope it helps you breathe better. Because I can't undo the rope around your mouth, sorry. I think the others would be mad at me if I did that."

He didn't move, only continued to stare.

Lyrrin looked over the crudely stitched saddle and pouches strapped around the wolf's midsection. She had only seen Kess and the wolf briefly at the slavers' camp, but she had instantly envied the strange, wild girl with how the two of them seemed to move almost as one.

She sighed. "You're worried about Kess, aren't you?"

His tongue flicked out through the tiny gap at the front of his snout, licking anxiously. A soft, barely audible whine came from deep in his throat.

"I don't blame you for what Kess did, taking Dracuni. That's not your fault. You were just being a good pup, doing what your friend wanted." Lyrrin's voice held a gentle weight.

The wolf's eyes held a flicker of recognition. They softened, and in an achingly slow movement, he brought his snout closer to her, sniffing at where her fingers still rested, not far from the offered handkerchief.

She didn't move, didn't twitch, as its wet nose bumped against her. Then it turned to the herb infused handkerchief and smelled it. A wary sniff at first, and then a long, rattling inhalation. With a soft whine, it lay its chin flat onto the ground, with its nose right over the medicinal fragrance.

Lyrrin reached out, letting her fingers dust over the very tips of the wolf's thick fur. "I miss my sister too," she admitted softly. "I'm really worried about her."

"Someone's coming!" The cry from Niskina made Lyrrin startle.

The wolf winced, but didn't move, as Lyrrin scrambled back to her feet and headed away from the shadows.

Benjin had his eyes squinted closed, lips trembling with each difficult breath. Niskina got to her feet from where she had been sitting beside him and pointed up into the crumbling stones that darkened as they rose higher and higher.

Lyrrin squinted, only making out the barest of movements, the slightest sound of stone shifting.

"Who's there?" Niskina called out, frowning.

There was no reply. No calls of welcome aid being promised, no ropes being lowered.

Aishena jogged over, with Yoskar and Brishan following. Caed brought up the rear, limping heavily.

"Are the others coming down for us?" Aishena asked. "We're going to need ropes, pulleys, a stretcher."

"Daymora would have told them. Only, I can't see ..." Niskina continued to frown.

They all stood in a circle beneath the hole, craning their necks in hopeful search of approaching relief.

The shadows flickered, and swifter than a bird, a figure flipped down from above and landed on silent feet in the space between them.

The brown-skinned woman with cold, age-worn eyes balanced effortlessly on the unstable pile of fallen stones. She had hair the color of burned wood, braided in small rows up the sides, and thick knotted bundles along the top, leading to a long, trailing whip of hair at the back that swung as she turned to take in the delvers.

She wore close-fitting armor of smooth, dully gleaming scales the color of smoke, and rested her hands on the hilts of matching swords, sheathed at her hips.

"Ma—" Aishena choked on the word.

"Lady Hjelzahn?" Brishan said at the same time. His face scrunched up as he turned, entirely confused, to Aishena and Yoskar. "You told me your mother had passed away."

Is that ... their mother? Glancing at Benjin again, she found him with his eyes wide open, round as the moon. Only Riony and Lyrrin knew about the slavers' plot to get the bounty on the Hjelzahn siblings.

The other children returned from being snatched up hadn't heard the details, so they had been unable to spread the news. Benjin said that was the only reason he and his siblings hadn't left the undercity entirely.

"*Hjelzahn?*" Caed whispered from the back, searching all eyes around him for answers, but nobody replied.

The woman didn't give any visual or verbal response to the discussion. She remained with her hands on her blades,

casting her gaze over each person in turn, eyes narrowing as they fell upon Brishan.

"What is she doing here?" Niskina asked.

Yoskar moved to the front of the crowd. "She's come for us."

Lifting his arms high, he grasped the end of the staff that had been stored on his back. He pulled it down in front of him and activated a burn rune on one of the crystals embedded in it in one swift motion.

The cavern lit up red as he held the weapon threateningly between Lady Hjelzahn and the group of fallen delvers and children.

The woman's eyes narrowed again, and she lifted her hands away from her weapons and into the air. "That's right. I'm here for my children."

An inexplicable shudder ran up Lyrrin's spine at the strange, flat tone to her voice.

"Yoskar," Brishan exhaled his name. "What's going on?"

"She didn't die." Yoskar didn't take his eyes off his mother for a second. "We left, we came here, to keep away from her, for the sake of our lives."

"Why under the stars?" The delvers' master turned to the woman for answers. "What does he mean?"

"I didn't expect to see you, Brishan. A fellow grayglim, keeping my children from me."

"Kverra, I'm not. I didn't know!" He took a step closer to her, but Yoskar warned him back.

Aishena seemed to have turned to stone. She was frozen mid-stride, with only her eyes turning frantically from Yoskar to her mother.

Lady Hjelzahn watched her daughter and Brishan closest of all. "Let me take them, and nobody has to be hurt."

"Why would anybody have to be hurt?" Niskina balked.

"We're not going anywhere with her!" Yoskar roared.

"I don't understand what's going on!" Caed cried and limped up to Yoskar's side. "I thought we were getting out of here. How is she here? Where are the other delvers?"

Yoskar's grip on his staff wavered, then he lifted it high before him again. "How did you find us down here?"

Lady Hjelzahn tilted her head and stared dully back at him with cold, midnight eyes. "A slaver told me they'd found you in the undercity."

"No, *here*! Down here in this hole!" Yoskar's voice grew frantic.

"A girl. In a tunnel. She was looking for help for you." The woman took a casual step down from the heaping rubble.

"Don't move!" Yoskar yelled.

"All right, everybody calm down. We can talk this out," Brishan said.

Yoskar shook off the words and spoke in a low, dangerous tone. "Where's Daymora? What did you do to her?"

This seemed to snap Aishena out of her trance. "Why ... what would she do?"

"Kill her!" Yoskar snapped. "She'd kill her, because she wouldn't want any more audience down here than there already is. She would have killed us already too if she thought she could take us all on!"

"Yoskar!" Brishan scolded.

"Where are the other delvers then? Where's the help that should be rushing our way right now? If Daymora made it to the top, why aren't the other delvers here? Unless something happened to her."

Aishena's mouth opened wide and she turned pleading eyes to her mother, an unspoken 'no' forming on her lips.

Benjin whimpered, and Lyrrin skittered quietly over beside him, dropping to her knees to squeeze his hand.

Lady Hjelzahn took another step forward, eyes glinting in the red glow of Yoskar's flaming staff. "Is that what Yoskar has been telling you? That I'm the killer? Did he tell you that I was the one who hurt your father and Neif?"

She focused on Aishena, and the delver seemed entirely hypnotized by her attention.

"He's been lying to you. Yoskar is the one who murdered them."

NINETEEN

"Bit? Bit by *a spider*?" Kess's voice went embarrassingly shrill. However, she was hanging from the back of a reckless idiot over a drop so deep she couldn't see the bottom. The rockface plummeted straight down into inky darkness.

"No," Pony groaned softly. "More like ... two spiders. Maybe three."

The leather and fabric between their backs was soaked through with sweat and felt as hot as iron laid under the midday sun. Kess could feel the muscles in Pony's shoulders tensing and shifting as she held their weight by her fingertips.

"What ... what does that mean?" Kess asked.

"You really don't know anything about cave spiders? You weren't prepared for the depths at all," Pony muttered.

"I hadn't expected to spend so long down here," Kess snapped back.

"It means that I don't know how much longer I can hold on. The poison, it's going to cause paralysis, spasms ... death, if the first two symptoms don't fling us off this cliff face first." Pony's voice was quiet and calm in the same way it used to be when she knew she was about to get a whipping, and it made Kess want to slap her.

Every part of Kess ached. The vest and straps holding her to Pony's back cut into her chest and thighs, and her core and arms burned from trying to keep a steady hold of the dragonling.

Now that she'd cut the bonds on the creature's legs, it had relieved some of the strain by actively clinging to her. It hugged close to her chest, front claws over her shoulders, and stomach pressed so close Kess could feel its heartbeat. And it hadn't attempted to bite her ... yet.

The intimate position left Kess questioning the instincts of the wild beast and left her feeling strange and disgustingly vulnerable.

It's still a dragon and is my dragon that I will tame and raise and ride.

If they didn't all die first.

Kess's heart rate spiked as she stared down into the abyss below her feet again. There were a couple of smaller projections in the rockface below and to their side, but otherwise it was a sheer drop into night-dark doom.

She could see Pony's hips and top of her legs too, see trails of glossy, red blood dripping from puncture marks through her pants. The dragonling mewled softly, and Kess found herself stroking its neck.

A few eyeball-sized bugs clung to the stone near them. Disturbed by the presence of dangling humans, the insects buzzed into movement, lighting up and flying away.

"Kess?" Pony's voice trembled in a way Kess had never heard before in her life.

Her throat dried up and closed and she couldn't reply.

"Kess! Listen. I need you to get Dracuni out of here, okay? You told me you could do it without me, and lucky you, now you get your chance."

I don't want to. The thought pierced too fast into Kess's mind. She gritted her teeth and gave her head a swift shake. She was being a baby. She was capable and strong. She could and she would get herself out of there and she didn't need Pony. Or anyone. Not for anything. She was always better off alone.

The sweat between them chilled as a drift of cool air puffed up from the darkness below their feet.

241

"Kess! Are you still alive back there or have you given up already?"

"I'd sooner acknowledge your intolerable self as the next rightful heir to Heithorn estate than give up," Kess hissed.

"There's the Kess I know. Right. You need to hurry. Help Dracuni climb up first."

"If this is some kind of trick ..." Kess tensed and wrapped her arms tightly around the hatchling.

Pony groaned breathily and it sounded like she head-butted the stone wall.

"Please don't be a stubborn ass right now. I need you to save Dracuni. She's special, you don't realize how special she is. Stop questioning and just help her up. Then I can help you climb up too."

"And you?"

"And then, if I can still move, I'll try to follow. Who knows, we might get a miracle, but you have no idea how my arms feel like dragonfire right now and I can't feel anything below my knees. *Please*, Kess!"

Kess wished for a second that her small vial of silvernix was with her, but she kept it in a pouch on Griskin.

"Don't you have some remedy? Some herbs to neutralize the poison?"

"Everything was ruined in the water." Pony readjusted

her grip, jostling all of them. "If I didn't know better, it'd sound like you were worried about me."

"I'm just annoyed at how long it's going to take to get out of here on my own."

"It will take even longer if you're starting from the bottom of this hole with all your bones busted. I can't ... mmmph ..."

There was a skittering of dust and pebbles, and one of Pony's hands slipped free. She cried out, and Kess gasped as they swung freely for a moment. With a colossal grunt, Pony threw that arm back up again and caught the ledge.

"Okay, okay!" Kess brought her hands underneath the hatchling's chest.

It was already wriggling into action as Kess pressed upward, giving it a boost as it stepped on her shoulders, then head. Filmy wings flapped uselessly over Kess's face.

"Come on, Dracuni. You can do it," Pony encouraged.

Kess lifted her hands as the hatchling climbed. It pressed its back feet into her palms, and she boosted it up from below. Angling her head back, she watched as it clung to Pony's bare arms and scrambled upward against the rock.

Kess realized her temple was so close to Pony's they were almost touching as they both arched their necks to watch.

Pony murmured, "Kess, I know you probably won't, but I have to ask. Can you do me a favor? When you get out of here, find my sister and ... just make up the most epic, ballad-worthy battle ever in which I died, okay?"

"You don't want me to tell her you died because you stole a cursed ornamental sword and made a mountain full of spiders angry?"

Riony's chest sobbed softly. "Yeah ... it doesn't sound great put that way."

Kess bit her bottom lip, as the hatchling pulled itself up over the ledge, tail swishing as it disappeared over the top. "I'll tell her."

Pony sighed so deeply she seemed to deflate to half her size.

"Okay, how do I get up?"

"Going to have to cut you off."

"What?"

Kess held her breath as Pony let go with one hand. She hung from the other, turning sideways away from the cliff while grasping around at her waist.

Something lit up bright yellow. She heard a slicing sound, and then the belt secured around Pony's chest was slid free. The glow stone on it bobbed, light flickering, as she tucked it through her other belt still at her waist.

"Should ... should I take that?" Kess murmured.

"Yeah. Yeah, probably." Pony's words sounded slurred. She thrust the belt and attached light over her shoulder,

and Kess reached for it. Checking the front of the vest Pony had given her, she found a couple of metal loops and tied the belt securely through them, so it hung close to her heart.

"Cutting now. You'll drop. Try to hold on, so you don't pull us both down, okay?"

"I'm ready."

Kess dropped startlingly as the first shoulder strap was severed. She yelped awfully and swung to the side still attached to Pony's lowered shoulder. Twisting, she grasped out, getting one arm around Pony's waist, before she jolted down farther.

The remaining rope between them tangled and pulled and Kess's momentum brought her spinning right around to smack face-first into Pony's chest.

The woman's shirt was torn, and her skin scraped. Rivulets of sweat ran red as they passed over ragged grazes. Over one of her shoulders, the edge of an old scar was just visible. Kess turned her eyes away from it as a stone formed in her throat.

Pony was breathing deeply and staring down at Kess as she hung from the cliff edge with one hand, and Kess clung to her. Her skin felt flushed hot under Kess's arms. The glow from the stone at Kess's chest shined up between them.

Kess stared back up into Pony's face, which used to be gaunt and square, but had grown into strong cheekbones and jaw. Her eyes still held that infuriating mix of indeterminable colors. It was still the face of the only person that had ever shown any kindness to Kess, no matter how much she'd been punished for it.

A tremor built up within Kess, and she couldn't fight how it rattled her teeth and hands.

Pony only stared back at her with a hard, determined gaze. Her free arm wrapped around Kess's shoulder on one side, pressing them in closer. Then she slipped the glowing stone blade between her skin and the rope and cut her free.

Kess's arms shot up around Pony's neck, clasping tight as her legs swung beneath her, her body no longer attached with anything but her own strength.

The yellow glow from the blade disappeared, and Pony reached down between their hips and tucked it away again.

"You need to let go now. I'll help you climb as much as I can." Pony licked sweat from her lips and winced as she grasped her free hand around a strong strap on the leather vest, holding Kess tight from that point at the side of her ribs.

It took all of Kess's strength to unlatch her fingers from around Pony's neck.

Pony pulled her in closer. Her red hair flopped over cheeks burned the same color from exhaustion.

Kess held her breath.

A small smirk emerged on Pony's face. "Wow, Kess. I never knew you were such a sucker."

Kess dropped.

She screamed roughly as she went down, caught, then swung on the end of Pony's arm. A small swarm of fire-bright insects around them took off again.

Banging against the stone wall in a rough arc, Kess lashed her arms out, trying to grasp on, and then she dropped again.

Kess never thought she'd be scared of falling. She was going to ride a dragon one day, and that was a fear she couldn't afford to have. But as the air rushed up around her, it felt as though all spirit and life rushed free through her throat as well, fleeing her body.

Then she struck stone faster than she should have. Breath whooshed out of her. She found herself on a narrow ledge, which only caught half of her, and she tumbled and almost went over again.

Scrambling, belly down, she clung furiously to the stone, fingernails digging in so hard they broke.

It took three deep, wheezing breaths to convince herself she hadn't died. Looking down, there was still a long way farther she could have gone. She had come to a stop, thrown like rubbish from Pony's grasp, onto one of the tiny jutting ledges she'd seen below them before.

Sounds of scraping rocks and pattering pebbles came from above. Kess angled up to see Riony pressing her forearms into the top of the cliff and lifting herself up with ease.

"It's okay, Dracuni, I'm fine. I'm here." The voice drifted down and stabbed Kess deep in her heart.

"What? What are you doing? You ..." Kess panted, half sobbing the words.

Riony faced away from the drop. Her shoulders sagged and she pulled a stone from her pocket. Tracing her fingers over it, the stone lit up a bright cyan.

She had a second light stone. But she ... she ...

"But you were bit! I saw it!" Kess shrieked.

"Yeah, it smarts, too." Riony touched her fingers to the puncture wounds on her hip, hissing as she made contact. "Lucky the spiders aren't actually venomous."

Kess turned cold all over.

Her voice was flat. "You tricked me."

"Don't take it too hard. No, actually do, you dragon-stealing gremlin. I mean, everyone in the depths knows cave spiders aren't venomous." Pony rolled her shoulders a few times and stretched them out. Bending down, she picked up the hatchling, and it curled up into her arms, tucking its head under her chin and trilling softly. "I've got you."

"And what about me? Are you going to leave me here?"

Pony cricked her neck and half turned. "Yeah. That's the plan."

"Go on then. Go!" Kess bit down the fury and tears in her voice.

The monstrous redhead didn't move. "You've got light ... You ..."

Kess rasped, "Don't worry, Pony. It's not like it's the first time I've been abandoned to die alone."

"Me either." Pony turned away again. Her voice echoed roughly through the cave. "I learned it from you, after all."

She walked away.

Kess rolled over onto her back on the tiny stretch of rock and screamed wordlessly into the darkness.

TWENTY

Benjin's hand spasmed, squeezing hard around Lyrrin's fingers. Her knuckles cracked but she didn't feel the pressure as she stared at his mother, numbed from the words the grayglim woman had just spoken.

Yoskar was the one who killed the Hjelzahns' father and sister?

Lyrrin never liked the eldest Hjelzahn sibling very much.

He was terse and commanding and never once cracked a joke or a smile. Benjin always said it was because he was very, very clever, cleverer than anyone else in all the depths, and so he knew all the risks that other people couldn't even see. And he had the responsibility to protect his brother and sister from those risks.

Lyrrin had told Benjin at the time that Riony was like that too but wasn't mean about it. She didn't treat everybody else as though they were their enemy, like Yoskar did. Yoskar even thought unborn baby dragons were worth killing on the chance their existence could lead back to hurting his family.

Lyrrin never agreed with Yoskar's severity. Even his grim sister seemed lively and friendly compared to him.

Especially now, as he stood poised to attack, the red light of his burning crystal staff glinting in his wild, furious eyes.

Could he really be the one who murdered his own family?

Aishena's face was stony. She straightened her back, rolling her shoulders as though preparing for a fight. Only her dark eyes showed her emotions—fear, confusion, betrayal. She turned that vulnerable gaze between Yoskar and their mother in equal turn. "What does she mean? Yoskar?"

"She's lying, obviously," he snapped. "She's trying to turn you against me, trying to turn the odds in her favor."

Around the rubble-strewn space, the delvers held wary positions. Niskina and Caed whispered to each other, equally bewildered.

Aishena's earlier confessions had given Lyrrin a starting point for the conflict unfolding before her, but it was still

all so confusing. Why would Yoskar kill some of his family, then put so much effort into protecting the other two?

It didn't make sense.

Yet all eyes were on Yoskar now, wary and assessing.

"Yoskar, lower your weapon," Brishan said in a soft, low voice.

Yoskar sucked air through his teeth and waved the staff, jutting it as he spoke. "She's lying! She's here to kill us and will happily kill every person here the very moment she thinks she has the advantage! Aishena ... You know, I would never hurt Neif. I would never ..."

A broken slab of stone shifted and crunched as Lady Hjelzahn took another step forward. "Look at him, he's ready to burn me alive, his own mother, here and now in front of you all. He's gone mad."

Lyrrin had to agree that it didn't look good. Yoskar was the only one with a weapon drawn, the only one threatening violence. Caed had circled around behind him as though ready to lunge in and take him down if needed. Niskina remained beside Lyrrin and Benjin, eyes locked on the conflict as she made comforting noises and patted Benjin's forehead.

His eyes were screwed closed, as though taking in just the words of those around him was too much, and he dared not even look.

Yoskar moved to match his mother's forward advance, closing the distance between them.

In a rush, Aishena leaped three big steps, positioning herself right in the middle of Yoskar and her mother's path. There was an athame clutched in each of her hands, not activated, but held so tight her knuckles whitened.

She lifted one and pointed it at Lady Hjelzahn, who halted her next step. "Why would Yoskar kill them? He's been looking after us, Benjin and me. He's done everything he could to look after us."

"Like I said, he's gone mad. Now why don't you ask the same of me? Why would I have killed my husband and child?"

Yoskar answered immediately. "She changed! You know she changed after her accident. You were the first to notice, Aish. You told me how she was so much colder during your lessons, that she didn't feel like the same person anymore. That's when I noticed the changes too; that's when I realized how bad it had gotten."

Aishena swung her attention from her mother to her brother, back and forth, mouth open and brows furrowed.

"Changed?" Lady Hjelzahn scoffed. Her eyes were still as black pools, staring her daughter down. "I am your mother and your master. Help me stop him, before he breaks our family apart even more. That's an order, Aishena."

She pleaded, "Mami—"

"Are you not still my prentice?" Lady Hjelzahn snapped.

"Mestra." Aishena bowed her head in a shimmer of steel hair. With a shaking hand, she lifted her other arm, pointing the second athame at Yoskar. But she didn't lower the one directed at Lady Hjelzahn. "I ..."

"Have you forgotten how to follow orders?" the woman in gray bellowed.

"Aish, she's lying to you! Don't let her get into your head. Take her down before she takes us down or move out of the way and let me do it!" Yoskar hissed.

Aishena winced and remained frozen, besieged by orders from both sides.

Lady Hjelzahn and Yoskar circled closer.

"Just hold on! Everybody stop for a moment!" Brishan growled.

"Maybe it was someone else!" Benjin yelled.

His sudden outburst startled Lyrrin. She grasped his hand, pressing his shoulder gently to keep him still as his body shook with harsh breaths, inflamed from his cry. He wheezed and squeezed his eyes closed as he forced air through his swollen throat.

Lyrrin's eyes widened as she understood him. "Benjin's right, it could have been somebody else who did it, not either of you! You don't have to fight."

Lady Hjelzahn's lightless eyes turned on Lyrrin, her face expressionless, unreadable. Lyrrin shivered, cowering closer to Niskina.

"Maybe ... you could be fighting each other for no reason." Aishena's arms remained raised, the crystal tips of the athames shivering in her shaking grasp. "What proof do you have, Yoskar? How do you know it was her?"

"I didn't see ... none, exactly." He pressed his glasses back up his nose and wiped his forehead with his free hand. In the hot glow of the burn stone, his skin glistened. "I saw other evidence, that she was a killer, that she was killing ... other people, dangerous people to kill, for no discernible reason."

Heirs. That's what Aishena had told Lyrrin. That heirs had been dying, assassinated by some unknown killer. And Yoskar thought for some reason that it was their mother. That was why he'd asked her to leave the first time, but she hadn't believed him.

Whatever evidence he'd had at the time, it mustn't have been enough.

Yoskar glanced at the others in the room before looking pointedly at Aishena. He seemed to be wavering.

"You're being a fool, Yoskar. You're mistaking the signs of my grayglim duties for sinister plots." Lady Hjelzahn's voice seemed laced with ice, and the barest hints of a smirk

raised her lips as she took another step forward.

"No! I took my suspicions to Fadda, to Lord Hjelzahn ..." Yoskar squinted his eyes closed and shook his head once, as though berating himself internally. "It was right after that when he and Neif were killed. I think he went to you, and you killed him for what he knew, as you would kill us too."

Aishena's shoulders dropped. "That's not enough. It *could* have been someone else, all along ... Fadda and Neif could have been victims of the heir killer. The *real* heir killer, out there somewhere, who was never our mother!"

Brishan grumbled at the term. "That's what I thought I was protecting them from. With all the news of heirs dying, with them telling me their parents were gone too, I thought I was helping to keep them safe from that, down here. Kverra, I didn't know you lived."

"I do, and I shall, as long as my son doesn't murder me. Trust I mean you no harm." Lady Hjelzahn grinned toward Brishan, but there was nothing warm in her expression.

"No, don't trust her!" Yoskar roared. "Please listen to me. If she's here for anything other than our deaths, then where is Daymora? Where are the other delvers? Where is the help that should have reached us?"

Lyrrin wasn't sure what was happening or who did what terrible thing to who. But they didn't have the time for accusations and arguments.

"Can you all stop fighting?" Lyrrin asked, pleading most with Aishena, still hovering stuck between her family. "You need to sort this out. Benjin's breathing is really bad."

He'd expended so much energy to call out and had gone limp since, just a low whistle of breath passing his ashy lips.

Niskina checked over the neck brace, loosening it from his swollen throat. "We really do have to get him help as soon as possible."

Lady Hjelzahn's gaze fluttered over the boy as though he was barely there. Brishan, Yoskar, and Aishena were all she seemed to care about, keeping her eyes on them.

"They're right. Enough of this fighting," Brishan said. He moved beside Yoskar and placed a hand on his shoulder. "Show us you aren't a killer and put the weapon down. We have to work together to get out of here."

Yoskar stared across at where Benjin lay panting on the ground, his face crumpled. With a grunt, he deactivated his staff, placing one end of it down, but still holding it upright like a warding shield.

"I'm not the killer," he said. "But I will do anything to protect my brother and sister. And I still don't trust her."

Aishena remained where she was, athames raised as a barrier between mother and son.

A soft growl caught Lyrrin's attention, and she peered

through the inky shadows toward the wolf. A slick, slithery shape dashed past the bound animal, rushing toward her.

Lyrrin let go of Benjin and put both of her hands out in front of her, gasping. The damp, clinging cave otter scrambled up her legs and started reaching its paws into her pockets.

"Butterfur?" Lyrrin breathed his name in quiet disbelief.

Riony! Riony must be somewhere nearby, and she sent Butterfur back to me for treats! Lyrrin clutched the cave otter so tight to her chest that he squirmed and nipped at her arms. It worked. Her idea worked.

For a moment, Lyrrin held her breath, waiting and hoping to see her sister following the otter's path toward her. She didn't come.

But if Butterfur had been down the channel after Riony and then come back again to Lyrrin, Riony had to be close.

She held the creature up on display. "Aishena, please! Put the weapons down. Look! We could find Riony, help Benjin. We could all get out."

Aishena's nose crumpled, but she held her stance. "No. Something isn't right. I feel ... I don't know who to listen to. I don't know who to believe."

"I'm your Mestra, first before any other," Lady Hjelzahn said. She held her arms wide and took a step closer. "You are the hand and will obey the voice."

"No! I know! But ..."

Lyrrin got to her feet, moving toward Aishena too. "What do you want to do? Forget about following orders. You can decide. You were right about the map! If Butterfur made it back, you must have been right!"

"What does an otter have to do with this?" Caed muttered from behind Yoskar. He no longer looked prepared to strike his fellow delver down and just watched the situation before him with a wrinkled forehead.

"Don't get any closer," Yoskar warned the advancing woman, his voice still edged like a knife. "Everybody stay still!"

"And lower those blades, prentice!" Lady Hjelzahn commanded, stepping within reach of her daughter.

Aishena's arms dropped, and she gasped as though it was a surprise to even her, as though her limbs had followed the order without her agreement.

"No!" Yoskar howled. He bolted forward out of Brishan's grasp, charging at his mother.

The sing of twin blades rushing from their sheaths echoed through the cavern. Lady Hjelzahn moved in swift flashes of slate gray, drawing, lunging, slashing.

Yoskar was there, between Aishena and his mother.

The flurry of motion ended as fast as it began.

Niskina screamed.

It took a moment for Lyrrin to make sense of the

shining length of steel emerging from Yoskar's back. It didn't fit there, jutting out crookedly, sheened in spatters of red. How had it appeared there so fast?

With a viscous, slurping whisper, it was gone again.

Then everybody was moving.

Niskina sprang to her feet, placing herself like a wall in front of Lyrrin and Benjin, pulling free a pair of her own athames. They lit up in a crackling burst of crimson.

Brishan crashed down on top of Lady Hjelzahn like a landslide. Legs kicked and tangled as they rolled. Their bodies danced across the shifting stones and Brishan came up onto his knees, pulling Lady Hjelzahn with him.

He pinned one of her arms, still grasping a blood-red blade, holding it tight around the wrist. The second short, curved sword was knocked free and clattered onto the broken rocks as he pinned her other.

The sudden movements and noise startled Butterfur and he dove into the safety of Lyrrin's shirt.

"What's happening?" Benjin rasped.

Lyrrin gaped, staring, unable to reply.

Yoskar turned a slow orbit, eyes flitting about until they landed on Aishena. His glasses slipped down, tipping off the end of his nose and clinking onto the ground. He opened his mouth, then fell.

Aishena lunged for him, trying to hold him up. His

solid chest crashed into hers, taking them both down. She cried out, and Caed limped to her in a rush, helping to roll Yoskar off her.

"Yoskar? Yoskar!" Aishena scrambled upright and into a crouch beside him.

Lyrrin held her breath, waiting for Aishena to say it was okay. Waiting for Yoskar to sit back up. In the combined light of the two delvers' glow stones, a gaping hole in Yoskar's leather armor glistened. A hole in the front to match the one in the back.

The sword had gone straight through the middle of his chest. Lyrrin felt as though she'd forgotten how to breathe entirely.

"Sparks!" Caed hissed. He glared, teeth bared, across at where Brishan held the grayglim mother.

"Get off me, traitor!" Lady Hjelzahn growled, but Brishan kept her pinned beneath his weight.

"Caed! Quickly! Help me." Aishena's hands moved in a flash, pulling bandages and bottles from the pouches at her belt. Her chest heaved and her eyes were wild.

Yoskar didn't move as she pressed a dressing to his wound. He didn't cry in pain. He only stared with unblinking eyes.

Caed caught Aishena's hands, stilling them from their futile work. He leaned into her, whispering. She shoved him, pushing him back. He argued in a crackle of breath.

"No, no, no," tumbled in a silent flurry from her lips. Aishena stared down at Yoskar, then touched his cheek, his neck.

Lyrrin's hands were shaking, and she patted them over the bulge in her shirt where Butterfur lay frozen in fear.

Because she'd seen bodies of people who were no longer alive before. She recognized that absolute stillness.

Aishena screamed out a long, broken wail, rocking back on her heels and staring up into the cavernous hole above them.

"What happened?" Benjin cried again more desperately.

Aishena leaned forward, picking up Yoskar's broken glasses and cradling them in her hands before squeezing her fist tight around them.

She turned dark eyes streaming with tears toward Lyrrin and her brother. "He's ... Yoskar's dead."

Twenty-One

Riony carried her precious Dracuni on one side and her precious replacement sword on the other and prayed to all her ancestors in the stars that she was heading in a direction that would save her from being stuck in these cursed depths forever.

Sir Butterfur was long gone. The cave otter had rushed ahead back when the avalanche of spiders fell upon them. Riony couldn't blame the critter. She would have run from the ravenous arachnids that fast too if she'd been able to. But it did mean she no longer had a compass to help lead her through the dark labyrinth of the Alderkin depths.

There was only one large tunnel leading away from the cavern with the deep pit—apart from the one full of spiders, which wasn't going to happen—so after picking up the sword and scrambling back up the slippery slope, she headed that way and hoped for the best.

She hobbled, making every effort to ignore the sharp pains of the bites in her legs, and the dull, shivering ache in her chest.

Her arms, at least, felt fine and strong and better for holding the weight of two things she loved.

Riony hadn't intended that taking the sword would help get Kess away from Dracuni. It had been a rash moment of unadulterated petulance that made her take the blade and not let it go. And there were moments when she thought she really had screwed everything up.

She was so sparking lucky there'd been a thin ledge just beneath her toes that she'd been able to stand on the whole time she put on her show for Kess.

And she'd been doubly lucky that paranoid goblin had fallen for the ruse.

Riony thus decided that the massive Alderkin blade was her new good luck charm. Unfortunately, the crystal weapon was far too big to hang around her neck the way she used to keep her acorn. It really was inconveniently large.

Dracuni fussed, wriggling about into a more comfortable position.

Riony dipped her head and pressed it to the soft scales at the dragonling's neck.

"I'm so sorry I let that monster get you. It's okay, you're safe now. We're getting out of here."

Other person? Dracuni questioned.

"What ... Kess?"

Where other person?

"She's not coming with us. She can find her own way out."

Dracuni rested her head on Riony's shoulder, staring back the way they'd come. She snorted, and her sense of confusion drifted through Riony's head.

In hole?

"She'll be fine."

Dracuni snorted harder.

"Okay, odds of her attaining a state of fineness are very slim. But I wouldn't put it past her. Plus, she kidnapped you, remember? It's better that we leave her."

Abandoned. Alone. To die.

The ache in Riony's chest shivered again. It was a horrible, sticky, guilty feeling that she had no time for. She willed the feeling away by summoning up memories of cruelty she'd suffered while under Heithorn ownership.

Only whipped by Kess's own hand once. Once. As if even once was forgivable. Sparks, Riony could take the beatings. It was the emotional and mental abuse that screwed her head right up.

And that one time Kess had taken the lash in her own

hands, that had screwed her up most of all.

We both hurt each other beyond repair that day.

Riony's eyes washed over hot and wet, and she shook her head. She'd gone too far into her memories. Needed to rein it back. Just remember enough that she didn't feel bad about walking away.

"Kess is only getting what she deserves."

Dracuni didn't make a move or sound.

Riony huffed, forcing the breath out between her teeth. "Okay, fine! I know it doesn't feel good. Sparks! But what else can I do?"

Riony's mind and heart raced. She hated every outcome laid out before her. She didn't want to care about Kess's death. But she felt all kinds of awful about being the cause, that she was a horrible person for leaving Kess to die. *Abandoned. Alone.*

She also worried that if Kess *didn't* die, she would just keep coming back and being a problem for her and Dracuni.

And *helping* Kess? Riony would rather scratch a dragon's balls with a short stick.

"We have to get away from her. We have to look after us now."

Dracuni mewled and blinked wide lilac eyes at Riony.

"Don't look at me like that. You don't know Kess like I do."

But that was Kess from eight years ago. The spoiled brat who rode Riony around like livestock and had her whipped for looking sideways.

The hard-edged, determined young woman, riding boldly on the back of a wild wolf—that was someone different, someone new. Cruel still, in all new, exciting ways, but there was something else there, hiding in the dull pain buried under the venom in her words.

Something that made Riony's heart reach recklessly outward, the way it once had in the rare moments she and Kess had found joy in each other's childhood company.

But Riony had always been punished for it.

There wasn't one time she'd shown Kess kindness that it hadn't come back to bite her.

You were the only one dumb enough to ever make that mistake.

The aching shiver returned.

"Ugh. Stop it!" Riony grunted at herself.

Dracuni lifted her head from Riony's shoulder. The unidragon sniffed at the air, then turned and prodded Riony with her snout.

"No. We're leaving. We're going home to Lyrrin and we're never thinking about Kessara Heithorn ever again."

Dracuni became more insistent, turning her head down and poking Riony's cheek with the point of her horn.

"Ow! That's sharp!"

Danger!

Riony's footsteps halted. She could hear a dull buzz coming up the tunnel behind them.

For a moment, she half believed that Kess had somehow already tamed a giant ghost snake and was riding it up the tunnel after them for revenge. She wouldn't put it past her.

But then the tunnel lit up. Like a sun chasing toward them, the glow grew closer as the buzzing intensified.

Riony gasped and threw her back against the tunnel wall as the swarm of glowflies hit. They filled the tunnel, rushing through.

The cavern she'd just left had been full of the large bugs, clinging to the ledges and walls. A few had been disturbed by her climbing but had only lit up and flew to a new spot close by.

They fluttered and crashed against Riony, even as she turned and sheltered against the wall, shielding Dracuni behind her chest. Thousands and thousands of glowflies streamed through like shooting stars. Something must have disturbed every single bug in that cavern. Something big.

Over the buzzing, a gut churning chorus of roars rumbled.

You do not go down a tunnel glowflies are flying from. You go down that tunnel, you don't come back alive.

Riony was running. She was running before she had time to put thought into action, her feet pounding the ancient stones beneath her through some drive of their own.

She was running back the way they'd come.

Dracuni clung tight over her shoulder, and Riony hefted the heavy sword in both hands, and they crashed through the remaining stragglers of glowflies.

One final fiery insect flittered through the air in front of her as she broke through into the large cavern. She skidded to a stop there, careful not to tumble down the slope toward the pit again.

Riony cast her gaze down that rough hill of crumbling limestone, silt, and dried stalagmites to the ledge and drop beyond.

Kess had pulled herself to the top and was clinging there, hair stuck against a dripping face, eyes large, grasping and clawing at the edge. Her chest was up on the flat ground, legs hanging behind.

Then with a sudden jolt she slipped back again, just her chin and arms above the edge.

Her head angled up, and she made eye contact with Riony. Terror and something too painfully like hope widened her eyes farther and she opened her mouth in a scream.

"REEEEE-OH-NEEEEEEEEEE!"

Kess.

A gargle of hideous roars rose from the darkness below, followed by the scrabbling of hard edges against stone.

Kess's wiry figure bobbed again, as though being plucked from below, and she fell back, disappearing into the pit.

Riony's heart seemed to stop.

The light from the glow stone Riony had left with Kess dimmed, then brightened again, coming back *up* from the dark maw of the pit.

She came with it, upside down. Her small form dangled, brought up over the ledge, hanging from one leg in the grasp of a nightmare.

A sickening tangle of bleached white bones, gleaming against the cyan light, worked both with and against each other, wrenching and crackling. Skulls and legs and fangs and claws, stripped of all flesh, were jammed into each other until there was no sense of where one skeleton ended and another began.

The mess of arms and claws tangled against themselves, fighting over the screaming woman in their grasp, like a ball of ants fighting over a dropped candy.

The huge conglomerate of bones swayed in the air like a toppling column, swinging Kess wildly. She writhed, steel hunting knife in one hand, trying to hack at the amalgamation of bones that had captured her.

In a scattering of chalky fragments, Kess flew free. Her body arced through the air in a stream of cyan light, then crashed into a cluster of limestone columns, cracking through them and disappearing under a pile of rocks and dust.

"KESS!"

Riony skidded and leaped recklessly along the slope, beelining across the cavern to where Kess fell. Silty limestone sand slipped under her boots and rocks dislodged and tumbled down into the abyss, eliciting more roars from below.

In a final burst of speed, Riony fell onto her knees and skidded to a halt beside the pile of shattered stalagmites and the small figure poking out between them.

She placed her sword down on one side and Dracuni clambered off, circling around on the spot and sniffing back at the pit behind them.

Bad, bad things.

Riony nodded distractedly and reached a hand for the still form in front of her. "Hey, are you still alive?"

Kess grimaced in reply, her whole face crumpling up. Her chest and arms lay free on the rough ground, but her legs were hidden beneath a pile of broken stalagmites and drip-columns.

Squinting up at Riony, she gasped her words. "You ... came back. Why did you come back?"

"Because I never could be very smart about things."

"I didn't think ... you'd ever come ... for me."

"That's what your amma said last time I saw her."

"How can you joke," Kess winced as though in great pain, "at a time like this?"

"Poorly and with inappropriate regularity. I'm sorry. It's ... my way of coping."

"You joke *all the time*."

Riony averted her eyes. "Weird."

Kess closed her eyes and shook her head softly, and Riony couldn't tell whether it was from pain or annoyance.

"Okay, let's get you out of there." Riony put her hands beneath Kess's shoulders and pulled.

Kess screamed, a violent, gut churning cry.

Riony swore and let go.

Panting and whimpering, Kess said, "I'm stuck."

Riony got to her feet and started hauling the rocks. The pads of her palms were grazed as she frantically grabbed and threw, grabbed and threw, small and large sections of shattered limestone. The debris cleared away, leaving behind something that left Riony's heart chilled.

A section of naturally formed limestone column, longer and wider than Riony, lay right across Kess's legs. With a rough snort, she gripped the end of it with both hands, braced her legs, and lifted with her whole body.

It barely shifted. Kess screamed again. Behind them

came a reply of a hundred roars at once.

"Sparks!" Riony stood back up and paced on the spot, breathing frantically. With a fierce shake of her head, she squatted to try to lift the column again.

"What are you doing?" Kess sobbed. "Just leave! Isn't that what you want? Leave and I won't be anyone's problem ever again!"

"I'm not sure even you deserve to die like this."

"I'm stuck!"

"I CAN GET YOU OUT!"

The column didn't budge.

"Why?" Kess's voice was the smallest, pitiful plea. "Why are you like this?"

A roar rattled the air around them, close this time, no longer filtering up from somewhere far below.

Riony turned slowly, scared to see.

A mountain of bones sprawled along the ledge, breaching over the top like a cresting wave.

And Riony could finally understand, in all its horror, what she was seeing.

Not just some strange, living pile of bones. It was a massive, moving tangle of revenants. Hundreds of them, human and beast and so broken she couldn't even tell what they once might have been, all picked clean to the white of their skeletons.

They must have come from above, like the one that had fallen on them.

And all had tumbled down there, into that pit, into a churning pot of cagey ribs and limbs that stuck into one another and knotted and bonded and held until they moved together as one immense, horrific creature.

The rat-king of revs.

And it was rumbling toward them on dozens of feet and claws.

It moved forward from three points, two armlike ropes of entwined revs on the sides, and the main mass of skeletons in the middle. There, three huge mouths roared again. Bears or boars or something else. Their blank, eyeless skulls were hard to identify.

But they formed a hideous three-headed face to the legion-born creature, with long, toothy maws snapping the air.

The conglomeration moved awkwardly, rattling and scraping as each of the hundreds of revs tried to act on its own within the confines of their bonded form. But they all moved with the same purpose.

To spill the blood of the humans.

Riony gritted her teeth and looked back up to the only tunnel that didn't lead to death by spider, now lying behind the approaching mountain of bones. She and Kess and

Dracuni were cornered down in the lower side of the cavern.

Turning back, Riony found Kess panting and pale. Dracuni fretted, dancing on her claws and staring up with round eyes.

Bad, bad, many bad things.

"It's okay. It's going to be okay." Riony pulled the cutting athame from her belt and activated it. It lit up with a yellow glow—still with charge, thankfully.

Squatting down, she pulled Kess's hand up into hers, then pressed the athame into it.

"Cut through the stone with this. If you cut it here, the section on your legs should be small enough to push off. Then we'll see about getting out of here." Riony frowned at the way Kess's skin felt so cold and clammy, how her fingers curled weakly beneath her own.

"Dracuni, stay back with her. Stay safe." Riony chewed her lip, then glared at Kess. "And you, I'm trusting you to look after her."

Kess gave a pained laugh. "Why would you do that?"

"Not very smart, remember?"

Kess shook her head, closing her eyes in an agonized wince.

Riony grabbed the hilt of her weapon, then pressed back up to full height, rolling her shoulders and neck.

"Where are you going?" Kess asked.

"I'm going to try out my new sword."

Riony turned, facing the conglomeration of death scuttling toward them. She lifted the heavy crystal blade up before her, as the mountain of bones lunged to attack.

TWENTY-TWO

They're not coming back, Lyrrin. Amma and Pabba are gone forever.

Lyrrin didn't remember much of her earliest years, when her family lived on the run as fugitive slaves through the dangers of the aboveground. But she remembered the happy times in the safe village they'd found and made their home in.

She was young, and she didn't have much experience with death, until their safe village was no longer safe anymore. She hadn't been able to understand that Amma and Pabba weren't coming after them when she and Riony had run. That she wouldn't see them again the next morning.

She couldn't understand that they weren't just out of

sight, just down the path, just around a corner, and would appear again with hugs and loving smiles at any moment.

I'm sorry, Lil Moon. I'm so sorry I couldn't save them.

And Lyrrin never did see them again. And Riony never called her Lil Moon anymore. That had been Amma's name for her.

By all accounts, Lyrrin had been an easy baby, calm beyond measure, never one to scream or fuss. But something changed the day Amma and Pabba died.

Tears and anger came fast to Lyrrin ever since.

As they did now, looking at Yoskar's unmoving body.

"Why? Why did you do that?" she shrieked at the cold, gray woman.

Her son ... he was her son!

"It was self-defense." Lady Hjelzahn lolled the words out lazily, still trying to wrench free of Brishan's grip. "He rushed me."

"Kverra!" Brishan said her name as a harsh admonishment.

"You didn't have to kill him!" Niskina growled from her defensive position in front of Lyrrin and Benjin.

Lyrrin tried to move in front of her and was pushed back. Benjin was paralyzed by the throes of breathless sobs.

"He was mad. It was the only way," Lady Hjelzahn said.

"Stop lying!" Aishena howled. She shot up to her feet and swayed on the spot, head hanging low and silver hair

curtaining her face.

Lady Hjelzahn stilled, ending her struggle instantly. Her dark eyes glinted as she stared, taking in the wary stances of everyone around her, the blades held high, the faces wet with salt water. Hers remained dry as chalk.

Lyrrin watched as the woman kept her eyes on Aishena the most, unconcerned with anyone else in the room. Not a flicker of attention or pity for Benjin, her youngest child, lying in the dirt near Lyrrin's feet, choking on his own grief. A chill shuddered through Lyrrin, and she clutched at Butterfur's warmth within her shirt.

There's something very, very wrong with this woman.

"You drew first. I saw you. You drew on *me*." Aishena pressed her knuckles to her forehead. "Yoskar was right. He was right about you! I should have listened to him. Now ... What do I do now? What do I do?"

"She drew on you first?" Caed rasped. He had remained kneeling beside Yoskar's body. With a snarl, he rose to unsteady feet and pulled an athame as long as a short sword. It brightened a pale green as he ran his thumb over the runes.

Niskina frowned at her father. "What do we do? Can you hold her until help arrives?"

Aishena pushed something into her pocket, then redrew her athames as well. "Help isn't coming. *Yoskar was right.*

Daymora is dead. Nobody is coming. No one is going to save us."

The corner of the grayglim's mouth lifted in a cruel smile, as though in confirmation.

"This is all sparking insane. We should tie her up." Caed gestured for Niskina to hand her cave silk rope over, as his and Aishena's were on the wolf.

Aishena laughed without any mirth. "She's going to kill us all."

"I didn't really want to." Lady Hjelzahn spoke flatly. From her motionless state, she twisted into sudden action. A foot booted out. A joint popped. Her arm slipped free from Brishan's grapple as though it had been held only by a wisp of web. An elbow cracked into his jaw.

He stumbled for half a heartbeat before he steadied and reached to grab her again. She pounced away from his swinging arms, landed near her fallen second sword, and kicked it up into the air. Her shoulders rolled and popped again as the blade flew, then was caught neatly in her hand.

She twirled the twin blades once. "It would have been so much easier if you'd let me take my children away to deal with elsewhere. Or if I could have removed the grayglim trained one from the mix before we started. But now I will have to deal with everyone the hard way."

Aishena remained slouched forward, staring down, as

though unable to raise her eyes to anything around her. "I should have listened to him. I should have ..."

"Kverra, you don't have to kill anyone! What madness has taken you?" Brishan circled around the woman, bringing himself back near Aishena and the others.

"Whatever it is, she's the one that needs to be put down!" Caed said.

Lady Hjelzahn didn't even flinch, just kept her gaze steady on Aishena and Brishan.

As though Caed decided that lack of attention on him meant he could take the opportunity to strike, he rushed forward, limping crooked and fast at the woman, his blade out in front of him.

Aishena peered up through her hair with a gasp. "No!"

Niskina took his lead, charging forward too. She was snatched from her path by Brishan, who swung her in an orbit around him and threw her back toward Lyrrin and Benjin. "Stay back! She's too dangerous!"

Caed thrust his long athame toward Lady Hjelzahn's side. It clinked against flashing metal. Then leather tore, blood sprayed.

Lady Hjelzahn didn't even blink as she lowered her sword again, and Caed dropped at her feet. He gasped once through a bloodied throat and then stilled.

Lyrrin felt frozen in place, as though her spirit had

already fled her body too, gone up to the stars to be with her lost loved ones, and her body had yet to awaken to that fact.

Her clawed hands were all that moved, flexing and closing, wanting action, but the rest of her could do nothing but stare with hot eyes at the lifeless bodies growing in number and the blood draining across the rocks.

This wasn't right. None of this was right! Lyrrin wanted to charge the woman too, join the fight against the remorseless monster. But she had no weapons beyond her claws, and they hadn't even been able to stop foppish Zade. And the grayglim woman was so much more. She fought like the touch of death itself.

Lyrrin wished she could fight like her sister, that she could swing a sword with strong arms and make a difference.

She wished her sister were here to do that for her.

But help wasn't coming.

There has to be something I can do!

"No!" Niskina's voice tore through the hollow space as she stared at Caed's body. She tried to charge again and was held back like a rabid dog on a leash by her father, feet scraping in place.

"We can take her. She can't kill us all!" she hissed at him.

"She *can*. You've never faced a grayglim, Nisk. Stay back and protect the kids. I'll handle this."

Lady Hjelzahn wiped the bloody blade against her thigh, staring coldly at them all.

Aishena shivered, shaking herself off and grimacing at Brishan. "You? You haven't been a grayglim since longer than Niskina's been alive. I will do it."

"You never finished your training," Brishan shot back.

"Then maybe between the two of us, we won't die immediately."

Brishan drew two athames of his own, lighting them up pale green, as Lady Hjelzahn strolled lazily toward them.

Lyrrin's heart pounded, willing her eyes to look away. She didn't want to see more. There was a cold, deathly finality in Lady Hjelzahn's dark eyes and unyielding approach.

She could kill them all.

But she hadn't. Not yet. And she hadn't tried to right away. She'd lied and waited until everyone had finally turned on her.

No ... that wasn't when. She'd struck as soon as she thought she could take Aishena out by surprise.

"Aishena! She's scared of you!" Lyrrin's words spilled fast and loud. "She wanted you gone first because you're her biggest threat."

Lady Hjelzahn swished a sword up to point at Aishena like a challenge. "Never once were you able to defeat me in sparring."

Aishena kept her eyes on her mother, but her eyebrows dropped, expression searching. "But now, I'm all that's left to protect my family. All the family I have left. I never beat you in the past, but then I wasn't fighting for my life and his."

A new confidence seemed to surge in Aishena, straightening her spine and pulling back her shoulders. Tilting her head, she drawled, "And now, I have my athames."

She lifted her arms and activated the crystal blades, one hot red and the other cutting yellow.

There was a flicker of hesitation on Lady Hjelzahn's face. But she didn't slow her advance.

"Lyrrin!" Aishena snapped.

Startled, Lyrrin blinked her wet eyes clear and swallowed the lump from her throat, her body coming back under her control.

"Go. Go where I showed you on the map. Find that giant sister of yours and bring her back here. We need another sword on our side." Then more softly, "Say goodbye to Benj and *run*."

Lyrrin wanted to say no. She wanted to argue because it didn't feel like she was going anywhere to help anyone. It felt like she was being sent away to run and hide because she was the only one left who had that option.

Benjin couldn't move. He could hardly breathe. He gulped tiny, infrequent breaths, his face red all over, eyes

scrunched shut and soaked in tears. Niskina hovered beside him, staring in horror at the standoff before her that could end at any moment.

Aishena was telling Lyrrin to say goodbye and run because she didn't expect the kid to get where she needed to in time to help anyone but herself.

Because she was too small. Too slow. Too useless.

But there was one more thing down there in the caverns that hadn't been counted on.

"I'll come back. I'll bring help," she whispered it, so quiet only Benjin would hear, if he could still hear anything. He didn't respond.

Plunging her hands into her shirt, Lyrrin pulled out Butterfur and placed him down on the ground. "Go. Go hide. Go home." *Just be safe, little friend.*

He sniffed at her once, then skittered up the cave wall, heading up the broken hole above them. Lyrrin was sad to see him go but didn't want to risk bringing him where she planned to go next.

Lyrrin ran across the rocks for the wolf.

She didn't know if it would help her. She only knew it wanted to find its rider as desperately as Lyrrin wanted to find Riony. And she knew it was fast.

Lyrrin crouched beside it in a rush. No time for careful movements.

It didn't flinch from her as it had before. It remained still, lying on its side, snout beside the laid-out handkerchief. Its breathing came clearer.

Good. It would need its sense of smell.

She held eye contact with the shaggy beast and took its front paws into her hands, then slashed clean through the rope binding them with a clawed finger.

The wolf exhaled in a huff and shifted.

The clash of metal against hardened crystal rang through the cave behind them.

Lyrrin reached for his back paws. Even as she tore through the ropes there, the wolf scrambled up to his feet, towering over her crouched form.

Light flashed through the cave—blood red, broken-egg yellow, sickly green. Colorful bursts mixed with dancing shadows. Rocks crunched and scattered. Metal sung and whipped through the air.

Lyrrin kept her gaze locked on the wolf, eye to eye. "We're going to find them. You're going to take me to find Kess." *And Riony.*

She reached out again and pulled off the rope binding his jaw closed. It could have stayed on. The wolf could have run with it on. It might have been safer for it to stay on.

But Lyrrin hoped that it would be the act of good faith that would win the wild wolf's trust.

As the ropes fell free, the charcoal-gray wolf whipped his head back. He straightened his legs, arched his hackles, and stared Lyrrin down.

She raised her hand tentatively toward the saddle. "Please, let me go with you."

The wolf bared its teeth and a long, low growl rumbled from deep within its belly.

TWENTY-THREE

That reckless, foolhardy idiot. That was all Kess could think as Riony ... Pony ... put herself between the churning mountain of bones and Kess.

She's only protecting the hatchling. She doesn't care ... Why did she come back? She came back. She left me. Idiot. She's going to get herself killed.

Kess's mind was a vortex of swirling thoughts, muddied with nauseous agony.

A chill ran through her, and she felt as though she were back in that ice cave, looking down as Riony lay bleeding, making the decision to leave instead of stay and watch her die. Instead of saving her life.

She'd gone back. With what intention exactly, Kess still

didn't know, but she went back into that frozen dragon lair … too late. Pony had already found her own way of saving herself and was gone.

Only Kess and Griskin and the acorn pendant tucked away deep in the wolf's saddlebags knew Kess had gone back.

Riony didn't know. *She had no reason to come back for me. She owes me nothing.*

A wave of darkness threatened to pull Kess's consciousness away. She bit her tongue to chase off the hollow feeling. She hardly felt that self-inflicted pain over the mind-scraping agony shooting up from her legs.

When she'd once compared herself to the fallen dragon-rider who lost the use of their legs, she'd felt lucky that she at least had feeling in her lower limbs, even if they didn't work right for her.

Now, she wished otherwise.

Now, she almost considered taking the rock knife Riony had given her and using it to hack those legs off to be free. She might have tried if she thought there was a chance the dull blade could cut through. Surely it wasn't going to work on the massive column that had her pinned.

Getting up onto her elbows, Kess jabbed the glowing yellow crystal at the stone to make that point. She gasped as it sank straight in, slicing like dragon-forged steel through silk.

Blinking hazy eyes, she tried again, slicing a long line

down through the rock. There was a smooth press of resistance as the blade slid along the stone, and the powdery dirt smell of crumbled rock.

Kess had seen how the humans of the undercity had used Alderkin artifacts, for lighting, for cooking, but she hadn't seen anything as powerful as this. This could cut her free ... one way or another.

A bolt of pain shot through her legs and Kess crumpled flat onto her back again.

Across the cavern, the revenant conglomerate roared, and Riony roared right back at it.

She'd scrambled up to the highest point of the slope, standing in the small globe of light from her glowing stone like a cyan star.

"Over here, you dumb jumble of body parts! Stars, you're ugly! If I wanted to see that many bones, I'd date men!"

Two of the three massive bear skeletons turned her way, gnashing at the air. They wrenched and pulled toward Riony, as the other large central creature continued to try to go the other way, toward Kess and Dracuni.

"That's right, up here! Come and get me!" Pony yelled louder, waving one arm high over her head. "Look at all these juicy bits you could be biting! I'm what you want! Come on!"

Her streaming shouts turned even more attention

from the sentient individuals within the mass her way. The majority headed toward her now, moving faster with the joint effort. It clattered and scraped up the slope toward her.

Kess's eyelids grew heavy. She watched as the first long, ropey tangle of skeletons reached for Riony. She lifted the massive sword and swung, skimming it just under the main bulk of bones, swiping through the fringe of peripheral limbs and sending bones pattering across the ground.

Caught in a faint haze, Kess wondered how Riony could swing that huge blade at all. If she could keep it up, maybe she could hack that monstrous mass to bits. Maybe Kess could just rest ... just close her eyes for a moment.

But it was clear even by the second swing that Pony couldn't keep it up. The sheer weight of that crystal weapon was visibly tiring her, and fast. The third swing went even lower, scraping along the ground.

With a grunt, Riony dodged to the side away from the scores of grasping hands and claws, ducking between a cluster of thin, cage-like stalagmites.

Kess's head felt hot and heavy, and her body felt terribly cold.

The hatchling mewled behind her.

The hatchling. My hatchling. My dragon.

She was so close to everything she'd ever wanted. A dragon for herself, right there, within her grasp. She

couldn't give up now. Nothing was going to stop her from achieving her goal. Nothing.

With a whimpering grunt, Kess pushed herself up onto her elbows again, leaning forward. Her arm shook and sweat streamed down her chest, and she pushed the glowing knife through the stone.

The crystal was short, only as long as her hand, and once she'd cut that deep, she had to change angles, slice in from the side to meet that first cut, pull sections out, widen the gap so she could reach in and cut deeper. Her stomach churned and ached from being curled to support her weight as she worked.

Acid rose in her throat as pain made her want to faint away and leave the agony behind. But she kept cutting, section by section, slice by slice.

Nothing—*nothing*—would stop her.

The hatchling moved anxiously around Kess, sniffing at where the stone rested on her legs, then stilling to watch the nearby battle, then clawing at the column. It baffled Kess that the wild creature hadn't turned on her, hadn't tried to eat her as she lay there at its mercy.

Kess had to push the hatchling aside twice so she didn't get too close to the magical cutting blade. She didn't want her prize hurt. *Until the taming ceremony.* Kess's face wrinkled as her chest clenched with confusing emotions.

"Are you through yet?" Riony yelled. Her voice was broken between deep, panting breaths. She weaved through columns and stalagmites, drawing the revenants after her. They smashed up against the rocks in their hectic efforts to grab her. Splintered bones rained onto the floor.

Kess opened her mouth, but only a painful grunt emerged. Her fingers bled as she scraped them at the cut rock, trying to pull the next chunk clear.

Riony jumped up to the flat top of a broken column, then skidded down the other side as a skeletal mouth snapped the air where she'd just been. "Not to hurry you, but playing keep away with this thing isn't as easy as I make it look!"

Kess nodded faintly. She was almost through. She could do this.

She was folded almost in half, trying to reach the furthest part of the stone to cut through. Her arm grazed the stone as she thrust it into the narrow split she had carved and ran the blade down the final length.

The heavy column shifted, and Kess cried out as the longer section, cut free, dropped the remaining height down from her legs beside her.

The small length left on her legs resettled, sending blinding stars of pain through Kess.

She took three deep breaths, her chest heaving, and

then she folded forward again and pushed against that stone. It shifted a fraction, and Kess thought she would wither away to nothing from the agony that motion caused.

The hatchling moved in beside her, matching her efforts, pressing her small front paws against the rock.

Lips shaking, Kess wailed and pushed with every last bit of strength she had, and the hatchling pushed too, and the stone toppled and rolled away.

Given a clear view of her legs, or what remained of them, Kess let out a harsh yelp. The sight flushed every bit of blood from her veins and replaced it with ice.

Blood darkened the thirsty stone all around her. Her legs weren't the right shape. The leather of her pants bulged and split and a mess of skin emerged through them, punctured with spots of horrifying white shards.

They were broken, both of them, in a way that wasn't ever going to get better. Tremors quaked through Kess's whole body.

It's okay. It doesn't matter. They didn't work anyway. It doesn't matter.

Kess gulped down a rush of tears. Her head swam. Everything was filtered through an oozing veil of pain.

Her hands lay lifeless at her sides, the yellow-lit blade in her limp grip.

A soft trill came from next to her. The hatchling was

there. Her hatchling. The unusual creature blinked those huge lilac eyes up at Kess, then pawed softly at her arm.

"We need to move. I know," she found herself saying in reply. Kess took an unsteady breath and pushed her palms against the ground, shuffling her body backward. Her legs followed, peeling and catching against the ground they had been pressed into.

A chest-racking scream sobbed from her as anguish fired through every nerve.

The rattle of revenants slowed their pursuit of Riony, turning to the noise.

"No, not over there! I'm here, you want me, you brainless bone bits!" Pony screamed even louder than Kess had. The mass turned back to her, like a field of wheat blowing in changing winds.

How am I going to move? How am I going to get us out of here? I have to get us out of here. She couldn't think through the pain. She wondered if she really should use the slicing blade to take off what remained of her legs. Whether that would hurt more or less.

The dragonling trilled again and bumped her arm with its snout.

"What do you want?" Kess whimpered. "I'm trying. I just need a moment ... then I'll move."

Talons tapping on the stone floor, the hatchling tentatively

approached her legs, sniffing then growling softly.

"Don't touch them!" Kess snapped, waving the creature away.

It skittered back, lifting its chin and tilting its strange one-horned head side to side.

Dracuni. Did they call you that because of your horn? She was such a strange dragonling, and Kess couldn't make any sense of its action. It moved back toward her, pressing in close until her head was tucked against Kess's stomach.

Dracuni turned up to look at Kess and whined a low, keening sound, then licked at the tears she hadn't realized were dripping from her chin.

Those tears came harder, as though shaking up from the depths of her spine until they poured free from her eyes. What was this creature doing? Was it feeling sorry for her?

It pawed and fussed, and Kess could only gape at it. Dragons weren't like this ... were they? She'd only ever known tamed dragons, or hatchlings so new they had barely peeled their eyelids open for the first time, awaiting their imminent taming.

But she'd been told, she'd studied, she *knew* wild dragons were savage, cruel, monstrous beasts. This hatchling couldn't be showing her sympathy. Nothing made sense.

Pain surged through her and her consciousness toppled toward darkness.

A thunderous bang startled her alert again and left the cavern shaking, as a long arm of the revenant mass smashed across the ceiling, knocking down a huge stalactite. It hammered to the cave floor, cracking into an explosion of boulders and dust. They rolled and smashed down into the pit below.

Riony leaped through that cloud of debris a moment later, chased by the middle section and three huge maws of shining white teeth.

"On your left!" Kess screamed, as the other arm swiped in, running on a clatter of skeleton feet and the swinging momentum of a hundred undead bodies angling toward their prey.

Pony braced, holding the heavy sword in front of her body like a shield. The skeletal mass broke like a tide around her and the blade, bones flying in every direction. Riony went tumbling too, down the slope after the broken chunks of stalactite.

Kess's warning cry had drawn the conglomerate's attention, and it turned her way.

Riony hit the dried remains of an ancient rimstone pool and caught the edge before going over. Getting up onto hands and knees, she slapped the ground loudly. "I'm still here, you dumb sack of bones!"

Her cheek was bleeding, red as her hair, and she brought

her sword up again just in time to take another hit. The very extremity of the mass's long arm whipped into her.

Riony turned the blade into it as it passed and smashed through, slicing the end clear off. A rolling tumble of bones flew like shooting stars through the air and crashed down onto the ground near Kess.

Most broke apart on impact, hailing across the cavern floor. Separated down into pieces small enough to end the shadowdragon's curse of faux-life that animated them.

But one larger cage of ribs, endless ribs and spine like a long whip, still twitched and turned. The skeleton raised the long-fanged skull of a serpent and turned to face Kess.

The massive snake skeleton curled and shook itself free of the remaining bones tangled within its splintered ribs, then rushed straight for her.

TWENTY-FOUR

Through the hail of bone fragments, Riony almost didn't see the revenant snake become detached from the cluster.

She could hardly track its path, as the massive arm made of too many creatures swung for her again, blocking her view. And she definitely wasn't going to get to that boney serpent before it got to Kess and Dracuni.

Help!

"Sparks!" She ducked low, flattening her body to the ground and rolling under the rev-king. The clawed and hard-boned feet that drove the 'arm's' momentum kicked and tripped over her, heavy from the combined weight.

Her ribs cracked and bruised.

Dracuni's fear pierced through her mind like lightning.

Breathing with pained difficulty, Riony tumbled up to her feet again on the other side and bolted toward the snake revenant. It was almost upon Kess, and still so far from herself. She considered dropping the heavy sword, currently resting over one shoulder, so she could run faster.

But it was the only protection she had from the flooding mass of bones throwing itself at her like a swarm of locusts on the last standing crops. She had those few random Alderkin crystals she'd pocketed, but she didn't know what they were and had only grabbed them as presents for Lyrrin.

The serpent reared, raising up, within striking distance. Riony could only see Kess through the cage of the creature's fillagree of ribs.

Kess pushed Dracuni behind her with one arm and raised the other, the bright-yellow glow of the cutting athame shimmering through the rev's pale bones.

It struck.

Kess slashed upward, crying out a high-pitched yelp.

Riony ran harder.

Kess and the snake collapsed in on each other. The serpent's skull lay on either side of the girl, sliced in two from the nape right up to its fangs.

The coiling length of its skeletal spine had lost all life, crumbling into pieces as the magic that had animated it and held it together was destroyed.

But Kess didn't move either.

"Kess!" Riony bellowed. She was a few long strides from the end of the snake's long tail.

Kess stirred, lifting her face. It was ashen, her eyes shockingly red against skin so bloodless it could have been as dead as the creatures they fought. Her head wobbled weakly on her neck, but she raised the cutting athame and sliced through that rev's skull again, for good measure.

She looks bad. Really bad. Not that she's ever looked particularly good.

The stone over her legs was gone, but Kess remained sitting where she was. Riony figured once she wasn't pinned, the stubborn goblin would have tied a leash around Dracuni and crawled herself out of there with her kidnapped bounty before Riony could stop her.

Riony could get them all out though. Now that Kess wasn't stuck, she could scoop her and Dracuni up and try to get past the conglomeration of bones. It was huge, filling half the rough slope of the cavern as it swung around trying to catch her, but they'd have a chance of breaking past it to the exit.

Riony might have one more good swing left in her, if

she could get Kess and Dracuni onto her back again and keep her arms free. She just had to get to them.

The rev-king's whiplike appendage crashed down in front of Riony, overextending and hitting the ground between her and the others. Shards of bone shot out from the impact and Riony skidded to a halt, bringing her arm up over her eyes.

The revs in that section were shaken but still moving, trying to right their joined mass and turn on the humans again. And now they lay between two options.

With a growl, Riony lifted the huge Alderkin sword and let it fall down into the cluster of skeletons. It was more of a drop than a swing. The sword was ridiculously heavy, and even carrying it around like a shield left her arms aching.

The hardened crystal cracked down through the boney tangle, crushing a couple of revs within the mass under its weight.

Each blow she did manage destroyed some of the massive multi-monster, but she couldn't keep this up much longer. Riony had the awful feeling that Kess was right, and the sword was purely ornamental and that she was going to die like an idiot holding a decoration.

But for now, all she had to do was keep the creatures' attention on her, and that crunching blow did the trick.

The armlike tangle of revs pulled away from Kess and curved toward Riony, sweeping across the ground. She

pulled the sword up by its hilt in front of her, the long blade tip scraping across the ground.

A skeletal claw slashed down her bare arm, drawing a scarlet line. Riony held her sword with one hand and punched that one particular rev in the skull with her other. There was a satisfying crack, but it and its joined companions didn't slow.

Riony dodged back, only to hear growling behind her. The triple-bear-headed central body of the conglomerate circled up behind her. It swept toward her from one side and the armlike section from the other, penning her in between them like a collapsing corridor of bones.

Riony ran up the slope between the two closing in walls of bone, trying to get to the end of them before they smashed shut around her. The bones clattered, grinding as the revs reached clawed arms and paws for her.

Lungs burning, Riony broke through the final fringes of bone as the two sides of the conglomerate closed up like a drawstring bag behind her.

A low, unseen stalagmite caught her foot and she tripped, going over and tumbling across the rough ground. Sharp limestone straws snapped under her and jabbed into her hips and arms. Rolling to a stop, she looked up.

Into the bared teeth of a huge gray wolf.

Oh, stars no, out of the rev-king's grasp and into the wolf's

mouth is not how I expected my day to go.

"Riony!" The small cry came from behind—no, *on top of*—the wolf.

It angled around, and there sat Riony's little sister, dwarfed within the fluffy coat of the huge wolf.

Riony's jaw dropped.

"Lyrrin? What in this razed earth are you doing down here?"

"Stuff has happened. Lots of very bad stuff!"

Riony frowned and her heart stammered. She'd abbreviated tragedy to Lyrrin that way herself before and was terrified at wondering what had happened to Lyrrin to bring her here on this wolf.

There was no light on Lyrrin, no glow stone brightening her and her ride. Wherever she'd come from and why, she'd done so alone, just her and the wolf, through the darkest depths of the Alderkin caverns. Riony wanted to snatch her up off the wolf into a crushing hug.

The rev-king roared behind her. The two sides had knotted together when they crashed into each other, a writhing mess of undead. The confusion as the revenants tried to reorient themselves within the larger mass bought Riony some time.

"What is that thing?" Lyrrin gasped.

"Yeah, we've got a bunch of bad stuff going on here

too." Riony hefted her sword back up onto her shoulder.

Lyrrin's eyes widened as she took in the weapon.

Riony turned to face the monstrous mess of bones again. "Can you ... are you controlling the wolf, or ...? Just try to get down to Kess and Dracuni. Get them on the wolf and get them out of here."

"Griskin?" The feeble cry echoed up the cavern.

The wolf sprang into motion, taking Lyrrin with him.

That answers that question.

The squirming cluster of revs had agreed upon a direction again, dragging their mass toward Riony. The wolf dashed, skirting the wall of the cavern to get around it, shooting like an arrow toward Kess.

Riony tried to chase after them but was brought up short by the second tangled long limb of the conglomerate looping toward her.

Riony's worn-ragged body rebelled, but she gritted her teeth, cricked her neck, pulled up the sword, and braced. As long as the rev-king's attention was on her, the others had a chance to get away.

The wolf reached the small pool of light from Kess's glow stone. It let out a low, mourning howl.

"Dracuni!" Lyrrin squealed, the sound echoing through the cavern.

Sister, sister! Dracuni thought with happy relief,

ducking her head out from behind Kess.

"How ... Gris ...?" Kess's voice was low and thick, barely audible over the grating bones lashing out at Riony.

"Oh no. I'm so sorry. Do you think you can get up onto Griskin?" Lyrrin asked.

There was such worried tenderness in her tone it made Riony's breath come fast. What was happening down there?

There was only a grunt in reply.

Her hurt. Her much hurt, Dracuni thought.

"I'll help lift. Three, two ..."

Kess screamed with such an acute howl of pain it made Riony bite her tongue bloody.

"I don't think she can move!" Lyrrin cried out.

Griskin growled, the reverberation mixing into the ongoing, echoing roars of the revenants.

"Hang on, I'm coming!" Riony bellowed back.

Heart hammering in her ears and nose scrunched from a war of emotions, she lifted her sword like a tower shield in front of her. Taking in the nightmarish swirl of bones before her, she tried to pick the thinnest section.

She ran for it, face-first, hoping she would plow straight through and come out on the other side with her sister and the others.

Sharp talons and jagged bones scraped up against her. It was like running through a thicket of thorns and

twigs. It gave way to her and the blade, at first, until her momentum ran out.

No, no, no! Riony wrenched at the bones entangling her, pushing her feet hard into the ground as she tried to continue her charge, but she was stuck tight.

"Riony!" Lyrrin called out.

"Don't worry about me; just get the others out of here!"

A snapping, skeletal canine jaw wormed through the jumble of bones toward Riony's face. She grabbed it through its eye socket and smashed it up into a rib cage above, trapping it away from her.

"Use the sword!" Lyrrin's voice broke through the clamor of writhing bones.

"Don't you think I'd be doing that if I could? It's too sparking heavy!"

"You have to activate the rune!"

"I don't know how!"

"I'm going to tell you how if you just listen!" Lyrrin snapped back. "Up from the bottom of the triangular line—"

"What's it going to do?" Riony tugged her hand free from the clutch of grasping bones and ran a finger over the carved rune.

"It's a float rune. Aishena said it's used for moving furniture and things."

"Sorry, *what*?"

Teeth of some kind closed on Riony's shoulder. She bit back a cry.

"Then up the short line, then down the longer line!" Lyrrin continued.

It felt like the weight of almost the entire rev-king had piled in on top of her now. Dozens of jaws tried to reach through the tangle, aiming for her flesh. Riony went onto one knee, pressed down within the violent, living graveyard.

With a grumble of desperation, Riony finished the sequence.

The massive weapon lit up with a cool purple glow. Riony felt for a moment as though her arms had gone numb, no longer feeling the pulling weight of the sword. Until she realized it was the sword that no longer had weight.

The clamoring mass of bones seemed to chew on her entire body, as though every bone of every revenant within the whole was teeth that could consume her.

From her half-kneeling position, she took a deep breath, then burst upward.

Riony brought the long blade up with her with magical ease, blocking a gnashing skull angling for her neck. She twisted, continuing her arc of motion, spiraling the massive weapon in a wide, spinning swing.

Bone fragments went flying. The revenants shattered around her, leaving her in a clearing of crumbled skeletons.

"Oh, sparks yes!" Riony grunted the words intensely. *I could swing this baby all day!*

The ends of her curly hair tickled her cheeks as they floated up around her face as though blown in a silent wind, and she felt light on her toes.

The swarming bones readjusted themselves, pulling in again.

Riony turned to the lowest point and pushed the sword tip into the ground like a vaulting stick, hoping to just break over the top of the skeletal mass as she leaped.

With a gasp, she flew airily high over the revenants, landing lightly on the other side. She snorted out a breath, and then let out a hearty chuckle. With a daring smirk, she turned to face the rev-king.

The fight suddenly felt a lot more equal, and Riony was ready to crack bones.

In the whirlwind of the battle, the thinner lengths of the conglomeration that had swung about like limbs before had both become entangled into the main mass. That surging, seething sea of bones scrambled for Riony.

She struck. With teeth bared in violent glee, she hammered the huge sword through the conglomerate. A whole section cut free, a mix of human and reptile skeletons. It rolled around behind her as she smashed again into the larger mass.

The smaller section moved more spryly, coming at her

back with a vicious growl. Twisting fast, she rammed the pommel into the largest skull of the group, then brought the rest of the sword around to half that section again.

The purple light glowed strongly and the sword swung easily, crushing the semblance of life out of the undead creatures.

But even with the new power of the activated Alderkin sword, it could take a hundred swings to take the monstrous mass apart, and a hundred more to finally put down all the individual parts.

Riony knew she'd try, knew she'd keep trying anything she could to get them out of there. But she wasn't sure she *could* keep throwing her aching body at the thing much longer.

Brishan's scolding voice came back to her.

Kid, listen, I know you're keen. But you've got to be more careful. You can't just deal with problems by throwing your body at them as though it's expendable. Because you'll spend it real quick down here.

Pure, reckless, relentless action had served Riony well in the past, but she knew her luck would run out one day. She had to be smarter ... which sucked for her. She always was more of a hit-things-till-something-worked kind of girl.

As the rev-king shook off the broken pieces Riony had laid waste to with her sword, exposing the central three bears, she opened her eyes wide in realization.

Maybe she just needed to get help from the people around her that already were smarter.

"Kess, give Lyrrin your light stone!"

"No! Why?" came the paranoid goblin's reply.

"Just do it! Lyrrin, can you add a burn rune on that thing?"

"But that will—"

"Yeah, I know exactly what it will do! Add it on and throw it to me."

Kess made some objectionable noises. Muttered arguing. There were some scrabbling and scratching sounds.

"Done, are you ready?" Lyrrin called out.

"Throw it!" Riony jogged back from the rev-king, giving herself some space and putting herself in position to catch the stone.

"It might be bigger than last time! The more charge left, the bigger the reaction." Lyrrin hefted the stone with her small arm. It arced brightly across the cavern.

"I love it when you give me good news!" Riony caught it in one hand.

"Okay, you disgusting butcher's boneyard. You want to eat something? Let's go." Riony charged toward the heart of the monstrosity, going right for the largest bear maw.

She carried her sword lightly in one hand, trailing it behind her as she ran, and activated the new rune on the already lit up glow stone with her thumb as she clutched

it in her other hand. It hummed with magic, growing brighter, and hotter, and brighter again.

With a thundering war cry, Riony leaped high. The three giant mouths of the bear skeletons snapped, and the hundreds of other claws and talons and boney fingers reached for her. She hurled the ever-brightening crystal straight down the throat of the largest bear.

The explosion shook the cavern, bringing down smaller stalactites. Burning fragments of bone sizzled through the air, crashing all around. The rev-king gave off a multi-mouthed roar as it crumbled in upon itself in a crackling bonfire.

Riony landed on the other side, half sliding, half running down the slope to throw herself over Lyrrin and Dracuni.

Boney limbs waved and lashed out from the flames, throwing embers. Chunks of stone and charred revenant bits pattered against Riony's back.

In a cacophony of mournful howls, the churning, sparking remains of the rev-king conglomerate tumbled down the slope and over the cliff edge, disappearing into the darkness below.

Underneath Riony's embrace, Lyrrin whispered in awe, "It worked."

A grin broke across Riony's face from ear to ear. She deactivated and dropped her sword, then lifted Lyrrin up under her armpits, holding her high and swinging her in a circle.

"You did it! That was amazing!"

A proud half smile didn't reach Lyrrin's worried eyes. She patted Riony's arms, pressing them down.

"We have to hurry. We have to get back to the others, fast," she said.

Riony put the girl back on her feet, a frown twisting her forehead. "Why? How did you even find us? Are we that close to the undercity? What's happening?"

Lyrrin's lips closed tight and she shook her head. With a deep breath, she said, "No. We fell too. Benjin is hurt really bad. Aishena and the others are fighting her mother who's a grayglim. Yoskar's dead. Jonna's dead. Caed too. Daymora, probably too."

"What? WHAT?!" Riony roared.

The rev-king suddenly felt like a million years ago. All the blood rushed from Riony's head. She grabbed her sword and turned to take up Dracuni too, ready to run.

Kess was propped awkwardly on one arm. The other held Dracuni around the neck, cutting athame shining yellow in her hand. She leaned heavily over the unidragon, breathing unevenly. Griskin pawed the ground next to her, growling up at Riony.

Her voice came out low and slurred. "I won't ... I won't let her go. I have Griskin again now. The dragonling is mine."

TWENTY-FIVE

Riony tightened her grip on the sword and prepared to pummel Kess close to death. It was only then that she got a good look at Kess's legs.

She already looked far too close to death.

Her hand around the crystal dagger shook.

Dracuni trilled a whimper. There was no fear coming from her, despite the magically sharpened blade near her throat. More worry, maybe even pity.

"Put the athame down. You're in no state for being such a stubborn, butt-faced jerk right now."

"No! I won't let you take the dragon. Then you'll leave me, leave me again." Kess's eyes turned, unfocused, lids drooping, despite how she kept her face angled toward

Riony. Sweat dripped from her pale skin. "I need … I need the dragon."

"You *need* to calm down before you pass out and skewer yourself."

A spasm racked Kess's wiry form. She opened her mouth in a silent cry.

Riony took a step closer, crouching in front of her. Griskin growled softly but didn't move. Riony laid the sword down beside her and lifted empty hands for his inspection. His gaze flickered between Riony and Kess and Lyrrin, and his growl became a whimper.

"No," Kess's voice was a weak plea. "Let me have her. I'll treat her well, I promise."

"You're planning on taming her," Riony snarled, but the anger in her tone was tempered with a gut-churning feeling she couldn't place.

"I can still be good to her. I have to … I have to have her."

"Like you were good to me?" Riony scoffed. "You. Can't. Have. Her."

Kess's face scrunched up with pain, her eyes screwed shut as she exhaled a whimper.

Riony leaned in and plucked the athame from her limp grip like picking a flower. She moved to deactivate it, but it sputtered out, yellow light dimming to nothing as it ran out of charge. With a sigh, she tucked it into her belt.

Dracuni mewled and skittered across to Riony's side, bumping her cheek against Riony's shoulder. Lyrrin let out a sigh and patted the dragonling.

Kess's arm swung weakly, trying to pull the hatchling back, then she slumped forward onto her elbows, face hanging just above the ground.

Help? Dracuni trilled, looking at Kess.

Riony breathed through her teeth. "Sparks, Kess. Where's your silvernix? Do you still have any? Is it on you or the wolf?"

Kess's head wobbled. "I need that for taming. I can't use it."

"You idiot! You are, very best-case scenario, going to lose your legs entirely. And much more likely, you're going to take your last breath any second now. Where's the silvernix?"

"No."

Griskin whined softly, lowering down onto his belly in front of Kess and nudging her as though expecting her to climb on. She wasn't going anywhere. She leaned there, face down, legs twisted horrifically behind, all her efforts required not to collapse entirely flat onto the floor.

"You can't see anything past your one stupid goal! You aren't taming Dracuni. I'll never, *ever* let that happen. And you won't be riding any dragon if you're dead!" Riony groaned and dragged her hands down her face, bringing them away bloody from the gash in her cheek.

"You never understood." Kess's voice was so broken Riony had to lean in to hear. "What being a rider means. It's the only way ... only way I can be worth something. I'll never ... give up."

Kess's arm slipped and she dropped lower, her body trembling.

Help? Dracuni questioned again.

"I'm trying to help her!" Riony reached for the pouches and bags strapped over Griskin's back.

The wolf's snout swung around toward her, growling fiercely.

Riony growled back at the beast, frustration swelling through her.

I help. Same as helped you? Dracuni thought.

Riony paused, then looked down at the hatchling, stunned. "What? No. You can't."

"What is it?" Lyrrin asked.

"Dracuni ... wants to help."

Lyrrin's eyes widened. She whispered, "She *can't*! Then Kess would *know*."

"Stop pretending you can talk to the dragonling," Kess murmured.

Riony ignored her, shaking her head at the unidragon.

"Kess and her problems, they're not your responsibility. She's got silvernix, somewhere. Maybe when she finally realizes she's not going to get any better without it, she'll actually use it!"

Kess's arm slipped, and she slumped lower. A long, low wheezing breath rushed from her.

She went down on one side, shoulder thumping onto the ground. Her head lolled, constellation marked cheek pointing skyward as her eyes stared, unfocused and watery.

"I'd treat ... her ... better ... this time."

Her body shuddered scarily.

"Kess. You dumb goblin ... KESS!" Riony yelled.

She didn't move.

"Kess?" Riony sprang up to her feet, her whole figure flushing with a horrible, gurgling energy. She paced hasty steps, eyes glued to Kess's unmoving form.

Her chest felt as though she'd swallowed one of Lyrrin's double-runed crystals.

"We need ... where's the silvernix? We need it!" she rasped.

Lyrrin made her own attempt to get close to Griskin, to search his bags, but he was on the defensive now.

But while he growled at Lyrrin and stared her down, Dracuni slipped closer to Kess.

I help.

"Dracuni ..." Riony's lips wavered, unsure what she intended to say next.

This moment ... It should have been like waking from a nightmare. It should be a celebration, to see the cause of her torment perishing. A sigh of relief that Riony and her loved ones would no longer be hunted.

But all Riony could see in front of her now was a girl who had suffered her whole life and was now dying in agony.

If Kessara Heithorn wasn't already dead.

Griskin seemed to have noticed a change and turned away from warding off Lyrrin. He whined and pressed his head against Kess's belly.

Riony fell hard onto her knees beside Kess and Dracuni. She couldn't say anything, didn't know what to do. Didn't know how to feel.

Dracuni bobbed her head once, then ducked it down low, bringing her horn sharply across her front leg. The sparkle of opalescent fluid spilled from the cut.

Riony chewed her lip and held her breath, as the unidragon pressed her bleeding leg against Kess's sweat-beaded forehead.

A soft sparkle of light glimmered where they met, and Kess drew a harsh gasp of air.

She convulsed, her body contorting in the grip of the unseen force. Her breath hitched and a brilliant light suffused the cavern.

The air itself shimmered all around her body, radiating out through her flesh, an otherworldly luminescence that cast eerie shadows across the rough walls.

Riony, Lyrrin, and Dracuni were bathed in the ethereal glow as they silently watched the unfolding magic.

Griskin loosed something between a groan and a whine and backed away from the glaring light.

Kess's back arched off the ground and her mouth and eyes opened wide and round. Her hand shot out, finding Riony's nearby. Kess's fingers latched tightly around hers as her eyes closed again.

Deep, disturbing sounds of mending permeated the air. Bones seemed to snap into place, flesh knitted back together, wounds sealed as if sewn closed by invisible hands, as shimmers crackled and bolted all over Kess's body.

As the light dimmed, Kess lay still, her chest rising and falling in a peaceful rhythm. The cave returned to its natural shadows, the magic of Dracuni's blood receding like a retreating tide.

Kess's eyes opened again, and she stared at the ceiling as she took a few long breaths. Then, scowling, she snatched her hand away from Riony's as though it were acid.

She launched upward, hinging at the waist into a sitting position. Grasping at her legs, she stuck fingers through the tears in her pants. With a wince, she adjusted her sitting

position, and Riony saw a flicker of disappointment on Kess's face when her legs didn't follow the rest of her body on command.

Kess turned from her legs to those around her, gaping. "How ... did you use my silvernix?"

Riony only pursed her lips. A slow, heavy settling of relief combined with sickening concern weighed upon her. Because she knew it was only moments before the clever gremlin added things up.

Kess's shrewd gaze cast over Griskin's undisturbed packs, the lack of bottle or vial in anyone's grasp. Then it turned slowly to the hatchling beside her.

She lashed a hand out, grabbing Dracuni by the front leg, staring with wild intensity at the smudge of silvery blood there.

"Back off!" Riony had the inactivated athame in her hand and aimed at Kess in a flash.

Kess dropped Dracuni's leg, more in wonder than in obedience.

"You ... you said she was special. When you were pleading with me to save her, you said that. I thought it was part of your trick."

Shrugging, Riony muttered, "Had to add some truth into the show. Figured it would sell better."

"What is she?" Kess leaned toward Dracuni again.

Riony pushed her back by the shoulder. "She's not yours."

Dracuni skittered over to Riony, chin held up. *I help?*

Riony scooped her up into her arms.

"You did help. You did good." She murmured the words low, for Dracuni, but didn't know herself whether they were true. There was nothing good about Kess knowing Dracuni's secret.

"You really can communicate with it too, can't you?" Kess sighed out the words, as though they were the most tragic thing she'd ever said.

Riony nodded once.

"And you, you too?" Kess threw to Lyrrin.

"No, just Riony can." Lyrrin pouted.

Kess pressed her fingertips to her temples. "This ... how is any of this possible? Even dragonriders who have been with their steeds their whole life don't have that sort of connection. I've heard rumors ... but this ... and her blood! She bleeds silvernix!"

"I am aware of that fact," Riony said carefully. She kept Dracuni held tight to her chest. "That's why it's so important that she's protected. Why I have to protect her. If the wrong person got her ..."

Kess's eyes flittered, as though every thought passing through her head showed through them. Her forehead wrinkled and she gave a firm nod. "You're right. She has to be protected."

"I won't ... sorry, what?"

"You're *right*. This is huge, far bigger than me getting myself a dragon to ride." Kess clicked her tongue, and Griskin shuffled toward her, low on his stomach. He licked her under her chin, and she leaned into him for the shortest moment before her face hardened again and she climbed up onto his back.

Riony got to her feet as well, still cuddling Dracuni tight, wary of Kess, returned to full health and reunited with her dangerous steed. But the goblin didn't attack. She ran her hands up the wolf's neck, buried her fingers deep into his fur, and sighed.

"Can we go and help the others now? They need us!" Lyrrin bounced on the spot, distress making her small body jitter.

"Right, yes." Riony shook herself and reclaimed her crystal sword.

"Benjin really needs Dracuni, too. If Dracuni is okay with that."

"Dracuni felt it was worth saving this monstrous sack of bones, so I'm guessing she might be okay with helping your friend."

I help! Dracuni butted her snout into Riony's chin.

"Did I hear you say Lady Kverra Hjelzahn is there, fighting her children?" Kess asked.

"She's trying to kill everyone!" Lyrrin cried again with urgency.

Kess's face scrunched up. "Why?"

"I don't know! But she's so fast, and her swords—"

"She's a grayglim, the most elite of royal guards, spies, and assassins. We'll be lucky if anyone is still alive by the time we get there."

Lyrrin whimpered, and Riony shot Kess a withering look. "We're going, and we're going to get there in time to save everybody. Because that's what we do, right? Big dreams, bold deeds."

"Big dreams, bold deeds," Lyrrin repeated, her blue eyes sparkling.

Kess rolled her eyes. "If you do want to save anyone, we need to get back there fast. Griskin can do that. But he can't carry all of you."

She stared down at Lyrrin. "Honestly, I'm shocked he let you ride him at all. But I could take the kid again, and Dracuni. Get them out of this haunted hole and go help the Hjelzahn brats."

"I don't know ..." Riony steadied her stance, leaning from foot to foot, as though that could somehow steady the turmoil of her insides at this version of Kess in front

of her, offering her help. What was even happening?

But there was no chance Riony was letting Kess ride off with the two things she loved the most. "Lyrrin could go on Griskin, take Dracuni back to Benjin to help him. I'll carry you again."

"No way am I letting you split me up from Griskin again. I'll take them. You and your heavy ass and heavy sword will have to catch up."

Riony hefted her newfound love up in front of her, staring at the facets of the crystal blade and the rune carved into it. She smirked.

"You know ... I think Griskin actually will be able to carry all of us."

TWENTY-SIX

"Do we even know we're going the right way?" Riony took up most of the makeshift saddle in the middle of the wolf's back.

She held her sword above her head, lit up and weightless. She sat lightly in the saddle, gripping tight with her other hand so she didn't float right off, but still took up the majority of the space.

"Griskin knows," Kess replied flatly. She leaned over Griskin's neck, squirming farther away any time Riony shuffled too close on the galloping wolf's back.

Griskin had raced along one long tunnel, turned into a smaller one, went through a broken wall into Alderkin chambers so rich they made Riony's mouth water, up two large flights of stairs, and was sprinting down a small corridor with multiple intersections and doorways.

Riony figured they must look ridiculous, all of them stacked onto the wolf's back like that. But it was also exhilarating. Griskin was fast and strong and pounced with agile precision through the Alderkin depths.

Even if Kess never did get her dragon, surely this was almost as good. There was a clear bond between Kess and the huge wolf. Maybe not the strange mind-speak Riony had with Dracuni, but still some kind of silent, mutual communication.

Riony's arms and chest remained tense, ready to strike Kess down at the first sign the goblin was turning on her, but part of her sparked with hope.

Kess could have tried to grab Dracuni again after she was healed. She could have ridden off on Griskin without Riony and Lyrrin, left them to run more slowly back to Aishena and the delvers. But she chose to let them ride with her. She chose to help them.

Riony's head practically throbbed with the conflicting emotions whirling in there. Could she ever trust Kess? Could she ever forgive Kess?

Why do I even care? All I have to do now is ride with her and hope that isn't a bad idea.

Riony would do what she had to do, as long as it got

them where they needed to be in time.

"Are we close? We had better be close." Riony squinted into the long corridor ahead.

Lyrrin, clinging on behind her, with Dracuni pressed between them, said, "I'm not sure. It was dark on my way to you. But it didn't take long, so we should be there soon."

Bouncy! Dracuni thought.

"Someone's still alive and fighting," Kess said.

Riony frowned, confused how Kess had drawn that conclusion, until a few moments later the sounds of a frantic swordfight resonated toward her.

With a final, growling leap, Griskin burst into a cavern piled in crumbled debris and lit up with a rainbow of scattered athames.

The shear amount of rubble gave Riony pause. Her sister had come down through that. One of their number didn't survive that fall, and it was a miracle—plus some small testament to the delvers' skills—that number wasn't higher.

Dancing across that landslide of broken stone, Aishena and a woman in gray dragonscale armor traded blows almost faster than Riony could keep track. Dual swords of bright steel met glowing athames of red and blue in cracking blows.

Brishan stood a few paces beside the combat, stretching and rolling an arm that was dripping blood, then moved

back into the fray.

In a twirling flick, Lady Hjelzahn disarmed Aishena of the blue athame, and it clattered across the floor. Aishena's belt, normally stuffed with a long row of the crystal daggers like a toothy dragon's maw, was empty.

With those three focused on their battle, nobody but Niskina saw the approach of the wolf and its riders. She crouched beside the small body of Benjin, one hand on his shoulder, one hand on an athame.

"Off," Riony whispered to Lyrrin. "Take Dracuni, take cover."

Kess turned her head to Riony's words but said nothing.

Her sister slid from the back of the wolf, the unidragon clutched against her chest. They were across the long room from Benjin and another large archway leading into a more decorated space, and Lyrrin pressed herself to the wall, creeping along it in the shadows.

Riony decided she needed to make a bigger entrance.

Letting go of the wolf, she let the weightlessness of her sword carry her. She crouched up onto the saddle, then leaped off into the center of the room, landing with a crash onto the pile of shattered rocks. She swung the massive glowing blade in a full circle in front of her, then pointed it toward the battle.

"Will all murderers in the room please drop their

weapons, or do I have to break some more bones with my fine new sword? I'm honestly okay with either option."

The Hjelzahns' mother's scowling attention flicked toward Riony. Aishena grinned ferociously and in a move that won her a larger portion of Riony's heart, she took the advantage to slash her burning athame toward her mother's throat.

Brishan took his chance from the side as well, striking with a pale-green athame toward her shoulder.

Lady Hjelzahn threw herself into a vaulting backflip before either blade touched her skin. Landing out of reach, she raised twin swords in a guarded stance, assessing the additional threats that had appeared.

Kess and Griskin padded up from behind Riony, prowling forward to join the standoff. The wolf's head was low and his throat rumbled. Kess took in the space with narrowed eyes.

From her vantage high on the tumble of rocks, Riony could see the bodies lying all around. Jonna, body twisted and broken from a fall, face covered in a delver's scarf. Caed and Yoskar, left where they had fallen, soaking in pools of their own blood. Her lips curled into a furious snarl.

"Drop your swords now before I shove your eyes down your throat and make you watch as I jam every inch of this beautiful blade through your chest." Riony flexed, holding her huge sword in one hand only, and pointed it at the grayglim woman.

She clearly had no experience with float runes because she stared at Riony with a horrified awe. Still, she didn't drop the swords. She stood like a statue, only her eyes moving, face twitching, as she recalculated her odds.

"I can still take you all," she muttered, not even sounding winded.

Kess and Griskin stalked closer to the woman, and Riony opened her mouth to warn her back. She was getting too close, and those swords looked mean sharp.

But then Kess angled Griskin back around so that he was facing Riony, Aishena, Brishan, and the others.

"You don't have to take everyone down," she said in a hard, dull tone. "Because I'm going to help you."

Riony's blood turned to ice. She growled, "Kess ... what are you doing?"

Lady Hjelzahn tilted her head, taking in the wolf-rider. In a voice that gave Riony shivers, she asked, "What do you propose?"

Kess plucked a couple of bone throwing daggers from sheaths on Griskin's saddle and pointed them across the space to where Lyrrin and Dracuni inched along the wall.

"I'll even the odds for you and whatever your end goal is. And I get to keep that hatchling over there."

An overwhelming, reverberating hum built in Riony's ears, and her breaths shook through gritted teeth. After everything they'd just been through … after everything!

"Kessara," Aishena gasped out her name. "She wants to kill us, all of us, that's her goal. Then she'll kill you too. You can't—"

"I can look after myself. I will get what I want, and this is my chance."

Lady Hjelzahn nodded curtly. "I prefer those odds. You have a deal."

The chill in Riony's veins reversed, flaring up with the heat of flowing lava. Every part of her felt hot, shuddery, ruinous with overflowing fury.

She couldn't even speak, couldn't even think of a single cutting word to hurl back at the awful goblin that could do nothing but hurt her and whip her when she was down. A curdled mixture of hatred and charred hope ground through her guts.

In a roar of rage, Riony threw herself and her sword at the girl and the wolf.

Griskin pounced to the side and the sword crashed down beside him, shards of soft limestone scattering from the warning blow. A bone dagger whistled through the air. Riony twitched back. The sharp blade skimmed across the side of her neck, leaving a sting. Kess wasn't playing. She was throwing kill shots.

This wasn't some ploy. Even in her fury, Riony had hoped, had wondered if Kess was lying, to get closer to the murderer in their midst. A trick to take that grayglim woman down.

When will I learn? When? She'll never be kind to you!

Riony bellowed, wordlessly, madly. Something broke painfully in her chest.

She swung again, scooping the blade from the ground in a hail of stones and sweeping it up to cleave Kess through the middle.

Kess wasn't the only one going for blood now.

The wiry girl ducked low against Griskin's back, the blade skimming across the tangled braids on her scalp. The wolf lunged, getting within arm's reach of Riony, snapping sharp teeth at her hands. She had to dodge back, give herself space to swing again.

Kess's throwing daggers rushed at her in a flurry of pale streaks. Riony deftly blocked two with her sword, but the next found its mark, sinking into the flesh of her upper arm. The slim blade remained stuck, protruding from her skin. Riony ignored it.

The pain only fueled her determination, her grip on her sword tightening.

How could you? How could you!? The words burned

permanent scars of repetition in Riony's mind.

She thundered, "I'll never let you have Dracuni. You'll have to kill me first!"

"I know." Kess dropped the words, heavy and emotionless, into the air.

More throwing daggers sliced through the air. Riony met the flying blades head-on, sword raised as a shield, bones pinging off as they hit. The impacts reverberated through her arms.

Each dagger throw was a threat she couldn't ignore. Kess's onslaught forced her to pivot and dodge, every step a calculated dance of survival.

Another found purchase in her thigh, hilt jutting out awkwardly. The pain of it was no more than a fly bite compared to the uproarious turmoil shredding Riony from the inside.

Riony didn't slow. In the barest moments of reprieve as Kess sought more blades, Riony bore down on her with ferocious sweeps of her sword. It whirled in blinding arcs, a tempest of glowing crystal that forced Kess to remain constantly on the move. Griskin's swift footwork countered Riony's brute force, keeping them just out of reach.

Neither yielded an inch. They each fought furiously, for their very lives, for everything they wanted and cared for.

An unsteady slab of stone shifted under Griskin's paws

and he had to dodge toward Riony instead of away to stay clear of the resulting landslide of rubble. She brought her sword hammering down, flat edge toward his snarling head.

Kess swung him around, taking the blow across one of her legs instead. The sword tip traced a line through the ragged leather covering her calf. Blood spilled from the wound, and Kess spat a curse.

Beside them, somewhere, somehow, came the singing clash of steel on crystal. Riony couldn't understand it at first because the only thing in the world right now was her blinding fury, and Kess, and Kess's imminent death.

Then Aishena's cry reminded her that other people existed. "Get to Benjin! Help him!" It was the cry of a sister, desperately trying to save her younger sibling.

"I can't!" That was Lyrrin.

Riony blinked, eyes clearing slightly from the red haze that had flooded them.

Across the cavern, Lyrrin and Dracuni were pressed into a corner, with Aishena and Brishan in battle with Lady Hjelzahn in front of her. Across the other side, Niskina stood over Benjin.

The fight with the grayglim was a whirlwind of motion, each movement precise and fierce as she clashed with Aishena and Brishan. It took both of them to even keep her at bay, and she still had time and attention to lash out toward

Lyrrin every time the girl tried to edge closer to Benjin.

"Let me help!" Niskina paced, stepping forward and back from the flurry of blades.

Riony narrowly dodged Griskin's teeth on her wrist and turned her full attention back to him. Kess had only a single bone dagger in her hands now, clinging to it, making Riony think it might be her last. She pressed forward, aiming a blow for the traitor's head.

Kess rolled away, hanging sideways from the saddle before righting herself and bringing Griskin back around to attack again.

The flurry of the other battle moved closer, and a nearby squeak from Lyrrin proved she was being forced along with it.

"No, Nisk! Stay back!" Brishan cried.

"Stay with Benjin!" Aishena added.

"You're at a stalemate, but the three of us could best her."

A thunderously loud clash of weapons sounded and Brishan grunted. "You've never fought a grayglim, you don't know—"

"I can still do what's right!"

Through the corner of her eye, Riony saw movement as Niskina ran into the fray.

And then Brishan made the most horrific choice Riony had ever seen. He turned his back on Lady Hjelzahn to bodily push his daughter out of the battle.

He thrust out with both hands, slamming them into her chest and knocking her onto the ground, across where Benjin lay. Air whooshed out of her, and she lay there, winded, gasping for breath.

Lady Hjelzahn's twin blades met around Brishan's neck and scissored clear through.

The ringing of that steel upon steel turned into a piercing scream from Niskina that shook through the cavern. She wailed a long, sharp note of grief that cut Riony deeper than Kess's blades.

Every part of Riony tensed, and her face scrunched in on itself.

Brishan ...

Master Brishan, who was going to give her one last chance to be a delver after her spectacular screwup. Who was going to be so impressed when she had come back the next day, followed orders, and done everything she could to be the perfect delver because it was all she'd dreamed of, all she and her small family needed to live comfortable and safe.

And Riony felt a venomous guilt to even think that, to see Brishan die and to feel the loss of her own dreams slipping away right before her eyes.

Niskina had lost her father, and Aishena had lost her

brother, and all the other delvers' families had lost them, and Kess ... Kess remained. Kess could have changed things. Worked with them to stop the murderous Lady Hjelzahn.

But instead, she ruined everything in Riony's life, the way she always did.

In that fraction of a heartbeat, as Riony grieved for Brishan, and all the dead around her, and the death of all her dreams, Griskin lunged, jaws snapping shut around Riony's leg.

Pain radiated through Riony's body. She cried out, staggering on her other leg. Griskin tossed his head, yanking her with him, teeth closed like a vise through her flesh and grinding against bone.

He pulled Riony off her feet and sent her rushing to meet the ground. She cracked down on her back in a puff of dust, crooked shards of stone jabbing against her. The long Alderkin sword tumbled out of her hand. Bone daggers, still pierced in her arm and leg, jarred with agony at the impact.

The wolf's snarls echoed in the air, a victorious proclamation. Kess, panting and bloodied, glared down at Riony, one final dagger in her hand aimed for Riony's heart.

TWENTY-SEVEN

Griskin thrashed his clamped jaw, as though trying to pull Riony's leg clear off at the knee. She bit off a scream, breathing through the pain. Searing agony shot through Riony as his teeth tore through her muscle with each swing of his head.

Kess toyed with the slim bone dagger in her hand. Her lips curled.

"You don't have to die," she said. "Let me take the creature, and this will end."

Riony gave a feral growl. "Counteroffer—you drop dead and let the world be a better place without you in it."

Kess lazily rolled her eyes.

Brishan's body had only just crumpled, headless, to the

floor. Aishena exploded into action, putting her mother on the back foot for the first time in her wild brutality.

Niskina lay where Brishan had pushed her, paralyzed by breathless sobs. When Lady Hjelzahn disarmed her daughter of her athames, Niskina's sobs stilled, her expression fierce. She threw crystal blades in to replace those dropped. Aishena fluidly plucked them from the air, still alit and glowing red hot.

There was still some life in each of them yet, and Riony would keep fighting until Kess sank that final dagger into her heart.

She twisted, throwing her arms out, trying to reach her dropped sword so she could swing it back in the wolf's face. She needed to detach its teeth from her skin.

The sword was out of reach, sliding away from the ends of her fingertips. Instead, she found Yoskar, lying nearby, eyes staring lifelessly back into hers.

A silent sob clogged Riony's throat, blocking her breath, as though her body was already preparing to join him in death.

But in death, the stern delver offered a glimmer of relief for Riony.

She wrapped her fist around Yoskar's crystal-studded staff, pulling it from his cold fingers and swinging it for Griskin's jaw.

Out of reach, Griskin kept her pinned as the staff whooshed through the air near Riony's knees, far shorter than the huge sword.

Movement behind the wolf-rider drew Riony's attention, and she glanced toward it. Lyrrin stood there, a few steps back from the wolf. Dracuni was down on the ground, curling anxious circles around Lyrrin's legs, as the young girl gestured with both hands in a grabbing motion.

Her lips silently mouthed, *"Throw it to me."*

Kess's head began turning to follow Riony's line of sight.

Riony shot her gaze back at Kess and clenched her teeth beneath a smirk. "What's the problem, Kess? You're about to have everything you wanted. Don't you have the stomach to finish this? Just like you didn't have the stomach to whip me yourself? Your parents aren't here to do it for you this time, coward."

"You always behaved as though you wanted to die." Kess snapped back to face Riony. Hesitation flickered over her pointy features. "I'm glad you're so eager. That will make this easier."

Riony swung the staff again, weakly and too far from reaching her target. But it was only for show, to keep Kess's eyes on her.

"Go on, then! Have the guts to follow through on one damned thing in your life, you self-serving, two-faced goblin. Kill me! You want your dragon, then you have to kill *me*."

On her third swing, Riony let the staff fly.

Kess dodged the flying weapon, scoffing at Riony's missed attempt.

And the staff landed where Riony intended.

She didn't know what Lyrrin was going to do with it. Something clever, probably. Add more runes onto one of the stones and make another flash bomb? Fire bomb? Riony braced herself for an explosion. She trusted Lyrrin to make it work. She should have trusted her all along.

But she was also prepared to go out along with Kess and the wolf if that's what Lyrrin had to do to keep herself and Dracuni alive.

The clatter of a hot, red dagger turned Kess and Riony toward it. Aishena's last athame spun across the floor, knocked from her grip.

Lady Hjelzahn's twin blades cracked through the air like lightning, chasing her daughter across the space with swing after swing. Unarmed, it was all Aishena could do to keep herself out of reach.

Kess nodded as though to herself, then glared down at Riony. "It's over. Wish I could say it had been a pleasure, Pony."

Her arm pulled back like a striking serpent, the bone dagger glinting in the cyan light.

And then a small figure came flying through the air behind Kess, bellowing a high-pitched roar like a miniature barbarian.

Kess turned too late, and Lyrrin brought the crystal-studded end of Yoskar's staff down over the back of her head.

It hit with a thudding crack. Lyrrin landed in an awkward tumble by the wolf's flank, and momentum carried her all the way up to Riony's side.

Kess slumped, dangling down over Griskin's neck. The wolf growled gruffly, unlatching its teeth from Riony's leg and backing off. He lifted his head, bobbing it up and down as Kess's body lay limply over his neck, as though trying to stir her.

Riony pulled herself up into a sitting position and grabbed for her sister.

"What was *that*?" Riony asked in awe.

Lyrrin shrugged bashfully, holding the staff in a hug to her chest. "I asked myself what you would do. I was trying to be more like you, because normally you do the saving."

"Lil Moon," the long-unused affectionate term slipped out, hurting Riony's heart with its appearance. She swallowed and continued. "You don't have to be like me. You're so much cleverer. Bashing someone on the head with a stick should be your last resort."

"Maybe. But also, I didn't want to do something that might blow you up. Maybe we can both learn from each other."

Riony ran her fingers over Lyrrin's cheek, then patted her hooded head.

With a great, sighing groan, Riony got to her feet,

leaning heavily on the leg that didn't have a dagger and teeth marks in it.

"Sword. Dracuni," she said, tucking her fingers in a beckoning gesture.

Lyrrin ducked to grab the weapon, eyes wide with excitement as she lifted it easily over her head to place it back into Riony's grasp.

Griskin snarled as Dracuni galloped past to join them. Kess's arms worked, trying to press herself upright, but her head flopped and she swayed.

As Riony lifted her glowing Alderkin sword his way, the wolf lapped his tongue nervously and backed into the shadows.

Hurt? Dracuni trilled and stood on her back legs, front paws reaching up to be held.

"I'm okay, I can handle this." Riony winced as she hobbled her first step. "Lyrrin, take Dracuni over to Benjin and Niskina. I'm going to help … Aishena!"

The silver-haired delver was down on her back, her mother standing over her, blades raised and ready to strike.

"You always were too easy to disarm. You would never have made the grayglim ranks if you can't even keep hold of your weapon." Her voice was strange, filled with a cold flatness, at odds with the heart-racing battle she'd just ended. "You have to die, regardless. Every last one has to die."

"It's lucky, then, that I kept my hands on one more

weapon." Aishena moved in a flash, tugging a long, thin athame out from her chest armor.

She didn't even activate it, just struck the sharpened crystal upward. It plunged through a gap between the scaled armor, deep into Lady Hjelzahn's gut.

The blow knocked the woman backward, and she folded, falling in a rumpled heap.

One steel sword then another fell, *clang*, *clang*, out of her hands.

Aishena spun her legs above her, then brought her body up with the momentum in a liquid motion. She snatched up the twin blades, pulling them back away from the twitching body of her mother as though worried the grayglim would strike out at her with them again.

Riony limped as quickly as pain allowed over to Aishena's side. "Are you okay?"

"For someone who just killed their own mother, I'm perfectly fine." Aishena kept her face down, shadowed by the fall of her hair.

"I thought you were done for. Nice trick with the hidden weapon."

Aishena tilted her head and shrugged. "I've been keeping one concealed on my person at all times since you suggested it while we were chained to that cart."

"Stars *damn it*, you're hot," Riony gushed.

Aishena flickered a dull look toward Riony, then turned her eyes again to the two bloody swords in her hands and the body of her mother lying before them.

Which continued to move.

No blood spilled around the athame lodged into her intestines. The woman twitched, then opened her eyes. One hand snatched at the hilt of the crystal dagger with terrifying speed.

With a great, spasming tug, Lady Hjelzahn pulled the long athame free from her stomach. It came out clean. The wound remained dry.

"Um ... That isn't normal," Riony said.

Aishena was already stumbling backward, horror stretching her features.

Lady Hjelzahn rose to her feet.

"No, no!" Niskina screamed.

"We have to get out of here!" Riony stared upward at the ragged hole above them, leading up and up and up. She was in no state to climb. Maybe she could hold off the unsettling gray woman while the others did.

There was an archway behind them, opening into a shadowed, cluttered space. They'd have to go past Lady Hjelzahn to go for the other tunnel they had come from, even if they preferred to face the rev-king again instead of her. Riony was fifty-fifty on that.

"Lyrrin, the gateway! Activate it!" Aishena yelled.

"The what?" Riony asked.

Lyrrin was already running through the archway, carrying Yoskar's staff and Dracuni, who bobbed over her shoulder.

Riony raised her sword, prepared to square off against the grayglim woman, to buy time for whatever it was Aishena and Lyrrin were planning.

Lady Hjelzahn straightened, glaring down at the tear in her armor. Something that looked uncomfortably like intestine poked out through that hole. With indelicate fingers, the woman pressed it back in again.

"*Nope*," Riony muttered and hobbled speedily toward the archway.

The weightlessness of the sword helped carry her, and she jabbed the tip into the ground, using the length like a crutch as she hurried after the others.

Aishena was beside Niskina and Benjin. She lifted him with as much care as time afforded. "Come on! Snap out of it!" she scolded to Niskina, then hurried after Lyrrin.

Niskina remained, gasping sobs her only movement.

Riony detoured a few steps to grab the sobbing girl's hand. Then she continued on, dragging Niskina with her.

She limped through the archway into a room that would have been everything she'd wished and dreamed

for a long time ago, that very morning.

Now all she wanted was to live and save the few remaining lives around her.

"Is there a way out through here? Where's the gateway?"

Riony could only see adjoining rooms, all dead ends.

Lyrrin was crouched on the ground in front of a huge geode slice that towered in the center of the Alderkin riches. She traced the complex rune at the base, and then another symbol to the side lit up.

Lyrrin touched it with ungloved fingers, and the inside of the geode shimmered with magic. The air contorted and changed, coalescing into a sparkling image that seemed familiar to Riony.

"Hurry! Go through!" Aishena commanded. She didn't wait for a response. She strode straight into the enchanted image, the touch of magic glimmering over her, and Benjin, limp in her arms.

"Are we sure ... is this safe?" Riony gulped.

Glancing behind her, Lady Hjelzahn's legs juddered into movement, breaking into a run toward them.

And at her side, a charging wolf. Kess squinted, leaning crookedly as she rode.

"Sparks!" Riony growled.

Lyrrin, and Dracuni in her arms, both looked up at her, questioning.

"Go!" Riony nudged them toward the strange gateway. They twinkled through it, visible still on the other side through the veil of glowing magic.

Then Riony dragged her aching body and Niskina after them.

A frisson of energy washed over her, making her skin prickle in goosebumps. For a moment, she couldn't breathe, her head spun, and it felt as though a rush of wind blew straight up into her rib cage and out the top of her head, taking all her bodily contents with it.

She stumbled out the other side into the crumbling interior of an Alderkin shrine.

Riony's bad leg caused her to trip on the uneven floor and she fell. She let go of Niskina in an effort not to bring her down at the same time. Landing on her hands and knees, Riony flipped herself over as fast as she could, grasping again for her sword as she stared back through the strange glowing portal at the two deadly figures racing her way.

Lyrrin stooped beside the large geode they had just tumbled through, scrabbling her hands around in the leaf litter and dirt at its base.

In the water-ripple image of the room they'd just left, the wolf leaped.

Then the light went out.

TWENTY-EIGHT

Kess's head thumped with blinding pain, but she could still see her prey right in front of her. Everything was blurry, but the strange space between the huge, glowing crystal window rippled and whirled the most.

Still, she could see Pony down on her back. The brat who'd given her the cowardly blow from behind was there too, and behind them, Dracuni, the creature she'd do anything to claim.

Griskin was in midair when the light faded in a zing of magic, and Kess's quarry disappeared before her eyes.

She and the wolf went through the middle of the massive geode and landed alone on the other side.

Griskin whined, sniffing at the ground and finding nothing.

Searching with her eyes, Kess grunted, "Where are they?"

A wave of pain washed through her skull at the use of her voice. She reached her hand back, feeling the rising egg on the back of her skull. The kid hadn't hit her very hard, just enough to cost her everything that had been within her grasp.

It's your own fault too. You shouldn't have hesitated. You should have put Pony down, once and for all.

Kess scrunched her hand into her hair around the swelling wound, seething anger out in a long breath through her teeth.

It wasn't fair. How dare that ... that monstrous, traitorous, intolerable oaf have the one thing Kess always wanted? How dare *she* have a dragon, and at the same time something that was so much more than a dragon?

Dracuni ... Kess should have known from the name, from the strange, singular horn formation and coloring. But how could she have known such a creature could exist? She still didn't understand how it did.

She only knew she had to have it.

Kess spoke the truth when she agreed Dracuni had to be protected. Every blight-bitten fool in this razed world would be after the thing if they knew what it was. And if that unblessed idiot Pony couldn't even keep the secret from Kess, she was in no position to keep that creature out of someone else's hands.

Kess wanted the hands that laid claim to the priceless hatchling to be hers. More than anything. Certainly more than the crawling, awful sense of familiarity that had crept into her during her time spent with Pony.

The way they had fallen back into that strange semblance of their old relationship brought every childhood emotion back to Kess in an unwanted rush. The mutual torment, the shame … the longing.

As a slave, Pony had never truly cared for Kess. Never could. And in a life where Kess existed knowing no care from anyone, she despised that sense of desire for care from someone so beneath her.

It would have been better if Riony had never been part of her life.

Now her target was gone, who knew where, and she had no leads or idea where to start next.

Why did I hesitate?

It was just a life, one life, that stood between Kess and everything she wanted. It should have been easy. Kess should have never allowed Pony's life to matter to her.

The soft crunch of a footstep twitched Griskin's ears, and Kess turned to see Lady Hjelzahn approaching.

"What happened to them?" She glared from the circle of crystal at Kess.

She'd lost her twin blades, but now held a long, thin

crystal dagger.

The one that had moments ago been plunged into her stomach.

Kess shivered and backed Griskin away slowly. "They must have used some kind of magic."

"Invisible?"

"No, Griskin would smell or hear them if they were still here. I think they are ... gone. Somewhere else. The view behind them through the crystal was a different place, an overgrown ruin. They might be there."

"Could they come back?"

"Would you?"

"Hmm." Lady Hjelzahn turned midnight-dark eyes toward the archway and the hole leading above. Then returned them to Kess, adjusting her grip around the crystal knife.

Kess eyed her hand. "We could continue to work together until we both have what we want."

"No, I see no value in that."

"We part ways here, then." Kess leaned over Griskin, spurring him into motion, gaze still locked on the approaching grayglim.

"No. You won't leave this place." Lady Hjelzahn moved to stand directly in front of Griskin, showing no fear for the beast whose shoulders stood almost as tall as hers. She ignored his growls, gaze locked on Kess.

"Whatever is going on between you and your children, whatever all of this was about"—Kess gestured to the bodies, sapped of their warmth on the floor of the caved-in area—"it doesn't have anything to do with me."

"I can't leave any witnesses." The grayglim burst into motion. Twisting past the wolf's biting teeth, she lunged the crystal blade toward Kess's chest.

Kess muttered a curse as it clipped up against one of the many steel rings on the harness-like vest she'd been given. The hard metal diverted the strike sideways. The force behind the blow bruised her ribs but didn't cut through.

"Gris, go!" Kess cried, and he bounded away from Lady Hjelzahn's second lunge.

Letting the wolf take control of their path, Kess turned back, eyed up her target, and let her last bone dagger fly. It sank neatly beneath one of the woman's collarbones.

The throwing daggers Kess carved from bones were small and thin, but punctured into a chest like that, they could still breach a lung, stop a heart.

Lady Hjelzahn plucked it out, clean and dry, and tossed it to the floor.

A gut-deep disturbing dread filled Kess. She leaned over Griskin, urging him on faster. They raced out of the rich chambers and up the pile of debris.

Footsteps pounded after them.

Reaching the summit of the landslide, Griskin jumped.

Lady Hjelzahn leaped after them, her fingertips brushing the end of the wolf's tail.

The nimble wolf landed on a small ledge, all that remained of the floor above.

He kept going, kicking off the wall there to bounce higher, scrabbling onto the next level, and then the next.

Beneath them, stones pattered down, disturbed by their climb.

Kess couldn't hear the grayglim, but a quick glimpse back showed the woman climbing after them.

She was fast, but Griskin was faster.

Floor after floor, he jumped from ledge to ledge. One gave way, crumbling beneath them, but his agile feet brought them pouncing safely to the other side and up again.

Kess held her breath and forced herself to look down. Neither heights nor depths should scare her. She could no longer see the murderous woman behind them in the dark pit, spotted with dimming crystal blades, scattered amongst the bodies far below.

Griskin's side bumped into a wall, and Kess hissed when the cut on her leg collided with the stone. The cut Pony had drawn with that ridiculous sword stung but wasn't too deep. It would heal on its own. She'd had worse.

And maybe Kess could even entertain the idea of using her silvernix, since soon, she'd have it in plentiful supply.

Griskin brought them leaping up one more level, and above them, Kess found a solid ceiling. She recognized the room as the one she and Riony had broken through the wall of into the water channel.

The tunnel leading out was a mess of debris and crumbled stone, almost blocking the exit, but there was room enough to squeeze through.

Griskin led the way, and Kess rummaged through her saddlebags for any remaining weapons, shaken and worried the unnatural grayglim woman was still after them. Nothing turned up. She was going to have to replenish her supplies once they were out of this awful underground tomb.

Griskin's breathing was heavy, and she let him slow his pace as they moved through the shadowy tunnel. Lady Hjelzahn was long behind them in the climb. They should have a few moments to recover, and were almost out into the larger, inhabited cave. Reaching down, she pressed both hands into the thick fur of her wolf's neck.

Blessed sun, it's good to be back on Griskin again.

He trotted nimbly down the unlit passageway. Kess couldn't see anything, but she could feel the wolf's sure motions, the turns of his ears, the twitch of his snout, as his keen senses led them confidently through the dark.

Soon, the sounds and smells of the undercity were noticeable for Kess too, and they came out into a lit area near the pungent fungus farms.

She leaned forward and gave Griskin a pat on his jowls. It was then that she noticed the small parcel of fabric tucked into the strap collaring the wolf's neck.

"What's this?" She pulled out the soft, thin cloth and unwrapped it. Within, the crumbled remains of dried herbs sent a strong whiff of fragrance into Kess's airways.

Griskin snuffled and pawed at his nose.

"Is this why you're not as sniffly anymore?"

Kess took another tentative breath. The bright, minty fragrance shocked a nostalgic memory free. She'd smelled this mix of nose-clearing herbs before. Delivered to her by Pony, back when they were children and Kess was sickly, and Kess hadn't even asked that favor from the slave.

When Kess's mother found out Riony had given her peasant's herbs as a remedy, she'd been furious. Peasant's herbs, for a Heithorn! Not that they had enough silvernix to spare on common sniffles by that point or would have spent any more on Kess even if they had.

Riony had been whipped for it. Told she needed to understand her place.

Somehow, those lessons never stuck.

Kess learned. She learned to share less of her and

Pony's activities with her parents. It didn't seem to slow the whippings though.

Kess wondered whether they were taking out the disappointment they felt toward her inadequacies as their daughter on Pony instead. That wild Rolanian slave who had all the qualities of strength and vigor a Taen dragonlord should display and their own child lacked. Pony was the perfect surrogate for all their spite.

And she ... she just took it.

Kess shivered and refolded the handkerchief and moved to tuck it into one of the saddlebags. Then with a scowl, she tossed it onto the floor. She didn't need it. Griskin didn't need it. They were leaving these caves for good, because as big of a fool as Riony was, she must know she couldn't come back here safely.

Kess turned Griskin toward the main thoroughfare of the cavern. There was no point now hiding her presence, slinking through the shadows as she'd done before.

The refugees of the undercity rushed to clear a path for her and the huge gray wolf she rode on.

The people muttered and stared at her passing, and a gaggle of squealing children built up behind her, daring each other to get closer.

Kess ignored them, pressing on toward one of the main exits.

She wasn't sure where she was going, only that somewhere out there was everything she wanted.

Dracuni. The creature may not have been the strong dragon she'd hoped for. Kess didn't really know what she was or how she would grow. Whether it would ever prove to be an effective steed.

But that didn't matter, because Dracuni was something far more valuable.

How ... how did Riony come upon this creature?

A living creature with unicorn blood.

The concept thrilled Kess beyond comprehension. Even if there were any true unicorns still alive, the value of each one enough to turn commoner into a noble, Dracuni would be worth ten of them. A hundred of them.

Never had a unicorn been able to be kept in captivity. They would wither and die within hours of being captured. They had to be bled and bottled as fast as possible to save every drop of the precious silvernix.

But that strange hatchling, it was living under a human's care, with them, possibly even bonded to them. Kept as easily as keeping a tamed dragon.

It had bled for Kess and still lived to bleed again another day.

Kess flinched at the memory of how the small critter had looked at her with some animal version of pity, had

done that for her, to save her.

It didn't matter. She owed the creature nothing. Debts were not earned by wild creatures. The value it offered Kess came before anything else.

And she could do as she said and be a good master to it. She'd at least treat it far better than anyone else who got their hands on it. Maybe she wouldn't even have to tame it.

She could be good to the creature and still get what she wanted from it in return.

Kess could buy a whole hatchery of her own with even a fraction of Dracuni's blood. She could buy an entire dragon army.

When Kess arrived at the mammoth stone doors of the exit, she smirked at the carved unicorns adorning the stone. She shot a glare at the guards, and they hastily pressed the mechanism.

Stone ground against stone, and the smoky chill of aboveground air blew in. Kess rode out into the darkening night, as determination set inside her like molten steel plunged into water.

She would find Dracuni.

Then nothing would be out of reach. She could have anything and everything she ever wanted.

And if all it cost to get that was killing Pony ... she wouldn't hesitate again.

TWENTY-NINE

Riony dropped her head back and it bounced on the broken tiles of the Alderkin shrine floor. "If somebody can confirm we have at least a few minutes before the next thing tries to kill us, that would be wonderful. My heart is ready to give up on me."

Dracuni nuzzled up at her side, sniffing at the blood dripping from the thin knife jutting out of her arm. She rumbled gently, low in her throat. ***Much bad hurt.***

"Yeah. Much bad hurt," Riony agreed.

Lyrrin stood above them, staring at the geode gateway, still deactivated. "I don't think they are coming through. They don't know how to work it. I think we're okay. Except for Benjin."

Groaning, Riony rolled to one side, then crawled up to her feet.

Aishena kneeled across the small space, beneath where a tumbled down wall and ceiling let moonlight in from above, the damaged ruin strangely familiar. She had Benjin in her lap and was staring down at him with motionless grief.

"It's his neck. It's broken, swollen. He's barely ... I can't tell if he's breathing." She looked up at Riony, and although her face was still, her cheeks were streaked and shining. "Lyrrin said you had silvernix. She said you can help him."

Riony turned on Lyrrin. "You told her *what*?"

"Only ... not everything ... only that you could help. We have to help him, don't we?" Lyrrin fidgeted her hands, free from their gloves.

Secrets were spilling as freely as the blood had.

"How? How am I supposed to help? Without them knowing? And it's not even up to me." Riony took a stumbling limp closer to Aishena and her brother, hoping there would be some other way to handle this problem.

Oh, he looks really bad.

"What do you mean it's not up to you? Who is it up to?" Aishena asked.

Riony bent at the waist, groaning gruffly. She pressed fisted hands against her temples. This was all wrong; this was all too much. "Sparks!"

She hated this. She hated that she held the knowledge that could save Benjin's life, and she wanted to, so badly. But doing so meant trusting everyone here with Dracuni's secret.

A secret that had already been revealed to the most dangerous person possible. *Kess.* Riony seethed at the mere intrusion of the goblin's name into her mind.

That harm was done, and Riony could already feel the repercussions coming to kick her ass from down her path ahead.

But whatever the consequences, she couldn't let Kess live and Aishena's brother die.

Riony crumpled down onto her knees in front of Aishena and Benjin. She stretched her arm out, bringing Dracuni in by her side so the dragonling could see the injured boy.

"I can't help. But Dracuni can. If she wants to."

Aishena frowned, and silent tears rushed from her eyes again. Riony knew she must think her mad and her brother lost.

Hurt? Dracuni nuzzled Benjin's hand with her snout. He didn't respond.

"He is. He won't survive on his own."

I help?

"If you want to. Only if it's okay."

Aishena stared aghast at the one-sided conversation.

"Is she going to help?" Lyrrin asked softly as she joined them.

Dracuni bobbed her head and moved lithely, bending her long neck and bringing a claw up to her horn. There was the slightest scratching sound, harsh in the breathless silence as everyone stared at the creature. Even Niskina's sobbing had stilled at the bizarre tableau before her.

Aishena gasped as the shimmering blood became visible.

The unidragon pressed her bleeding claw to Benjin's hand.

Riony's shoulders slumped. It was done. There was no coming back from this. She remained there, kneeling before them, as Benjin's body flushed with the brightness of starlight.

Aishena held the boy tight as his body twisted and twitched, the healing magic rushing through his failing system, repairing what was broken. Her mouth hung open and dark eyes glinted with the magical glow.

Then Benjin stilled and opened his eyes. When he raised a hand, desperate and seeking Aishena's crying face, she wailed loudly and brought him up into a crushing embrace.

The siblings held each other, crying thick tears of combined relief and loss.

Riony took a shaky breath and wiped her eyes.

"What about you?" Lyrrin asked softly. "You look like

a pincushion made out of raw meat."

Riony smirked. "I *feel* like a pincushion made out of raw meat."

She grabbed the narrow hilt of the knife puncturing her arm and pulled. It slurped out, tight from the suction. Riony saved her whimper for when it finally popped free. Staring at the sharpened length of bone, Riony scowled and snapped it in half.

She tossed the pieces into a shadowy corner of the ruins, then adjusted her sitting position to work on the one in her thigh. She hoped she still had a bandage in one of her pouches. Probably contaminated with olm-pool water, but it would have to do. They couldn't go back for other supplies. They had what was on them now and nothing more.

The second dagger dragged through her skin until it was out and Riony discarded it with disdain. Looking at the mangled lower half of her leg and the teeth marks through her boots, Riony figured she'd need more than a few bandages. Maybe one of the other delvers would have something she could use to bind her wounds.

Dracuni returned to her side, blinking lilac eyes as she tried to climb into Riony's lap.

Riony let out a low groan. "Just a moment, little one."

Hurt too?

Riony shrugged. "Nah, it's nothing. I'll be okay."

Dracuni's toothy mouth opened in a scolding warble.

A tear spilled from Riony's eyes. She pressed a hand to Dracuni's cheek and whispered, "I promised I wouldn't ..."

Snorting warm air near Riony's hand, Dracuni pushed her snout against Riony's fingers until she dropped them in her lap. And then the dragonling pressed her claw into it. The tiniest shine of silvernix remained there and absorbed brightly into Riony's palm.

Riony pulled the beautiful creature up into her lap as the ethereal brilliance enveloped them. She let a few hot tears fall against Dracuni's neck as her physical wounds healed, but the ache in her heart remained overwhelming.

"Thank you." She breathed the words near Dracuni's ear.

Aishena watched with pained eyes as the glow around Riony subsided. "I have so many questions."

"Yeah. I thought you might. And I'll get to them. Just ... let's take a moment to recover first."

Niskina slapped a hand against the ground and glared through puffy eyes. "A moment? To recover? We have *lost family*!"

Riony ran a hand into her hair and tugged at the red strands. "I know. I'm sorry."

"We've lost more than our families. We've lost our home," Aishena said flatly. "Again."

Riony looked at where the end of the ancient Alderkin shrine had collapsed, opening to the forest around it. "I don't think we're far away, though."

"We could be anywhere, anywhere in Elundrae. Yoskar said ..." Aishena choked on the words.

"No, I'm pretty sure ..." Riony stood up, bringing Dracuni with her, unwilling to let go of the hatchling that had signs of fatigue catching up to it fast. She stepped out the vine-shrouded doorway and looked around. "Yep. Apple tree. Remains of our fire. This is the shrine we stayed at, just down the hill from the Alderkin depths."

For some reason that made Aishena start crying again.

"If we want to go back, I think we can just use the gateway again. It might work from this side too." Lyrrin closed in on it, pointing to the rune she'd cleared off at the bottom.

"Whoa, no!" Riony said. "I'm not ready to face what might still be on the other side."

"We *can't* go back," Aishena said. Benjin was squirming and griping in her hug now, but she refused to let him go. "That place, it won't ever be safe again, from *her*."

Riony knew Aishena meant her mother. But it was again Kess's name that stabbed at her heart.

She swallowed away the remaining shreds of fury and tried to think about what was ahead of them now. "Niskina

could go back. There's no reason she couldn't go home. We can help her back to one of the entrances."

With a sob, Niskina turned her face toward the ruined stone wall. "I can't go back there."

The grieving young woman closed off again, staring blankly at the ground and coughing through her tears.

Benjin was whispering to his sister within their tight bubble, and she spoke hushed words in return, the only one Riony could make out, over and over, was *sorry*.

The energy of Dracuni's blood still zinged through Riony, but she also felt tired to her marrow.

She lowered herself down, sitting with her back against the doorframe of the shrine. Dracuni drooped, curling up on her lap with a snuffle.

Riony reached an arm out, and Lyrrin took the hint and hurried into it.

"How are you holding up? Today was ... intense doesn't quite capture it. Unreasonably hectic? Catastrophically tragic? Just plain shitty?"

Lyrrin coughed a small laugh. "You really can't stop with the jokes."

"Who said I was joking? Those were all fair descriptions. And I do want to know how you're feeling."

"I cried already. I'll probably cry again." Lyrrin took Riony's hand in hers, tugging on it so that arm that looped

around her pulled tighter.

"That's okay. Cry as much as you need to."

"But I also feel good because I still have you and Dracuni." Lyrrin frowned over her small smile. "But also bad that I feel good when the others lost more. And ..."

"What is it?" Riony prompted.

"I left Sir Butterfur behind." Lyrrin's tears came again. She pressed her head into Riony's shoulder, thankfully now free from daggers or holes caused by daggers.

"That little furry menace? He'll be fine. The caves are his playground, and I'm sure he'll miss you, but he'll survive without us."

Lyrrin made a sad noise and buried her face farther.

"And you know what? He was how I found my way back to you. Or at least, most of the way, until you found me. You were so clever to send him after me. Sparks, I wouldn't have survived today without you. I'm so happy we're still together too."

Lyrrin's small body shook for a moment, then the sobbing slowed. Riony rested her head against her sister's.

"Riony?" Lyrrin's voice was small and hesitant.

"Yeah?"

"Did ... did my mother have hands like mine?"

"No. Why?"

"Never mind."

Riony's eyebrows twisted, but she didn't question her sister further.

She didn't have anything else to offer either. She hadn't had the chance to question Kess more about the guest who'd given birth at Heithorn estate to find out anything more about Lyrrin's mother's identity. She wished she could give the kid more answers.

Not that I could have trusted a word that came out of that horrible goblin's mouth anyway.

The ghost of Kess's weight on her back made her twitch. She shouldn't have gone back into that revenant-filled cavern. She should have left Kess to die, the same way Kess had done to her.

Riony grasped the muzzle tied to her belt, tearing through the soaked leather straps. She scrunched it in her fist, then threw it into a shadowed corner to join the knives.

Her throat burned dry from the embers of her fury. And from the utter shame that she had, for even a moment, thought Kess could act on something other than selfishness. And how there was part of Riony that bruisingly wanted that to happen.

Riony rubbed her knuckles over the middle of her chest, as though trying to massage the ache beneath her ribs. Everything felt broken. Everyone felt broken. Her, Aishena, Niskina, the kids.

Could she trust these crushed souls with Dracuni's secret? Could she even trust them to keep themselves in one piece in the dangerous aboveground life they'd been thrust into?

Maybe not, but Riony would do her best to keep them all alive.

They'd all lost too much. She didn't want to lose anyone else.

Except maybe Kess. That was one life she was ready to strike off.

The zealous greed in the wolf-rider's eyes scared Riony. If she'd been a threat to them before for wanting a baby dragon, what would she do now that she truly knew what Dracuni was?

Did she just hear a wolf howl? Or did she imagine it?

A shiver rattled her bones. "I'm not even sure if we can stay here overnight."

She was met with silence and sobs.

Riony looked at the ruined and crumpled faces around her. "I mean … it's probably okay. One night. There might even be a couple of apples left for us. We can move on tomorrow, hit up what remains of that slavers' camp, see what we can salvage from there."

Aishena turned her chin up, as though expecting orders. "And then?"

"Then ... we take it day by day. We find a new home. We will."

Lyrrin cuddled close to Riony's side. Dracuni snuffled a soft snore, head on her lap. Everybody else—Aishena, Niskina, Benjin—looked to Riony with worn, anguished expressions.

"There must be somewhere out there that can be safe for us. For all of us, together."

For those of us who remain.

To Be Continued
in
Rise Of the Dragon Sworn

GLOSSARY

Including pronunciation guide

CHARACTERS

Riony Eyfarr (Ree-OH-nee AY-far) – Rolanian, Daughter of Eylin and Farrad, born when servants to the Gyrstein Dragonlords, then sold on as a family to the Heithorn Dragonlords, and since living as fugitive slaves. Trained as a midwife and herbalist. Sword enthusiast.

Lyrrin Eyfarr (Li-rin AY-far) – Daughter of "The Guest", an unknown dragonlord woman, and an unknown father. Taen and Elgarthan? Has some unusual features. Likes animals and magic.

Kessara Heithorn (Kess-AH-ra High-thorn) – From the once wealthy Heithorn dragonlords with strong dragon riding traditions, estranged. Taen. Rides a wolf.

Kife Heithorn (K-eye-f High-thorn) – Elder brother to Kessara, dragonrider. Taen.

Dracuni (Drak-YOU-nee) – Unique hybrid between unicorn and dragon, created from the use of silvernix on a broken dragon egg, and something more?

Griskin (Griss-kin) – Large gray wolf, male, for some reason abides Kess's company.

Aishena Hjelzahn (AYSH-en Hyel-zarn) – Delver, Middle sibling of three (remaining), fifth generation heir, grayglim in training. Taen.

Yoskar Hjelzahn (Yoss-kar Hyel-zarn) – Delver, Eldest sibling of three (remaining), fifth generation heir, Alderkin rune expert and academic. Taen.

Benjin Hjelzahn (BEN-jin Hyel-zarn) – Youngest sibling of three (remaining), fifth generation heir. Taen.

Kverra Hjelzahn (Kv-errar Hyel-zarn) – Grayglin warden and wife to Vori Hjelzan, fourth generation heir to the Dragon King. Taen.

Brishan Ulfaran (Brish-arn OOLF-ah-ran) – Taen ex-grayglim, Master of the delvers.

Niskina Ulfaran (Nissk-EE-nah OOLF-ah-ran) – Half Taen, half Rolanian. Brishan's daughter.

Yeonard Draekhan (Yeh-nard DRAKE-arn) – Dragonking, ruler of Elundrae. Taen. First to tame a dragon.

Sir Butterfur Spelunkychunks – A cave otter. Food motivated.

GENERAL

Alderkin (ALL-der-kin) – a secretive and powerful race of elven humanoids. Masters of rune crystal magic. Extinct.

Alderkin Depths – Massive underground cities once inhabited by the Alderkin. There are five known Alderkin Depths across Elundrae.

Alderkin Runes – Magical symbols carved into crystal items, which, when somehow charged, allow for a range of magical functions. The runes must be traced in the right sequence and direction of strokes in order to be activated and deactivated.

Alderkin War – A twenty-year war between the Alderkin and the Dragon King's forces, ending thirty years prior to the events in these books. Prompted by the human's slaughter of unicorns, and the Alderkin's attempts to protect them.

Athame (Ah-Thahm-Ay) – A dagger of varying size, made from crystal, and powered by various Alderkin runes for utility or combat.

Breachers – Undercity dwellers who brave the aboveground world to scavenge resources, highly dangerous but sometimes required.

Delvers – Undercity dwellers who brave the dangers of the Alderkin depths to salvage useful artifacts to be sold in the undercity. A risky but lucrative profession.

Dragon Glass – Glass manufactured with the use of dragon's fire to melt the base ingredients.

Dragon guards/riders – Those trained to ride dragons, generally for combat purposes. Either born to or hired by Dragonlord families who own the dragons.

Dragonhold – A building with multiple facilities for dragon keeping and raising, including hatchery, stables, and training areas.

Dragonkeeps – Walled in cities protected by dragons. The Dragon King has built and gifted a dragonkeep to each of his first generation heirs.

Dragonlords – Those who have the riches and resources to own their own dragons. Not necessarily royalty.

Elgarthans – A sea-faring race, pale skinned, they will visit and trade with Dragonkeeps for the riches of steel and glass provided through dragon labor, but rarely remain in Elundrae due to the dangers.

Elundrae (Ell-Un-Dray) – The continent in which the story takes place. Nearest neighboring country being Elgartha, across the seas to the East.

Rebel Riders – Title of a popular serial fiction, published and distributed in chapters.

Revenant/Rev/Shadow Revenant – Any undead creature raised by the Shadow Dragon's curse. Generally defeated by fire or dismemberment.

Rolanians – Once ruling large cities throughout Elundrae, most Rolanian settlements were destroyed as the Shadow Dragon curse spread through the land. As very few Rolanians became dragonlords, they had to buy into protection from those who had dragons, often at the cost of their own freedom. Generally presenting with a warm array of darker skin tones, and hair ranging from blonde, through reds and browns.

Shadow Dragon – a cursed and mysterious creature of smoke and sadness that brings the undead blight to the land of Elundrae. Wherever the Shadow Dragon touches ground, the dead rise.

Silvernix – Unicorn blood. Miraculous healing qualities, a single drop can cure a body from near death. Can only be stored in dragon glass, otherwise loses potency within minutes. Opalescent liquid.

Taens – Generally dark-haired and light-to-mid-brown skin-tones, Taens were once a warrior like clan of horse-riders, taking residence through the north-west of Elundrae. When the Dragonking rose to power, Taens became favored and more likely to become dragonlords, and soon became the dominant race across the land.

Taming – The ceremony in which all dragons are subjected to in order to be domesticated, similar to a lobotomy. Performed not long after birth on dragons bred in captivity. Utilizes silvernix in the process.

Undercity – A human settlement, established in the large upper cavern of the Central Alderkin Depths, as a refuge from the dangers of the aboveground world.

Unicorns – Ethereal, horned horse-like creatures. Driven to extinction in the race for the riches of their blood.

Herbs

Carrowmy – culinary.

Corpsefoot – used for contraception, dangerous in high doses.

Genjermint – sleeping tea.

Hennen – for hair dye.

Morass Mercy – powerful sedative with bad side effects.

Plumeberry – tart, seedy berries, poison detox.

Shillgrue – to condition leather.

Tinctoria – for hair dye.

Weftweed – a sticky (both in appearance and sap production) antiseptic.

Dragons
Natural subspecies

Etherflame – Plains dragons. Golds and reds, large size. Fire breathing for clearing grasslands/cooking herds, and big wings for hovering. Blood itself is flammable and is aerosolized in breath weapon. Most common dragonrider mount.

Seasong – Sea dragons. Silvers, greens, blacks, largest size, big lungs creates big surge of air/sound to stun schools of fish, and bigger mouth for feeding. There are tales they once sang, but never have in captivity or once tamed. Mostly used for interbreeding and beasts of burden.

Snowshimmer – Mountain dragons. Whites-blues, medium-sized, fast build for snatching up rare prey. Big talons, lightning breath attack, rare and solitary. Used in industry for power and interbreeding.

Treedart – Forest dragons. Yellows, browns, purples, camouflaged scales. Smallest type, with concentrated fire bolts for individual prey. Considered pretty basic by breeders and dragonlords, mostly used for interbreeding. Main/only dragon still in the wild because of size.

Dragons

Interbred selective breeding species

Etherdart – Etherflame/Treedart cross. Medium size, tough but slow, big fireballs. A basic combat dragon.

FlameSongs – Etherflame/Seasong cross. Largest size, high-capacity fire-breathers, used mostly for industrial uses, not used as mounts because they can spontaneously explode.

Seashimmer – Seasong/Snowshimmer cross. Large size, cold, icy breath used in ice making and food storage industry.

Shimmerdart – Snowshimmer/Treedart cross. Small size, with small ball lightning darts, dangerous for single targets but not great against mass undead, bred for speed as scouts/communications/assassinations.

Snowflame – Snowshimmer/Etherflame cross. Medium-large size, white "liquid" fire, fast, considered a great dragonrider mount, but short lifespan as breath weapon deteriorates their health fast.

Treedart/seasong – don't interbreed successfully.

ANIMALS

Bantam Ferrets – Mouse sized ferrets.

Bovin – A large (twice human height) buffalo or yak style creature, docile, used to be in large herds that supported wild dragons. Moved into farming for captive dragons.

Carrion Birds – Massive scavengers with a cry like a wolf's howl.

Cave Otters – A large sized otter with specially adapted claws that allow them to climb sheer walls easily, pale colors to match limestone surroundings.

Cave Spiders – Head-sized spiders, nonvenomous.

Dreer – Deer with Armadillo like scales, that grow as large as giraffes. Also popular prey for wild dragon populations in the past.

Glowflies – firefly-like bugs, finger sized, live in large swarms and light up when disturbed.

Mouse Deer – Cat sized deer with fangs.

Olm – Just like real olm, but larger than human size and carnivorous.

Owlettes – Cave dwelling owls that feed on small rodents and insects within the caves, the size of a small hand.

Rope Worms – Just a worm, but much larger. Delicious when fried.

ALDERKIN RUNES

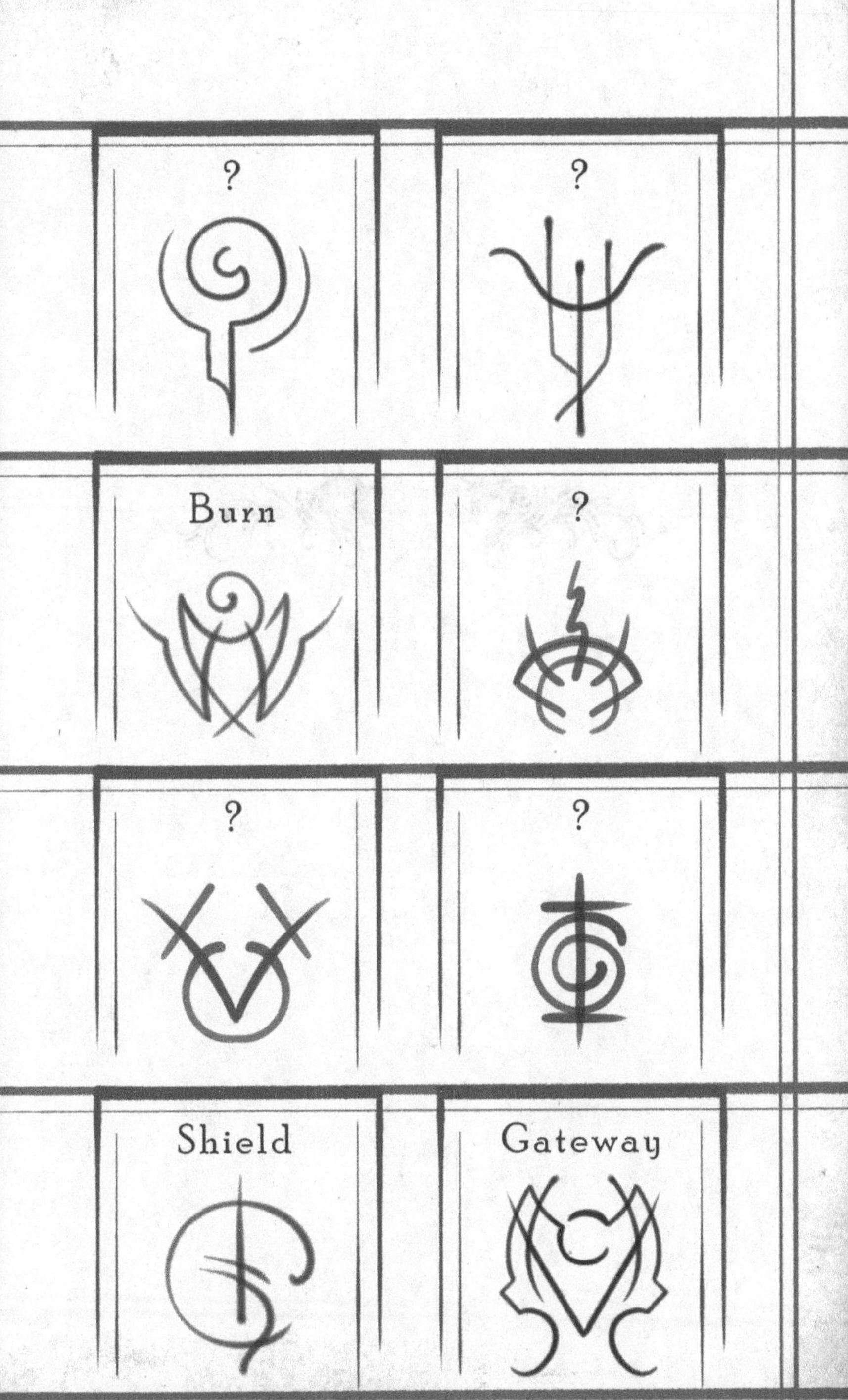

?
?
Burn
?
?
?
Shield
Gateway

About the Author

Professional daydreamer, Selina A. Fenech writes "adorably dark" Epic and Urban Fantasy for teens and adults. Filled with sweet and quirky characters, laugh out loud moments, and perilous adventures, her magical worlds are perfect for readers who love daring twists and happily ever afters.

A cancer survivor determined to live life to the fullest, she is an escape room enthusiast, avid gardener, foodie and self-proclaimed geek, residing in Australia.

In addition to literature, Selina applies her unique take on the dichotomy of light and dark as a professional fantasy artist working under the name Selina Fenech and has published many illustrated books, oracle decks, and colouring books.

Find Out More About Selina

OFFICIAL WEBSITE:www.selinafenech.com

Memory's Wake Trilogy

A modern girl lost in and hunted in a fairy tale world.
An illustrated young adult portal fantasy with
Arthurian and Victorian themes.

Empath Chronicles

Teenagers with superpowers fueled by emotions ... what
could go wrong? A young adult superhero romance.

MORE BOOKS BY SELINA A FENECH

Beshadowed

You have been lied to. Werewolves, vampires, ghosts ... they aren't what you think. What is really lurking in the dark? A spooky urban fantasy.

Heartsblood

Her blood is irresistible, but is it worth the cost? A vampire romance for adults.